— or —
Trouble Is Her
Middle Name

Also by Audrey Couloumbis

Getting Near to Baby

The Misadventures of Maude March

Say Yes

Summer's End

MAUDE MARCH
ON THE RUN!

— or —
Trouble Is Her Middle Name

AUDREY
COULOUMBIS

RANDOM HOUSE NEW YORK

Copyright © 2007 by Audrey Couloumbis
Jacket illustration copyright © 2007 by Robert Papp
Map art copyright © 2007 by Bryn Barnard
Some jacket and interior fonts copyright © 2005 by The Scriptorium,
all rights reserved. For information on these fonts go to www. fontcraft.com.
All GreyWolf Free Fonts are copyright © R. Gast, GreyWolf WebWorks.
All rights reserved. Used by permission.

All rights reserved.
Published in the United States by Random House Children's Books,
a division of Random House, Inc., New York.
RANDOM HOUSE and colophon are registered trademarks
of Random House, Inc.

www.randomhouse.com/teens
Educators and librarians, for a variety of teaching tools, visit us at
www.randomhouse.com/teachers

Library of Congress Cataloging-in-Publication Data
Couloumbis, Audrey.
Maude March on the run!, or, Trouble is her middle name /
Audrey Couloumbis — 1st ed. p. cm.
SUMMARY: Due to a misunderstanding over her involvement
in a botched robbery, Maude, with younger sister Sallie, hides out
at the home of an uncle, but when she is discovered and arrested,
the orphaned sisters flee, trying to clear Maude's name.
ISBN 978-0-375-83246-8 (trade) —
ISBN 978-0-375-93246-5 (lib. bdg.) —
ISBN 978-0-375-83248-2 (pbk.)
[1. Adventure and adventurers—Fiction.
2. Frontier and pioneer life—Fiction. 3. Robbers and outlaws—Fiction.
4. Sisters—Fiction. 5. Orphans—Fiction.]
I. Title: Maude March on the run!
II. Title: Trouble is her middle name. III. Title.
PZ7.C8305Mau 2006 [Fic]—dc22 2005036133

Printed in the United States of America
10 9 8 7 6 5 4 3 2 1
First Edition

NAZ *STOP* THIS *IS* THE PERFECT PLACE
TO WRITE DOWN ALL THE THINGS I
WANT YOU TO KNOW *STOP* TROUBLE
IS I LEARNED ALL THE BEST *STUFF*
FROM YOU *STOP* FORTUNATE ME *STOP*
LOVE, MOM

MAUDE MARCH ON THE RUN!

or
Trouble Is Her Middle Name

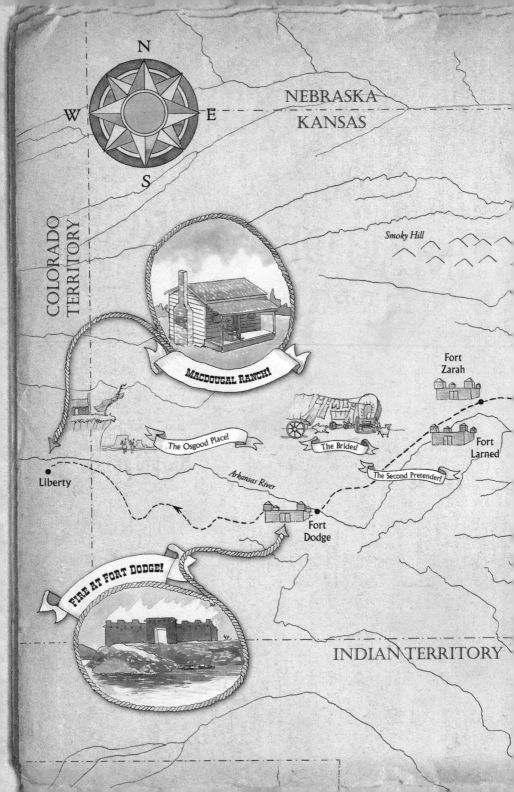

N

W E

S

NEBRASKA

KANSAS

Smoky Hill

COLORADO TERRITORY

MACDOUGAL RANCH!

Fort Zarah

The Osgood Place!

The Brides!

Fort Larned

The Second Pretender!

Liberty

Arkansas River

Fort Dodge

FIRE AT FORT DODGE!

INDIAN TERRITORY

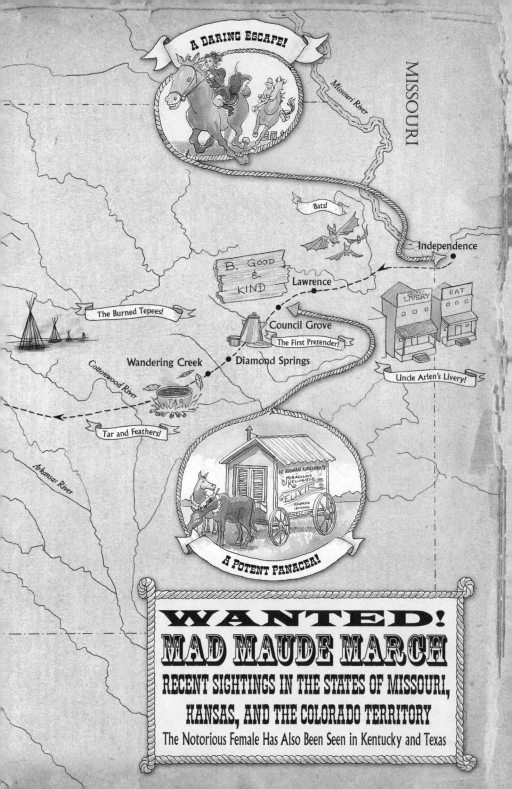

ONE

THEY SAY MY SIXTEEN-YEAR-OLD SISTER PASSES FOR A man and shoots like an outlaw, and I cannot argue it, since she has done both in her day.

Maude has been called a hardened criminal, and of this I must tell you, do not believe it. People say a great many things and only some of them are true.

This afternoon I watched from across the street as my sister was arrested. She made a small figure in her plain dark dress, her arms pulled behind her to cuff her wrists.

"Maude!" I shouted.

She didn't hear my voice over all those so filled with excitement. I felt my blood rush toward my feet, leaving me so dizzy and breathless I nearly sat down. For the crowd only saw my sister as a fugitive from the law, accused of being a horse thief, a bank robber, and a cold-blooded killer.

It'd been five months since we found our lost uncle Arlen and settled into a new life with him in Independence. I had begun to believe she might never be discovered to be the infamous Mad Maude, even though a dream came to me over and over, in which I opened a sack to find oatmeal cookies and

1

two train tickets. I always found the oatmeal cookies tasty, and there was no sense of being short of time to catch a train.

The dream flashed behind my eyes as Maude stepped into the sunlight, head held high, the law on both sides of her gripping her at the elbows. I'd never told my sister about this dream, not even that recent time she tried to talk me out of my determination to be ready for just such an occasion as this.

We were getting dressed for the day ahead of us, which was also my twelfth birthday. "When do you plan to go back to looking like a girl?" she said to me. Unlike my sister, I hadn't yet taken to wearing skirts again. Maude said of course I must, as soon as my hair grew in nicely. So long as I could wield the scissors this fate would not befall me.

"It doesn't matter how you dress, Sallie," Maude said. "They might still find me out. Then again, they might not. I'm meanwhile missing the sight of my little sister."

"I'll whisper it into her ear," I said. "See if she don't surprise you one day."

"*Doesn't,*" she said. "Is that a few bristles I see under your nose? Why, it looks like the beginning of a mustache."

"It's a shame I didn't ask your admirer, Mr. Wilburn, for a shaving lesson," I said. "That fellow had mustache material growing out of his ears."

Maude whopped me with her feather pillow and we were occupied with battle for a time. As soon as she wasn't looking, I touched my upper lip to be sure she was teasing.

I had begun to think she might be right about one thing—that we might never need to make a sudden run for it. But past events had impressed upon me how fast things could go wrong, and how different life might be after they did. Because of this, I kept some handy items for life on the trail in a sack in the loft. This meant fewer necessaries than you might guess. A horse and a canteen can get you through most anything.

The heroes in the dime novels I read were always planning ahead this way. Maude did not read much and so didn't appreciate this fact. That sack prompted her to remind me of a Bible story.

Three kings were in the desert and couldn't find water for themselves or their horses. They put their troubles before the prophet Elisha, who said to them what the Lord told him, which was, "Make this valley full of ditches.... Ye shall not see wind, neither shall ye see rain; yet that valley shall be filled with water."

Even though it didn't make good sense to those kings to dig ditches, they did it, and sure enough, a big flood came and filled the ditches with water. Which meant you have to get ready for what you want.

"Or in this case," Maude had said, "don't get ready for what you don't want."

Maybe she was right, for a scant hour after Maude was arrested, I was taking stock and judged myself to be as ready as anyone can be for an event that will spin their lives in an unexpected direction.

My plan, in case of Maude's arrest, had always been to go in like a confused younger brother looking for his sister, arguing a case of they had mistook her for this other one. I had half a chance, for no one appeared to have noticed Maude had a younger sister, let alone an unexpected brother.

Only as I was riding to the sheriff's office, I knew why people resorted to packing a gun—in case that first plan didn't work out the way they hoped it would.

The way I saw it, I might could breach the doorway when there was only one lawman on hand. Then, in case he didn't believe my story of they had the wrong female and release my sister to me, I could try to get the drop on that single fellow.

I could see flaws all over this thinking.

One, Mad Maude and the Black Hankie Bandit, both notorious outlaws, were stuck in the same jailhouse. It might never come a time when only one lawman stood on duty. I could be waiting outside till I took root and sprouted leaves.

Two, once me and Maude were on the run, they would know to watch for her traveling with a boy. We had already been two boys, so they'd watch for that as well. And girls couldn't travel on their own without someone wondering why.

Three, the likelihood of getting myself shot.

It might could happen I'd get shot and killed some time or other, but if it was because I'd packed a gun, Maude would never let me rest. From every side, this was flaw enough to quit right there, if only my sister wasn't in the jail.

I did wish myself taller and wider and more truly a man. For in front of the jail, I couldn't step forward smartly. I stood shivering like winter had come back all of a sudden. My heart was pounding so hard I stopped hearing the sounds in the street.

I saw a man-on-his-horse-shaped shadow glide into the alleyway nearby. It gave me a start, but it also got me on the move. Uncle Arlen had once said to me that I was not truly the criminal type. I didn't care to be the proof of his statement.

I let Maude see me heading into the sheriff's office, directly beneath the window where she stood. Like something in me knew the exact way, tears started to flow.

Making a loud, obnoxious crying noise, I walked inside.

TWO

LOOKING BACK, I KNEW I OUGHT TO HAVE SEEN THIS
turn of events coming. It didn't help one bit that the hero in
every dimer I'd read had much the same thing to say when
they messed up. For a sign should be read as carefully as a
book.

I'd seen a new wanted poster just lately, offering a reward
of three hundred dollars. The picture was bad and the partic-
ulars weren't awful particularly right, but Mad Maude March
was printed at the top. It looked like news of her name being
cleared didn't travel as fast as tales of her exploits.

Without thinking about how Maude would take it, I'd
carried that fresh news straight to the supper table. For a fact,
the picture was the worst of the thing. It made Maude out to
be past plain, and leaning toward downright ugly. Maude took
the insult of it right to heart.

"Burn it," she said.

"Where did you get this?" Uncle Arlen wanted to know.

"On the ground," I said, "where somebody dropped it."

"Who would carry a wanted poster around?" Maude said
as if we didn't all know the answer to that: the law.

"Maybe some fellow who thinks you're pretty," Marion said, and caught a swat for his trouble. Being he's some younger than Uncle Arlen, Maude didn't treat him with the same respect.

"I don't care to be made fun of," she said.

I said, "He don't like it when anyone else makes fun of you." But that poster lit a fire under her.

"I've thought it over," she said. "I'd rather tell them my story and be thought a liar than too chicken-hearted to show my face."

"You haven't thought it over long," I said. "You've only had that poster in your hand for a minute."

Only worry for Uncle Arlen kept her from walking into the nearest sheriff's office and telling her right side of the story.

Then, in one Sunday morning at the livery, I saw four separate men with badges on the vests they wore under their coats. Later in the same day, while I ate noon dinner over at George Ray's restaurant, I heard the name of Maude March come up in the conversation of three men who made me think of boat rats.

Boat rats being what a person living near the river took a broom to at least once a week. Now and again it happened a rat tried to run up the broomstick. These fellows were that feisty, and not more appealing, either.

They talked like they were friends of the Black Hankie Bandit, who had been jailed earlier in the week. Two of them didn't sound like they were in favor of this.

The one said, "Hankie done his share of wrong, but he don't deserve hanging," and the other one agreed, saying, "That feller got shot twice before, and it didn't kill him."

The third one wondered aloud where the James boys were these days. This I understood entirely, for the James boys did a fine job of taking the law's mind off other matters.

Then came the mention of Maude. "What do you hear a that one?" one of those two said. "Wan't she in Mississip last I heard a her? I ain't heard nuthin about her lately."

"A flash in the pan," the other one said.

I wasn't happy to hear my sister, Maude, made light of, and I was glad when the first one didn't care for it, either.

"How would you know?" he said. "You been out there in the middle a nowhere with me, and I didn't hear word one about her or anybody else. What I didn't hear, you didn't hear."

"All I'm saying is, if she'd done anything of note, we would've."

"She coulda peeled a strip a land off this continent to rival the Oregon Trail, and we wouldn't know."

The argument was getting a little heated when the third fellow spoke up again. "She could be anywheres by now. I don't listen to them papers. Wouldn't surprise me one bit if she was sitting right in this here restaurant."

While I was noticing this one was a thinker, the other two looked around the place. Some of the patrons were locals, more of them were dusty travelers, and a few of each of those were mighty suspicious-looking.

The most innocent face in the place was coming to their table carrying a tray full of eats. They didn't look at her.

Her name was Maude March.

It's hard for people to grasp the fact of Maude being a

young woman with a respectable demeanor. They think she must enter every door with teeth bared, guns drawn, and coattails flapping in an unnatural gust of wind.

They also don't think of a rough-and-ready outlaw combing her hair into a crown of bright curls. This was a great relief to Uncle Arlen, for he wasn't in favor of my sister working right out in the open. He fought her on this point, but her stubborn streak won out.

All unawares of the rats' conversation, Maude gave them their dinners. When she came over to me, I said, "Can you get out of here for a couple of hours?"

"As soon as these fellows eat up," she said. They were scooping food into their mouths as regular as shoveling coal into a furnace.

Listening to those fellows talk, I'd learned a few more lawmen were coming to town to say their piece at Black Hankie's trial. I wanted to tell Maude of this.

I said, "Quarter of an hour?"

She said, "Saddle up our horses, why don't you?" Lately Maude liked to ride out to the edge of the prairie and stare across it like someone in love.

I first went on down the street to treat myself to a new dimer. I worried back and forth between Powder Keg McCarthy and Hardweather Hampton.

I didn't anymore read them as the innocent I once was. I could see through the adventure of them, oftentimes, to the wearing part. I knew the sick feeling that came with the danger. When everything came right in the end, I took particular satisfaction in it.

As I paid up, Mr. Palmer, at the counter, said to me his usual piece of advice: "Son, those things are a waste of your hard-earned pennies."

I walked away from the counter a happy man. It had taken some doing to get to the point where people didn't see through my disguise and know me to be a girl right off.

Outside, a pack of boys were running behind a wagon of squealing piglets. I ran along with them as far as the livery. Maude hurried across the street ahead of us, the flurry of her new petticoat ruffling the edge of her skirt.

Maude had taken to riding sidesaddle, with one leg hooked over the saddle horn. I admired the look of this myself, and didn't worry about her taking a fall, for that sorrel she favored was not one for sudden starts.

Once the city was behind us, the sky made a great room all around and the prairie a thick carpet. Blocks of yellow lay over the grass like quilt patches. Maude had a weakness for flowers. Only when we rode among them did we see they were bright tiny flowers on a weedy stem. No good for picking.

I said, "There's a fresh mess of lawmen in town for a trial."

"I know it," she said. "I stayed in the kitchen all morning to bake cookies. When that ran out, I told the other girls I didn't feel like taking orders but wanted only to carry the plates out to the tables."

My eyebrows raised over this.

"Don't worry," Maude said. "Not many people look at me when the food is being set before them."

We didn't get off our horses until we had a grassy field all around. I couldn't see wasting free time by staring. While I stomped down a cleared space and began to read, Maude stared westward.

The unbroken line of the horizon fooled the eye. Something seen clearly could turn out to be much further away than expected, or clouds seen at the distance could close over your head so quickly you had no chance to find shelter.

THREE

"It's like an ocean, the way the grass moves like water," Maude said after a time.

"It's just an awful lot of grass," I said back to her.

"An ocean is just an awful lot of water," she said, "but it's special because of that."

I didn't reply to this. Hardweather Hampton had just been charged by a buffalo and, of course, not a tree in sight.

Not knowing of his desperate situation, Maude said, "It still troubles me, Sallie, that we're running from the law."

"We ain't running," I said. "We're at Uncle Arlen's."

"Hiding, then," she said, and made the hard little sound of biting a fingernail. "Although there's little difference."

"What choice do we have?"

"My stomach was knotted up all morning, Sallie, till I got over expecting to be noticed."

I let Hardweather fend for himself for a minute. "Maude, we have to think of Uncle Arlen—"

"I am thinking of him," she said, and made a series of little biting sounds.

She didn't used to bite her nails and would not have tolerated such a habit from me. Myself, I wasn't picky about my nails. I wouldn't have been picky about my sister's, but for she had bitten them down to the quick. Her fingertips looked puffy and too new, like they hadn't grown used to the light of day.

"We're hiding under his roof, Sallie. If I'm found out, he's guilty, too. Marion said so."

I pulled a handful of grass, not liking the sound of this. Maude tended to think quick. Maybe because of this, she didn't think long.

Our friend Marion tended in the other direction, and—he was fond of pointing this out—he was not dead yet. This was saying something, for Marion Hardly did used to go by the name of Joe Harden.

He was the actual hero of those Joe Harden stories that were so popular before the rumor of his death got around. I started this rumor deliberate.

"I wrote that letter to the sheriff, explaining everything," I said. It was a long, long, long, long, *long* letter. It took me two months to write that letter, and near as much paper as a book. Some parts brought tears to my eyes.

The doubtiest part was telling how it happened that, at the bank robbery, me and Maude had simply shown up at the wrong time. As for Willie, it was the fullest truth that while Maude had grabbed her rifle when the shooting started, she didn't fire off a shot on the day he died.

We had yet to hear how our story was received.

Maude shrugged. "What if the sheriff didn't believe what you said in the letter?"

"We sent the money back," I reminded her. "That ought to have swayed opinion somewhat."

Besides which I told only two small lies: that we had no way of knowing whose shot killed Willie, and that Joe Harden had breathed his last. They were small lies, because "lies" is a strong word for a fib that was meant to put things right.

There was nothing to be gained by telling them I killed Willie by accident, so I did not tell them I shot him at all. Things happen in this world that cannot be properly understood unless you were there in the midst of them.

I doubted they'd believe Joe Harden had changed his ways for once and for all. I told the sheriff it was because Joe died that we came to have the money from a bank robbery in our possession. I said here it is, every dollar, would he please see to it that it got back to that bank in Des Moines?

Of course we couldn't tell the sheriff where he could write back to us. We had to keep our eyes open for a newspaper from Cedar Rapids, announcing Maude's innocence.

I went back to my book to find out if Hardweather could outrun a buffalo. Lucky for him, there was a prairie dog hole about to slow that big fellow up.

"I think we need more than a letter," Maude said to me, turning away from the prairie. "More than giving them the money."

"What could be more convincing than the money?"

"I don't know," Maude said. "Something that doesn't make people feel like they're just taking our word for it."

On the ride back to town, she said, "I hear people talking over at George Ray's. They talk of Independence as the far edge of the East, rather than the near edge of the West."

I could not disagree.

"I'm thinking we ought to move further west, Sallie."

14

This was the last thing I expected to hear my sister say.

Only a year ago, it would've been me, dreaming about driving cattle to someplace woolly wild, like Abilene. Now I had every hope of clearing my sister's name. I wasn't anxious to go further west just yet.

"I'm surprised at you," Maude said. "I thought you'd like this idea."

"I like it just fine." Though I didn't feel quite as eager to leave Independence as Maude did. I had not had my fill of being part of a family again. "I'll ride with you when the time comes. But right now we have to find out how our letter was received."

She swept this idea away with a motion of her hand. "The trouble is, newspapers from Cedar Rapids don't often make it to Independence."

"Let's don't rush into anything," I said, sounding very like Marion.

"There must be a place where we could live without worry once more," Maude said.

FOUR

M AUDE WENT BACK TO GEORGE RAY'S, AND I TOOK
our horses back to the livery. Marion stood in the arch of
the barn door, selling some fellow a horse.

Three good ones were standing there for a look-over. I
brought our horses to a stop nearby. One of the finer things of
working in a livery is the horse trading.

As I pulled the saddles off my horse and Maude's, Marion
named the buyer a fair price. He said he would do some more
looking around.

"Hey, Marion," I said as the fellow left.

"Hey yourself," he said. "Glad you're back to lend a hand.
We've gotten eight more horses in here in the last hour. Some
folks're coming in for a big trial."

"A lot of them are lawmen," I said, wanting to sound
knowledgeable.

"That's true," he said. "But we were expecting it, your uncle and me. Quit worrying. Maude looks different now."

Well, there was no one left for me to tell about these lawmen but the chipmunk that lived in the back room, and likely

it had already heard all about them from the horses. "What do you need me to do?"

"I'll toss some hay into a couple more stalls," Marion said, reaching for the currycomb. He waved it to include the boarded horse with ours, saying, "Make them all look like going-to-church-on-Sunday," and held it out to me.

"I'll take the stalls," I said, feeling some contrary.

"Suit yourself," he said with the air of a man who has made the better end of a trade.

I got the pitchfork. "Where is Uncle Arlen?" I said to Marion before I started tossing hay, for the place was quiet when I came in, no sound of metal ringing.

"He got a piece of mail," Marion said. "Came from somewhere out west, I believe."

"You don't know where Uncle Arlen went?" For there was nothing coming from out west that he considered to be good news.

"B'lieve he went over to the telegraph office."

I readied the next two stalls. Tossing hay is not careful work and doesn't take it out of you in that way, but it's enough labor to empty the mind entire. I didn't give the matter any more thought.

When Uncle Arlen did come back, he brought with him an astonishingly large man who wore pants that were held up by a piece of rope pulled over one shoulder. "Beef here is going to do the smithing for a time," Uncle Arlen said to Marion, pretty much ignoring me.

Uncle Arlen thought nothing of letting me go around dressed as a boy, but he hated letting the schoolteacher think I really was one. I won my point by telling him so long as he encouraged Maude in her disguise he had to let me have one.

It looked to me like he hadn't yet decided what to tell Beef.

Beef didn't ignore me. "And this young'un?" he said, and put out a huge paw in greeting. We shook, and before an awkward silence could fall, he said, "I see you like to dress in boy clothes. My sister used to do the same."

Uncle Arlen looked more surprised than me. "Sallie's the name," I said, putting my fists on my hips the way even boys are told not to do. "How did you know so quick?"

"I cain't rightly say. I reckon I'd've taken you for a boy, if not for all those years with my sister."

"All right, then." I was fooling everybody else I cared to fool.

But I still didn't know why Uncle Arlen wanted him. "How is it Beef will be doing your job?" I said to Uncle Arlen, then looked at Beef and said, "No offense intended."

"None taken."

"A friend needs me out in Colorado Territory," Uncle Arlen said. My sister came into the livery just in time to hear this, carrying a covered basket over her arm.

"You can't go west," she said to him.

I agreed. "You don't run into nothing out there but trouble."

He said, "That's exactly what I expect to find."

Maude's mouth drew into a firm straight line. She had never, to my mind, looked more like our aunt Ruthie. People say pioneers are the ones with the unmarked graves, and Uncle Arlen had come close to proving the rule more than once.

Uncle Arlen introduced Maude to Beef, who turned pink and called Maude "Miss" and wiped his paw on the bib of his pants before shaking hands with her. He didn't see right through *her* disguise.

Uncle Arlen and Marion walked with Beef to the back of the livery.

"He knew me for a girl right off," I said. I lifted the cover and peeked into the basket. Pie.

"Dried cherry," she said, of the kind. "Uncle Arlen's favorite."

My sister's hand with baked goods had come to George Ray's attention when he could not get a cake to rise but in a lopsided way. He thought to make her the baker, but she would only consent to do it a time or two each week. Until this week, when so many lawmen had ridden into town, and she took to baking every day.

"George Ray must think he's died and gone to heaven," I said.

"George Ray has a whole congregation who act like they feel the same way," Maude said. "I hope I haven't roped and forever tied myself to that bake oven. There's a hot summer coming on."

I said, "What do you make of this? Uncle Arlen surely won't ride alone."

"He doesn't sound like he's taking *anybody* along, Sallie."

She was right. As I listened to him telling Beef who needed a plow blade repaired or a length of chain forged, which horse needed shoeing, Uncle Arlen kept saying I could help with one thing and another.

After a time, Uncle Arlen turned the livery over to Beef. We went back to the house some earlier than usual, and Marion came with us.

19

Uncle Arlen had built the place himself, two rooms up and two rooms down, and he was proud of it. Me and Maude had called it home for five months, starting last December.

Maude took up peeling potatoes for supper. There was hardly any talk, except her saying we ought to put eggs to boil with them. Marion hauled fresh water, and Uncle Arlen stirred the fire.

He was particular about the stove, using birch to get the heat up quickly and a piece of oak to make it last late into the night. Seeing him fuss with it, I said, "Aunt Ruthie missed you worst in winter."

"I doubt she claimed to miss me," he said.

He had me there. Truly, when she missed him, it was more in the nature of a complaint. He thought Aunt Ruthie never forgave him for coming along and robbing her of her place as baby of the family before she had tired of it.

I said, "I think she liked you better than she would admit."

"I'm sure of it," Maude said. "It's just younger brothers are a trial to their big sisters, as Sallie is to me."

I didn't feel I was *enough* of a trial, for she kept me busy, doing one thing and another. Wrap up a wedge of cheese, chop up the last of the ham with some pickle.

These were things we did every day, more or less, and I didn't mind it. This time I knew Maude was making things ready for a journey we weren't a part of, and it bothered me awful.

Once Uncle Arlen had gone upstairs to pack a bag, I said to Maude, "You don't need to make yourself so agreeable."

"I'm not agreeable. I'm cooperative. Look it up if you don't know the difference." She had bought me a dictionary for my birthday and didn't lose an opportunity to tell me to look something up.

Uncle Arlen came back down, and Maude asked if there was anything special he liked to have to eat on the trail. He asked for corn bread sweetened with molasses and went down cellar, where he kept a wad of money hidden in a jar.

"You don't need to cooperate before you've lost the argument."

Maude splashed water, tossing a naked potato into the pot, and said, "We haven't got an argument."

Marion glanced at us. He sat with a burlap sack half filled with walnuts, cracking them into a wooden bowl. As if to no one in particular, he said, "There are things between men you can't interfere with, and debts is one of them. Debts are binding."

Maude said, "You see? Girls don't have an argument."

I said, "Then I think you should go back to your boy clothes."

I was glad to have the distraction when a boat rat scampered away from the heat of the stove, its tail scraping snakily over the boards of the floor.

Maude, quick as lightning, snatched her rifle from up top of the flour cupboard and shot it dead. She was careful to do this only when Uncle Arlen was at home, letting him take the credit with the neighbors.

I picked it up by its tail. "You ain't going to be able to shoot a one of these all the time Uncle Arlen is gone, or it will make the neighbors think," I said, and carried it out to the alley.

I did like to have the last word on a matter.

FIVE

GATHERED AROUND THE TABLE FOR SUPPER, WHEN WE ordinarily gave an account of our day, Uncle Arlen spoke first. "You've heard mention of my friend Macdougal."

Marion looked up from his plate. "The one who found a camel on the Texas plains?"

I said, "Does it need shoes?" And under the table, Maude kicked me in the shins. I wouldn't be run off. "Camels are said to carry men like horses do."

Uncle Arlen ignored this. "Macdougal started a cattle ranch a few years back. I may have told you."

"No, you didn't," Maude said. For someone who'd only this afternoon been talking about going west, she was spider-quiet. I figured her for biding her time.

Myself, I thought of that dream of train tickets and oatmeal cookies. "I believe you could make your distance by train now," I said, "and no danger of Indian attack."

"There's an idea," Marion said. "Been a while since you rode like you were shot out of a cannon."

"I'd never sit down," Uncle Arlen said. "I'd pace the whole distance. Might as well ride easy."

Maude had stopped eating and was biting her nails. She said to him, "What kind of trouble is he in?"

"I'm not real sure."

Our uncle had somewhere picked up a way of talking that told the high points but didn't fill in a lot of detail. This was fine if the person talking to him was in a great hurry. Otherwise, getting the whole story out of him was like picking buckshot.

I said, "What's it *likely* to be?"

With a little shake of his head, he told us, "Macdougal sat it out through drought and windstorms and Indian uprisings, and never called them trouble."

"Sounds like he might should've called the cavalry," Marion said, and was rewarded with a hard look from Uncle Arlen.

"You said you would never go west again," I reminded him. "You said it didn't agree with you."

"Let's don't get alarmed," Uncle Arlen said. "A turned ankle can be an emergency when you got a place to take care of."

Me and Maude and Marion glanced at each other around the table, all of us sure it was worse than a turned ankle.

Maude said, "When are you going?"

"Before first light," he said, and this confirmed our worst fears. He was in an awful hurry to get to the man if he wasn't in any real trouble.

"I'll ride with you," Marion said.

"Me too," Maude said at the same time I did.

"I can't take you girls," Uncle Arlen said. "George Ray counts on Maude. Beef needs you, Sallie, and Marion, both. He won't know which customers are paid up and which ones to collect from."

"You must have someone along to watch your back," I said.

"Not necessary," Uncle Arlen said. "If things are awful bad there in Colorado, maybe I'll just bring Macdougal back with me."

I pulled out my big guns. "He must be a special friend, if you leave your family behind to visit with him."

"Once a man saves your life," Uncle Arlen said, "he's family."

I opened my mouth to ask about Macdougal saving Uncle Arlen's life, but Marion said, "How long you figure to be gone?" Maude had gotten up to cut the dried-cherry pie, but she stilled, waiting for Uncle Arlen's answer.

"It's about three weeks' travel as the crow flies," he said. "But I'm no crow, and I intend to travel good roads, so we'll see."

So it would be three weeks on the back of a horse getting there, and three weeks back again, and however long the trouble held him up. Two months maybe.

"The town is called Liberty," he said, reaching into his shirt pocket. "I've mapped it, if you want to have a look."

From this point, we were silently agreed to act like this was no different than when Uncle Arlen rode out to somebody's place to buy a horse. Like he'd be gone for the day.

I made up my mind to look at the right side of this. Uncle Arlen had said to me more than once it was a necessary part of living with other people to get used to the fact girls weren't always their own bosses. He'd said it a time or two to Maude as well. When I asked her how did she tolerate it, she said she had a place in her mind to go to.

I did not have such a place.

I looked over the map, drawn in Uncle Arlen's own hand on a piece of brown paper, and unfolded it, flattening it on the tabletop. He'd drawn a right fine map, marking the creeks and forts along the way.

I took out my pencil and made a copy.

SIX

M E AND MAUDE AND UNCLE ARLEN SAT AT THE table again the next morning, in the half-light of daybreak. We ate soft-fried eggs and yeast-raised biscuits made the night before, Uncle Arlen's favorite breakfast.

"I want to go with you," Maude said to him, and I perked up. "I don't feel safe here since Sallie came across that poster."

Uncle Arlen said, "Are you talking about *staying* out west?" He glanced up as he scraped the last bit of egg yolk onto a piece of biscuit. "You are."

"I should find out if I could get along there."

"You can't want to lead Sallie out of safety," Uncle Arlen said, "any more than I can take you into unknown danger. Can we talk about this when I get back from Liberty?"

I knew when a horse was dead and so did Maude. She sat at the table, worrying her thumb, while I smoothed my socks and pulled on my boots.

Marion had opened the livery by the time we got there, and he had a horse ready for Uncle Arlen. Me and Maude tied the bedroll and the sack of foodstuffs onto his saddle.

Beef was stoking the fire for a day of bending iron, and Uncle Arlen went back there for a word with him.

"I do hope you girls aren't prone to tearful good-byes," Marion said to us as we worked, "because I'm not much good at back-patting."

"Don't you worry about it," Maude said. "We'll pat each other's backs, and we'll pass you a hankie."

They went back and forth like this until Uncle Arlen got on his horse. "I don't like leaving you girls alone," he said.

Maude's chin firmed up. "Sallie and I can take care of ourselves. We've done it before."

Uncle Arlen looked like he might argue this but thought better of it.

We had no sooner seen Uncle Arlen out the livery door than those boat rats I had seen over at George Ray's came through it, quarrelsome as ever. They wanted to put their horses up with us, reminding us there was a little excitement in town—the trial of the Black Hankie Bandit.

They were only the first of the day. Independence was a busy place, with wagons backed up waiting to turn a corner. But the trial made things worse than any day I'd seen so far. I had to skip school to lend a hand; not a sacrifice. I hoped for a long trial, although many others said they expected to see a hanging that day.

Black Hankie had murdered someone, but the fish were biting and the judge wanted to see it done right soon. A sign had gone up in the window of the courthouse:

HANGMAN WANTED

This made for a general feeling of justice having triumphed, but when those three fellows came for their horses, their spirits were clearly flattened.

Marion was called out to collect a horse, and during this time Beef showed a horse to a sharp-looking fellow, but didn't sell it. I listened in and was convinced Beef knew horseflesh as well as how to bend metal.

As for the buyer, I noticed a line of dirt under his fingernails. This didn't fit with his clothing, which could have cost more than the horse he had in mind.

The business didn't suffer—Uncle Arlen had been right about that much—and I was sorry he wasn't here to see the cash box overflowing.

There had been one sour note to the day. When Marion and me went over to George Ray's to eat, Beef rented out Silver Dollar with a little rig. It didn't surprise me to learn the sharp-looking fellow had come back to strike this deal.

The rig was meant to be rented, along with a horse to pull it, that part was fine. But Uncle Arlen would never have put his favorite horse in the traces.

Marion swore over it up and down.

"Why, then, ain't Arlen riding that horse, if it's his best?" Beef said to me.

"He meant to trade horses all along the way," I said, "to stay on a fresh one."

After a bit, Marion calmed down. "I'm feeling the weight of my responsibilities," he said to Beef, and my breath caught. "But anyone could have done it."

Beef said, "I know it."

"You don't have to worry about me and Maude," I said, once Beef had gone back to the anvil.

Marion looked at me. "What do you mean?"

"We don't want to be a heavy responsibility," I said, and because he appeared to take offense, I steered away to another subject. "I think it grates on Maude that she isn't her own boss."

"I don't know anyone more their own boss," he said. "She has George Ray bent over backwards to get her to bake a pan of cookies."

"It ain't the same thing." I knew this was true, but the difference was hard to put into words.

I hardly had a minute all day to take in the fact of Uncle Arlen having gone west that morning. To let it sink in that he was not coming home with us that night.

When Maude took me over to George Ray's for supper, I said, "I don't have an appetite."

Sounding like Aunt Ruthie, Maude said, "Eat up. I plucked the chickens this morning. You won't find fresher food being served anywhere in the city than right here."

I did eat, but I also thought of Uncle Arlen needing a better horse and coming back because he wanted only his own stock, such as Silver Dollar or that big sorrel Maude rode. I didn't really want a lame horse to befall my uncle; it was just Independence didn't feel so much like home without him.

Something else had been at the back of my mind all day, and I mulled it over now. I didn't like to be childish, but I wanted to hear myself counted Macdougal's equal.

I felt in my pocket for the copy of Uncle Arlen's map.

"We should have gone with him," Maude said, pushing her clean plate away. "I'm a better shot than he is any day."

"I'm going to tie my ankle to yours while we sleep," I said, for I didn't care to get left behind twice in the same day.

She offered a flirty smile. "I didn't know you for such a sentimental type."

"Don't go without me," I said. "I want your word on it."

"I swear it on my fingertips," she said, and kissed each of them on her right hand.

We didn't go home, but back to the livery, where Maude asked Marion to play a game of checkers.

To keep my spirits up, she gave me a dime out of her waistband and sent me over to Mr. Palmer's store. This was unusual generous of Maude, who didn't care for dimers, and who could hold tighter to a penny than Aunt Ruthie ever did.

I purchased that latest in the adventures of Powder Keg McCarthy, a soldier who'd found himself at loose ends once the war was over. I bought some pretty red-and-white candy sticks for Maude.

Maude took the candy gladly. While she and Marion played checkers under the brass Rochester lamp that hung from a beam, the sharp sweetness of peppermint brightened the livery air. I sat down to read by the lamplight and let their voices fade from my notice.

It so happened Keg was in Kansas, hired to protect a small town from some local rowdies. They didn't sound a smart bunch, the townspeople, that is, always fighting over who had the best hiding place or falling out of the barn loft or wandering off alone.

But Keg got the women and children together in the

church, which was the nearest thing to a fort they had, and told them to ring the church bell if the rowdies showed up.

"Sallie, it's time to go home." Maude was sliding the checkers into the box.

I helped Marion put feed bags on a few horses that were staying the night; eighteen more of them than we had stalls for.

"Your uncle didn't count on us having more horses than stalls," he said. "I'm going to hunker down against the wall out there and make sure none of those nags go missing from the corral before morning. Or at least we're paid for our services before they do."

I said, "I know what we can do—"

"You and Maude can't sleep in the loft," Marion said.

SEVEN

THIS NOTION TOOK HOLD OF ME. I KEPT WONDERING about me and Maude following Uncle Arlen by train out there to Colorado Territory. C.T., folks called it. If that letter came, making Maude a free woman, we could read it when we got back.

As things worked out, I had reason to look again at my copy of the map only two days later. Maude came across the street from George Ray's, bringing a jar of hot bean soup for the midday meal.

The day had been cloudy and oddly chill for April, and I pressed my fingers against the jar. "Sit with us," Marion said to Maude.

"Not today, I can't," she said. "It's busy as a hive over there. They made up their minds to hang Black Hankie tomorrow."

A boy came in then, bearing another message from Macdougal. He was a boy I'd been forced to whomp to cut down on his remarks about my name. One good thing about being a boy is never having to worry over being liked. One good whomp and everybody likes you fine.

"'Sfer Arlen Waters," he said.

Maude put her hand out, and he gave it over, never turning a hair upon hearing my sister bore a boy's name.

She opened the fold of paper and read aloud:

TOO LATE FOR ME STOP THEY HAVE THIS DAY STAMPEDED MY CATTLE SHOT MY FATHER BURNED DOWN THE BARN STOLEN MY HORSE AND KILLED MY DOG STOP I AM NIGH TO GIVING UP STOP MACDOUGAL

I grabbed the telegram and read it for myself. "Who are they?" I didn't like to think of Uncle Arlen having to face them.

Maude dropped to sit on a hay bale as if all her strength had left her. "Too late? Does that mean Mr. Macdougal wanted to stop Uncle Arlen from coming?"

"I have to go out there," Marion said. "Your uncle was expecting one more man to fight on their side and that man's been shot."

"We all have to go out there," Maude said.

"I don't know what I'm riding into," Marion said. "I'm not about to drag you girls into it."

"I am tired to death of being called 'you girls,'" I said to him. "It's only to kill the argument we have that anyone ever says it."

"Sallie's right," Maude said. "We're as capable as boys."

"More capable," I said, thinking of some of the boys I'd met thereabouts. They tended to look scruffy but could not necessarily hold their own in a scuffle. I had easily whomped a couple of them for speaking too admiringly of my sister. This would've embarrassed them a great deal more had they known they were fighting a girl.

"Your uncle would never forgive me if I took you along with me," Marion said.

"There is that," Maude said.

"Maude! Are we just to sit here like ticks on a cow while Uncle Arlen rides to a sorry fate?"

"Now, Sallie, don't take on like that," Marion said. "His fate isn't something you could change, even if you did catch up to him."

In her most outraged tones, Maude said, "You do expect us to sit here and wait like ticks on a cow! What kind of females do you take us for?"

"Now, Maude—"

"Don't you use that coddling tone with me," she said. "Sallie and I are making ready to ride. I'm going over to George Ray's to collect three days' pay."

I said, "I'll get our horses saddled."

Maude hurried outside to dash through a break in the rough stream of horses and wagons. I climbed to the loft.

I didn't have to look into my sack to know it held a tin cup, a pot, a long-handled spoon, my gun kit, a box of cartridges that were a match to Marion's gun, half a wedge of matches, my compass, my pouch with a few dollars in it, and an empty canteen. I checked this cache nearly every day, sometimes adding to the sum in the pouch, more often taking money to buy a dimer. Saving was not in my nature.

I threw the loop of the canteen over my head and climbed down.

"I guess somebody better tell Beef he's on his own," Marion said. He headed back toward the anvil. I took this to mean he would be coming with me and Maude.

These last words were no sooner spoken than a shot rang out across the street, lifting bits of the building's roof shakes into the air.

Horses startled.

I yelled, "Maude!"

Pedestrians scattered like pebbles.

EIGHT

Every living thing in the vicinity had jumped at the shot, and all up and down the street, horses were prancing, circling, trying to unseat their riders.

I ran outside, only to have Marion yank me back by my shirt collar.

"Don't go running over there, Sallie."

"My sister," I cried, near wild. "Maude!"

She came out of the door across the street, her arms pulled behind her, a burly man pushing her ahead of him. My head swam at the sight; I might could have fainted. He was the law, I had no doubt.

Maude's face looked burned from the sun, but I knew better. It was hard not to care when people you talked to every day watched you get arrested.

I drew breath to yell again, but Marion put a hand over my mouth and hauled me back into the dim of the livery. From there we watched the surge of the midday dinner crowd as they spilled into the street, making Maude the head of her own parade.

Behind us, the anvil rang like a warning bell come late.

"Marion," I said behind his hand, and he loosened me somewhat. "What will we do?"

"I'm thinking, Sallie."

"Well, what are you thinking?"

"Saddle me a horse." He hurried off after the crowd following Maude.

I was shaking as I brought out Marion's horse and mine, the only horse that belonged to me and Maude free and clear. By the time I had those horses tied to a rail so I could throw a saddle on them, the shaking had left me and I was thinking.

I brought out the horse Uncle Arlen let Maude ride, the big sorrel with a blaze on its face. Most of the lawmen who came to town for Black Hankie's trial were still in town. It didn't take much of a leap for me to figure on those fellows agreeing to hang my sister just as quick. Save themselves another trip.

There was no question of leaving her in there.

Beef came to the front of the barn, wondering what the gunshot meant. "You all going for a ride?" he said, seeing what I was about.

He had to give me a hand with the saddles. The horses weren't bothered by gunshots when we rode out to hunt, but they had been in the stalls all morning and so were in high spirits as well as somewhat startled.

"I couldn't stop in the midst of fixing that plow blade," Beef said, still talking about the gunshot, "but it sure got my curiosity up."

"Probably some fellow working off a drink or two," I said to him. He was a sweet fellow, and I didn't like to lie to him. I didn't care to tell him Maude had been arrested. He would find out sooner or later, but later was better.

I hoped he wouldn't think too poorly of us for keeping our secrets. He'd liked Maude a great deal.

"Where did Marion go?"

"To get Maude," I said. "We've been meaning to tell you. We're planning to follow Uncle Arlen."

"There's a good idea," Beef said. "I didn't want to say nothing, but I'm afraid Arlen used up a cat's nine lives on his last trip."

As we saddled the horses, I said, "Should anyone come looking for Marion or me, don't tell them which direction we took. If they ask after Uncle Arlen, say he told you he wanted to see his sister, Ruthie, back east."

"How long ago did you leave?" Beef said to me. He was a sharper nail than he looked.

I didn't want him to get into trouble unnecessarily. "Today will do well enough," I said.

As I tied my sack to the saddle horn, I noticed the jar of bean soup, which would soon grow cold. I pointed it out to Beef. "Maude brought you dinner. It smelled good to me."

"Much obliged."

I ran to the closet at the back of the livery for my shotgun, then snatched up the sack of Maude's own molasses cookies I'd put there early in the morning to keep them safe from the chipmunk. I didn't know how long Marion planned to sit outside the jail, but I didn't like going without a meal.

Seeing I didn't need any further help, Beef went back to fixing the plow. His fire had died down some, and he had no sooner started to work the bellows than Marion came in.

Beef kept his back turned to us, I noticed. What he didn't know he couldn't tell. My appreciation for him was growing by the moment.

Marion knew immediately why I was holding three horses. "You can't come with me, Sallie."

"What have they done with Maude?"

"She's in jail," he said, surprising me not at all.

"But what did you find out?" I said. "You must know something more than that."

"I could hardly walk in there and say, 'I'm Joe Harden, the one who robbed that bank in Des Moines, if you want to get your facts straight, and I'd like to know what you plan to do with my friend Mad Maude,' now can I?"

"What are we going to do?" I expected he'd been working on some story to give the sheriff.

In a dimer I read once, Cheating Charlie's brother got him out of jail by passing a red pencil through the barred window. Then going in as if he was a doctor, he pointed to the pencil marks on Charlie's face and said, "That fellow is sickening with something contagious."

I doubted Marion could pass for a doctor.

He didn't have much of a plan, either. "I'm going to keep an eye on that jail."

"I'm going with you."

"There's some things a man has to do alone," he said, and when I opened my mouth, he added, "There's other people who ought to let him."

"One by one my family is being carried off by unfortunate circumstances," I said. "I cannot stand still and watch it happen to Maude."

Marion got on his horse and rode out, his face set, determined.

I put a foot in the stirrup and slung my other leg over, driving the shotgun into the cloth boot at the saddle horn. I took the reins to lead Maude's horse. Used to the city life, he didn't get tetchy in crowds.

I rode out at a pace and spotted Marion just as he turned a corner. I kicked up my horse, anxious not to let him out of my sight for long.

NINE

I NEEDN'T HAVE WORRIED. MARION WAS WAITING FOR ME around that corner. He'd brought his horse to a halt right in the middle of the street. Horses had to make their way around him as if he was a boulder, with no complaint from the riders. This was no doubt due to the dark look on Marion's face.

"Don't give me any more of a fight," he said. "Time's a-wastin'."

"Then let's ride." I looked hard back at him.

He motioned for me to come closer, and I did, pulling my horse up alongside his. With a creak of saddle leather, he leaned in near. Although it was unlikely anyone could hear us over the noise of the street, he said into my ear, "I don't want you anywhere nearby if I break that jail."

"You're going to bust Maude out?"

"Shh!"

This was better than I'd hoped for. I lowered my voice to say, "Are you carrying enough firepower? You might have to kill a few lawmen."

Marion pushed his hat up off his forehead. "What kind of man do you take me for?"

"One who's thinking of jail-breaking my sister."

He turned his horse and rode. I followed him through the city, and I didn't fall behind. I knew better than to bother him with my questions. He still wore that dark look.

Left to my own thoughts, I wished that telegram had come the day before. Or that Uncle Arlen had consented to take us along. I started to wonder if it was the letter I wrote to the sheriff that gave Maude away somehow.

Uncle Arlen had said I should give it to someone riding out of town, let them mail it somewhere else along the line. I could not bear the thought of wondering when my letter might get posted, never mind worrying about whether it got lost entire. So I sent it from Independence.

Now I wished I had taken Uncle Arlen's part when he told Maude she ought not keep that job at George Ray's. Marion had taken Uncle Arlen's part.

Marion hadn't yet said one word to me. I'd been doing my best to look as if I wasn't speaking to him, either, but this was an effort wasted. He hardly noticed me.

We took up a position on the street.

The jailhouse was a two-story building with a brick front. It looked a lot like a hotel, except for the bars on the windows. I didn't see how we could take Maude out of there.

Some hours later, when full dark had fallen, we were still sitting on our horses about a block from the jailhouse. There were fewer people on the street than in daylight, but there was no letup in wagon traffic that I could see.

"I want to ride past that building a time or two, see how many lawmen are inside," Marion said, breaking his silence.

"Don't start up without telling me what you're up to," I said. "I want to be ready."

"I plan to study the situation a while longer," Marion said. "I can't make a mess of it, like that bank robbery I fumbled."

"You got out with the money," I said. "Even if Maude did make you send it back. It isn't your fault we walked in on you at a crucial moment."

"It's the things a man does not take into account that trip him up," he said.

"We need to think it through," I said to him. "How many lawmen do you figure we have to overcome?"

"*We,*" Marion said firmly, "are not overcoming anybody. Don't mess with me over this, Sallie."

"Do you want a molasses cookie?" I asked him, and held out the sack.

"Believe I will," he said.

"A boy can go nearly anywhere and never be noticed," I said as he took two cookies. "That's more than a man can get away with."

I took only one cookie, thinking to save the others for Maude.

"What do you have in mind?" Marion said.

"I can stand outside looking in, and nobody would think anything of it." He chewed thoughtfully through one cookie, and then he told me what I was to look for.

I handed him the reins to Maude's horse.

A few minutes later, I rode past the jailhouse. I took my

time, noticing an alley between the jail and the next building. No gates I could see.

There were brass lamps hanging from the ceiling on the first floor of the jailhouse, but the windows were cloudy. Dirty, most likely. I got off my horse and put my face right against one.

I spotted a back door. More than anything else, I saw this was just any old day to them around the desk. Others of us were having our lives ruined at their hands; they could at least put their games aside.

I rode back to Marion. I said, "There's an alleyway and a back door. I saw four on duty."

"I can handle four," he said, "if I can get the drop on them."

"*I* could get the drop on them," I said. "They were playing cards."

TEN

"YOU WAIT HERE," HE SAID TO ME, TAKING MY SHOTGUN.

"That doesn't seem like the right kind of weaponry to face down four pistols."

"It'll pepper them all if I have to let a shot go at close range," he said. "I'm counting on it none of them will want to catch a pellet."

"The fellow that had his back to the window faces the door you're going to use," I said. "He would be the one to watch out for." Behind these words, I was making up my mind to a thing or two.

It was what Uncle Arlen had said exactly: Once a man has saved your life, he's family. "Tell me the truth," I said to Marion. "Are me and Maude going to be orphans again?"

"Not if I have anything to say about it," he told me.

He rode away looking to me like a man who intended to live through something, which was as much as I could ask of him. Like I was feeling for a good-luck piece, I checked that Uncle Arlen's map was deep in my pocket.

When I was fair to certain I wouldn't run right into the back of Marion, I squared my shoulders and headed for the jailhouse. As luck would have it, I rode up just as Maude came to the window.

In the dark, I saw her shape only, with a pale light behind her. But it looked to me like she set her hands against the window sudden like.

I tied our horses to a rail and tightened the cinches on both saddles. Doing this, I realized how hard I was shaking. Even my horse had the jitters.

Not Maude's. That animal looked relaxed enough to fall asleep right there in the middle of the street. I wished some of that calm would rub off on me and my horse.

I looked back up at the window for a long minute and then made a motion with my arm like I was swiping at bugs in the air. But I pointed my finger, trying to make Maude know she would have to take her own horse and ride off that way.

I startled at what I guessed to be Marion's shadow slipping into that alleyway—I thought he would've been back of the jailhouse already. It wouldn't do for him to bust in without I had at least tried to provide some distraction.

A great howling rose up in me and I let it loose. I twisted the doorknob and nearly fell inside, making a noise to raise the dead. The deputy with his back to the door turned to me. "Here now," he said.

The other two deputies got up, laying down their cards, and the sheriff himself pulled me more into the center of things. I let out more of a wail than I meant to.

The first deputy said, "Is he bleeding anywheres?"

The back door flew open and hit the wall. It was like a gunshot, the way that noise stopped my breath.

Marion stepped inside, his hands in the air.

No shotgun. It might could've been a trick of his own but for the look on his face that said he had fumbled again.

My heart went out to him. I'd learned there was more to being a hero than the glory parts. The glory parts wore a little tarnish if you looked real close. It didn't make the hero any less of one.

Another fellow came behind him, short and tough-looking. I recognized him right away for the smarter one of those boat rats from George Ray's.

The other two stepped in behind that one, bigger rats, with guns and rifles pointing every which way. Those fellows were armed like porcupines.

The law stood quiet, expectant.

Even I went quiet.

The sheriff's hand drifted toward his gun belt. "Hands up! Hold 'em high," the little rat shouted. At the same time, another rat's rifle swiveled in our direction.

I screamed.

He didn't shoot but kept that dark eye trained on us. The sheriff stood undecided, his hand half on the draw.

Upstairs, someone pounded on a door.

That weakened the sheriff's already wavering resolve.

"Ain't nobody going to get hurt if you don't do nothing stupid," the little rat said. He looked ready to use his gun. He looked dead serious. With a nod, he sent one of the standing deputies back to his chair.

Motioned to him to hold his arms higher.

Another prisoner started thumping, and in the next moment everybody up there started a-banging on the doors. The fellow pointing a gun at us said, "Let's get on with this."

The little rat poked Marion hard in the back. "Collect their guns one at a time. Hold each of them by the barrel, and keep it up where I can see. Drop them in that there waste can real easy like. We wouldn't want one to go off by accident."

Marion did exactly that, and all the while the pounding didn't stop. It got louder and more measured, like some of them were switching from fists to boot heels.

Meanwhile, the little rat kept a sharp lookout for trouble; his gun moved to point at the next fellow in line for Marion's attention. As the last gun dropped into the bucket with a clatter, he said, "Good game, boys?" and swept the playing cards to the floor with his gun.

It did my heart good to see that.

The last rat snatched the key ring off a hook and said, "Where are you holding Black Hankie, poor innercent that he is?"

This fellow flicked an angry glance around the room, and I made good use of his attention when it landed on me. I still had one hand to my chest, and I pointed straight to where I had no doubt Maude stood behind a locked door, right above us.

The rat headed on upstairs, the keys jangling all the way. The little rat shouted to him, "Let them all out."

"You can't do that," the sheriff said. "We've got Mad Maude up there."

The gun-pointing-at-us rat grinned. "Maybe you'll just chase her instead of Hankie, once we're all out of here."

"We'll chase Hankie," one of the sitting deputies said in deep tones. "He's due to hang, and we wouldn't want him to miss the fun."

A kind of chill ran through me, making my teeth chatter.

The little rat banged him on the ear with the butt of his rifle, and the deputy yowled with pain.

With one foot, Marion scooted that bucket toward the back door. "Check their boots," the little rat said. "Make sure there's no guns hidden there."

"Take them off," Marion said, giving one of the lawmen a kick at the ankle. "Boots and britches, let's have them."

"Well, I won't—" the sheriff said.

But the little rat raised the butt of his rifle again. "You heard him," he said to the sheriff. Everybody wearing a star began to tug at their boots. To Marion, the little rat said, "Good thinking, pard."

I heard Maude's voice upstairs, sounding angry and confused. More than that I couldn't tell, for the pounding near drowned her out.

The first wild desperado, white-haired and toothless, came reeling down the stairs in his socks, looking like a leaf being blown by a strong wind, and left the door open. Maude couldn't be far behind.

"Son, you better get on your way," Marion said to me. "I don't believe your momma would like the kinda company you're standing around with."

I hated to leave just then, but I knew it would make things go more smoothly if I did.

"Hold on there, boy," the little rat said. "I want your solemn oath you ain't gonna run out there and sound an alarum."

"Nosir. My solemn." I started to back toward the door I'd come in by.

"You look like a trustworthy fella."

"Yessir." Two more steps and I stood on the boardwalk.

ELEVEN

NO ONE APPEARED TO HAVE NOTICED THE DOINGS AT the jailhouse. I shut the door and leaned on it. I couldn't hear the pounding outside those brick walls. I flipped the reins off the rail and got on my horse, trying to look like I had no place in particular to go, careful that no one would wonder what my hurry was. My blood was racing, and like my horse could feel it, he danced in place.

I backed him out into the wagon traffic and rode to the corner, telling myself I wasn't going to have a long wait. Indeed, I saw some action at the jailhouse.

The door opened and two men hopped out like rabbits, both of them carrying their boots. Didn't want to take time to put them on, I guess. They hurried off in different directions. No one paid them any mind that I could see.

That was three fellows jail-broke so far, and done without a single gunshot fired. As I watched for Maude, that very thought went round and round in my head, *not a gunshot fired*.

About the sixth time around, it was getting old and I began to feel a little ragged.

Then shots broke out.

At the same moment, Maude burst out of the door, her skirt swirling around the tops of her shoes.

I stood in my stirrups and saw clearly the way she ran and perched for an instant on the hitching rail and, with a flash of white petticoat, leapt onto her horse and kicked it into a run.

She was a sight to behold.

Me and Maude locked eyes immediately, like she knew right where to find me. She came at me at a gallop.

This didn't make her especially noticeable, because horses and riders alike had been startled by the shots and were jigging every which way. A frightened horse pulling an empty wagon racketed past me.

I headed my horse in the direction we ought to go.

More shots rang out.

I looked back and Maude was right behind me all the way. I did not yet know what the gunshots meant, only no matter how things turned out, Maude and me were embarked on a new twist of fate.

There was something wild in me at that moment, wild and even joyful, as my hair whipped against the back of my neck.

Much as if every horse on the street had heard a whispering in its ear, the traffic parted to leave a clear path for us. I picked up speed, and out of all the horses jog-stepping around me, I heard only the rough rhythm of our horses' hooves, Maude's and mine.

What a strange time for a memory to come to me, but there it was, me and Maude and Aunt Ruthie in the middle of a sunlit afternoon, daisies threaded through our hair, dandelion seeds a-floating as we spun about in dizzying circles.

I felt back then that my chest was near to bursting with happiness. I felt the same way now, completely lost in the run of our lives. I was near to flying.

Me and Maude were at the center of an adventure, after all, and I didn't mind it. For Marion was part of it, and Uncle Arlen wasn't all that far ahead. It didn't hurt there was no snow on the ground and months to go before we'd see another flake.

There was still a good deal of traffic abroad at the edge of the district, but no one looked at us. When two horses passed each other, the dust raised to choke a person.

We didn't amble, but we didn't push the horses hard. We knew to save them in case we needed to get some more speed out of them later.

Maude pulled up beside me, and I saw her usually neat hair was all afly. She said, "You weren't *with* those men."

My breath caught. I saw right off the flaw in our planning. Maude had strong notions about right and wrong, and jailbreak would just naturally fall into line with her idea of wrong.

"Marion and me had to throw in with them at the last moment, more like."

"What does that mean?" Maude said.

"It means we got there, and they got there at the same time, with a plan of their own," I said. "We couldn't ask them to come back later."

She shushed me and waited till we had a little distance between ourselves and any other rider. "It bothers me to think of you talking with them," she said.

"I didn't talk to them." Maude could be worse than Aunt Ruthie for wanting to be sure she had raised me to know better. But it did seem to me a jailbreak ought not to have rules of conduct. "They came in the back with Marion. He didn't look like he was on speaking terms with them."

Maude said, "I wish you weren't mixed up in this."

"I know that. But I couldn't leave you in there. Nor could Marion."

"It's still wrong, what you did, Sallie. What we did."

I said to her, "Did anybody get shot?"

"I don't know," she said. "I didn't hang around long enough to find out."

This made me grin. I didn't let Maude see it.

She said, "Do you think the sheriff and his deputies were doing the shooting?"

"I believe all their guns were in the waste can."

Maude said, "Chances are good they'd be gunning for the one that made them shuck their pants."

I flinched on hearing this. But I kept quiet. Maude might turn around and go back, and we couldn't afford a change of mind. I kept quiet for probably three minutes. Three long minutes.

I watched back along the trail.

"Marion won't come the same way we're riding," Maude said in the tone of a big sister who has done this a thousand times before. "He'll work his way around to us. Are we headed west?"

"Yep, we're following Uncle Arlen's map."

"He'll catch up," Maude said.

TWELVE

ANOTHER HORSE PULLED UP CLOSE BEHIND US AND stayed there. This wasn't so unusual, since lone riders at night did tend to clump together. Me and Maude let our talk die down.

It was a fair part of an hour later before we could talk freely again. Maude had been doing some thinking of her own. She said, "I saw you come in, and only a minute or two later this rough-looking fellow opens my door. Why didn't he open the other fellow's door?"

"How was he to know who was behind each door?" I said. I wouldn't admit to any communication with them at all.

"He acted like he knew me from somewhere."

"You waited on them at George Ray's," I said. "Besides that, the sheriff dropped a word about you being up there."

"Big mouth," Maude said of the sheriff. "As for those others, I served them beans and a slab of corn bread, and they wanted to break me out of jail?"

"They let you all out. They're Black Hankie's gang," I said in a near whisper. Voices carry on the night air, and another rider was approaching, going toward Independence.

"I believe he's an innocent victim of circumstance, like you. Black Hankie, I mean," I said when we were alone again. This may have stretched the truth, but I couldn't think of a better time to do it.

Maude waited until that rider had passed us by. "Where did you hear that?"

"I overheard them at George Ray's."

"I just wish Marion hadn't let you take part in this," Maude said.

"He didn't; I let myself in on it," I said, forgetting to keep my voice down. "We don't know for sure that Marion or Uncle Arlen is safe, either one. Don't be mad till you know for sure we ain't alone in the world again, for Pete's sake."

It could be argued we were foolish to stick to the trail, knowing a posse would sooner or later come down the same road. But we were sure of our direction, and we made good time.

The moon gave off just enough shine to make gopher holes of every pocket of shadow, which would've slowed us down considerable had we ridden off-trail. Low bushes looked very like something crouching there.

We continued a brisk pace and stayed alert. We rode till we hadn't seen anyone ahead of us or behind us for some time; we were near to being alone on the road.

The good side of this was, neither Maude's wild red hair nor her manner of riding were so likely to be noticed in the dark. Maude had gone back to riding like a boy. Once daylight came, she was someone who was bound to be noticed.

When we came upon a creek, we drew up to let the horses

drink. Maude said, "Someone had peed on the mattress. I couldn't sit on it."

"You couldn't stay in there."

"I couldn't have gone without you, either," Maude said. "Not even knowing Uncle Arlen needed my help."

"Our help," I said, and Maude grinned.

I thought things were going good, in a way. Maude was free and as ready as me to beat it for Colorado Territory. "I saved the last three molasses cookies for you," I said, and held the sack out to her. She took two and motioned at me to take the other one.

Maude said, "They talked about hanging me. Like the other one."

"Black Hankie, you mean." It bothered me to think of her listening to talk like that. "Did you tell them your reputation is undeserved?"

"I did," she said. "It gave them a good laugh."

"How'd they know to find you at George Ray's, do you think?"

"Somebody saw my face on the newspaper under their plate and realized I'd served them their dinner," Maude said.

I said, "It must have been an old one," for we had been living a quiet life at Uncle Arlen's. Maude hadn't shown up at the scene of anything more serious than the killing of a chicken.

"They had a paper, two weeks old," Maude said. "I might have been all right if I had ignored the fellow who called out my name."

"Maude Waters?" For she'd been answering to Uncle Arlen's and Aunt Ruthie's last name for some time.

"Maude March. I turned around, Sallie, and gave myself away."

"Anybody else would've done the same," I said.

"Not true." Her shoulders slumped with those words. "Or there would be more outlaws in the jails."

"Why would you be mentioned in the papers now?" I asked her.

"I don't know. They wouldn't give me time to read it." She brushed the cookie crumbs off her skirt in a ladylike way that didn't take into account she was sitting astraddle her horse. "This is my own fault. I used to be more watchful of the papers we were laying down."

"You can't kick yourself over this," I said. "You don't do nothing but wait on tables and go home and to church on Sundays. You are as proper as they come. Besides, you aren't the only person who papers the tables."

"I should have laid low," Maude said. "Uncle Arlen told me, and I didn't listen." She gigged her horse and trotted ahead.

"You couldn't have laid any lower if you had set up housekeeping in a rabbit burrow," I said, following her. For good measure, I added the argument she'd made to Uncle Arlen: "Somebody around us would've gotten curious about you if you didn't show your face."

Maude sat a little straighter. "That's true."

I kept watch for Marion, but we rode around anything that looked like a settlement and took no more apparent interest in other riders than to nod as we passed them.

As the hours crept by, we saw fewer riders.

Cloud cover rolled in somewheres after midnight, but

even with the moon in hiding, we had the benefit of some kind of reflected light. I thought it a strange thing that in full moonless dark, the earth could be read as light and dark shadows, the stomped-down trail being lightest and the shapes of bush and tree being darkest.

Some time later, Maude woke me.

THIRTEEN

"I CAN'T LET YOU SLEEP ON YOUR HORSE," SHE SAID. "I'M afraid you'll fall off."

She'd already struck out across the grassland, where we shortly came upon a dry creek bed deep enough to provide cover for the horses.

Coming off the horses, we stood a minute on sore feet, getting used to the idea of walking. I wondered sometimes why no one mentioned in dimers how long hours in the saddle made the feet swell.

We clambered down the bank by moonlight and by touch, where the horses might graze the greener grass. At least I suspected it was greener. It was silkier to my fingertips, and so I figured more tender fodder.

We wiped the horses down, turned the blankets over, and saddled them up again in case we had to make an escape. Maude said, "Maybe Marion will catch up to us here."

I heard a kind of rumbling noise.

I didn't pay attention to it right away. I was running a hand down my horse's leg, twisting a hobble to keep him from wandering off.

"What is that?" Maude said.

"Riders," I hurried over to the bank of the creek and climbed halfway up. There in the darkness, I saw three or maybe four riders, but we were far enough off the trail they didn't see us. This was likely very good luck.

"Posse?" she said.

"I don't know." I made my way back to where Maude stood soothing our horses. "It didn't look like enough men to be a posse."

Maude said, "I feel like we ought to hide, but then, we are. Hiding."

My stomach was churning, realizing we'd just had a close call. But then, maybe I was just hungry. I said, "I wish we had some cookies left."

"See, that's why you are convincing as a boy," Maude said. "Your stomach runs your brain."

We stood at a kind of attention until the only sounds came from the horses, and from Maude biting her nails. She said, "How many men do they send out, do you think?"

I tried to think of any chases I had ever read of in a dimer. "Eight or ten is likely," I said. "So they can split up when half the gang goes one way and half the other."

"Why would the gang do that?"

"So the posse will follow just the one set of tracks."

"You just said they take enough men to split up."

"It sounds pretty tricky when you read about it," I said.

Maude made a little "hmph" sound to herself. Probably she regretted asking me what I might have learned from a dimer. "They don't always have a dry creek bed to hide in," I said to her.

She said, "I'm getting worried about Marion."

"He knows how to shake off a posse."

"Are you sure he knew where to look for us?"

"He has surprised us before," I said, "passing us and waiting for us to catch up to him."

"Only once," she said. "Not right after breaking me out of jail, either."

I didn't have a reply to this.

The air had begun to look blue; morning wasn't far away. We settled ourselves in the knee-high grass, but I couldn't sleep. My mind was humming. I rolled over, hoping a view of the stars would quiet me.

There were birds calling to each other in low, sleepy voices.

"Are those wood doves?" Maude asked me.

"Are you thinking of popping a few?" I said.

"No."

I was glad to hear it. Maude's rifle was back there in the kitchen. Because Marion took my shotgun with him, we didn't have a weapon to our name.

"Beans are fine for a day or two, if we can get hold of any," she said. "I don't want to make a fire. Somebody might notice us. We aren't so well outfitted for this, are we?"

"We have my compass and the copy of Uncle Arlen's map and a canteen," I said. "We have horses and the fair chance of finding well water to put into the canteen sooner or later."

At this, Maude made a strange sound that might have been laughter. "You are a practical woman."

"At least it's not dead winter," I said. "We ain't likely to freeze."

"Don't say 'ain't' to me. It makes my teeth ache."

"They wouldn't do that if you wouldn't grind them together so."

"Are you asleep yet?" she said.

I wasn't asleep, and didn't think I would sleep. I'd forgotten what a busy place the grass was, the wind rustling through, the cautious passing of any kind of bug or small creature you could name. It never failed to leave me with a fellow feeling, for when we slept in the grass, we were living by much the same laws as them, where every moment might be our last.

"I'm an outlaw, Sallie," my sister said. "That can't be changed now."

I wanted to argue this. Wanted at least to say it wasn't true until now. For she was more of one now than she had been when she got out of bed this morning.

Me and Marion had acted to save her, never asking ourselves, was this what Maude would have chosen?

Maude was speaking low when she added, "I have been an outlaw since the day we left Cedar Rapids. It's time to know things for what they are."

"Then we're both outlaws," I said to her just as low. "We left Cedar Rapids together."

"No, Sallie," she said. "I don't think you are."

"Why not?" I said, and I was thinking, I'm the one who killed a man.

I didn't say it. Maude would rather I put it this way: "I was holding a gun that went off."

I didn't need to mince words with the truth. He was an awful black-hearted sort of man bent on killing someone else.

He had in mind no one in particular, just someone who wasn't likely to kill him back.

The long and short of it was, if I hadn't made the mistake of pulling on that gun by its trigger, he'd probably have done in someone more innocent than me by now.

I reminded myself of this every time I woke from a black dream of shooting him, feeling cold and damp. I thought about how, somewhere, someone would've been missing a loved one if he had his way.

Maude said, "You don't watch for things to go wrong the way I do, Sallie. It would break my heart if you did, so don't feel bad that you're still a little girl at bottom."

I knew myself to be as much an outlaw as Maude believed herself to be. If she thought it was pure chance I noticed her picture on a poster and didn't know I regularly watched for a badge under a man's jacket, then that was fine.

One thing Maude didn't need was a broken heart.

FOURTEEN

It wasn't with what I'd call a complaint that I woke up an hour or so later to feel a tenderness where I'd slept hard against a pebble. I was grateful I wasn't waking up to being chased. I wasn't waking up to look into the dark eye of somebody's gun. But I did wish I had kept bedrolls in the loft.

Maude had slept sitting up. I thought of a comb, first thing. Bad enough her hair was bright; she couldn't let it get into a worse snarl without drawing every eye to herself.

The horses woke now and again for a few minutes of grazing, the way horses will. The moon had sunk low in the west, and in the east, clusters of deep purple and night-blue clouds were outlined in a fierce orange light.

I sat in the center of a kind of silence, and yet there were small sounds all about me; something in me stretched to hear them. I missed this when sleeping in a bed.

A mosquito whined in my ear, and I lost my friendly feeling toward waking in the grass. I swiped at the air, suddenly itching from bug bites up and down. I had to scratch so bad I wondered if I'd picked up fleas or chiggers.

The creek bed was dry as powder, I already knew. There wasn't a smidgen of mud to spread on an itchy spot. I scratched quietly at each complaint. Yet I didn't fail to notice how green and clean the air smelled. It was a far cry from the way of people and horses living elbow to hock in the city.

I watched all around us for lamplight that wouldn't have been on two hours before. There were no windows, but there was a lone slow-moving buggy in the distance, just a dark silhouette against a lavender stripe of sky.

I saw when Maude came awake, not with a start but with a deeper breath. Like she'd never shut an eye, she said, "No sign of Marion." She sounded like she was telling me, but she couldn't disguise the hope in her voice.

"None."

"Let me have a look at your map," she said, and I handed it over.

The last couple of years, '68 and '69, had been real bad for fighting Indians, was the talk I heard around the livery. Some said the Indians finally understood these white men weren't just a parade passing through, but a whole lot of trouble come to stay.

Others said it had more to do with the railroads paying a bounty for buffalo skins—a mile-wide herd crossing the tracks in their own good time could put a nasty crimp in a train's schedule. Likely the Indians were angered at the sight of so much good meat going to waste.

Uncle Arlen tended to agree with the camp that felt Custer kept stirring them up. "A man can get used to most anything if he's let to make peace with it," Uncle Arlen said. "These people aren't being given anything but a hard time."

Plus there was Jesse James and Black Hankie and other fellows like them thick as fleas on a hound out there, according to the newspapers. To say nothing of the posse that was looking for us.

It was pure craziness to head west of Independence without guns and a sackful of bullets. But Maude was only thinking about the map. "This trail is as crooked as a dog's leg."

When Maude looked away I judged her to be perplexed. "Uncle Arlen set out on the safest route he knew," I said.

"What's that?" Maude said, staring off toward that rig on the horizon.

"Somebody riding through the night, like us," I said.

"No, I mean, behind him."

I looked, and after a minute or so I could see there was a big cloud of dust building behind the buggy.

"That's a posse for sure," I said. It could be nothing else, looking like a howler wind coming down the trail at daybreak.

"Let's ride," Maude said, starting up.

I yanked her back. "Don't let's move or they'll be following our dust cloud."

The buggy appeared to have stopped. Or maybe the speed of the other riders made it look like they'd swallowed it up. I could feel the slightest shiver in the earth beneath me, the thunder of horses' hooves moving over it.

There were more of them than eight or ten; there may have been twenty.

The men on horseback swirled around the buggy for a minute or two—a nerve-grating, teeth-grinding minute or two—no doubt questioning that fellow about whether he'd seen anybody else on the trail.

Then they rode on, still tight to the trail, still flogging their horses up to a dead run, leaving the buggy rider in peace. They also left him in a cloud of their dust. Then they passed by on the trail above us.

"We still have to eat," Maude said after a time.

"Let's go, then," I said.

"What if the posse doubles back?"

"We'll see them coming."

Maude gave me the look that's called skeptical in the dimers.

"You will anyway," I said, for she has eyesight like a hawk's.

She said, "And then what?"

"We'll get off the trail and make these horses play dead," I said. "In the tall grass, all we'll have to do is lay still till they ride by us again."

"I'd like to see that," she said.

FIFTEEN

I SAID, "IN A DIMER I READ, A POSSE DOESN'T GO BACK over the same trail, because it has looked there already. The men circle around another way to get back to town, covering fresh ground along the way."

"Let's hope these fellows read the same book."

For the hour it took to reach full daylight, the buggy was a near partner to us, sharing the trail. We rode just faster enough that, finally, it was a speck in the distance.

According to Uncle Arlen's map, we were taking the Santa Fe Trail southwest to Fort Dodge, where we would follow the north fork into Colorado Territory. When we came to the river, I knew we were in Kansas. We left the main road to take a well-traveled but narrow path that followed the water.

Now we had crossed the border, I hoped we could attend to other pressing matters. I said, "If a posse came riding up behind us, I wouldn't hear them over the rumble of my stomach."

"Don't think they won't come out this way," she said.

"I expect you're right," I said. "It would only be our word against theirs, if they claimed to find us in Missouri. But you did say we have to eat."

"I see some buildings up ahead," Maude said. "We might find something there." I could see nothing up ahead and had to take her word for it.

I told my stomach to be patient, and in a while I saw the buildings. Not much later, I could see there was a general store of some size, poised to take advantage of a crossroads.

We came up to one of the buildings from behind and stopped at a well to fill our canteens. This made it easy to take note of the activity around the store. We saw nothing posse-like, no undue excitement.

The smell of something cooking wafted on the air. Eggs, I thought, eyeing the chickens scratching in the next kitchen yard. We hadn't eaten but two cookies apiece since breakfast the day before.

"Have you got any money?" Maude asked me.

"Not much."

"Lucky I didn't keep this in my boots." Maude dug a few dollars out from under her waistband.

"Why's that?"

"They checked my boots, looking for one of those little guns," she said, counting over the bills.

"Lucky for you they gave your boots back," I said. "Some of those fellows to come out before you did were still in their socks."

"I told the deputy it isn't proper for a lady to go barefoot," Maude said, and handed the money to me. "I guess the main thing is to get something to eat right now, but whatever else you get, don't plan on a fire later."

"What about a rifle for you?"

"Not yet," she said. "If a posse stops us, I'm going to put

my hands up. You do the same. You have to keep your shotgun in its boot."

"I don't have my shotgun," I said, and ignored the question I saw in her eyes. I didn't want her getting mad at Marion all over again.

I shoved the money deep into my pocket. I had my own ideas about what was needed. A comb and a hat for Maude, for starters. "Maude, can we wire Uncle Arlen?" I said.

"He hasn't gotten to Liberty yet," Maude said firmly. "We can worry about what to tell him later on."

"Ride on a little ways ahead, why don't you? People might wonder if they see you waiting around like you don't want to go in." Her hair looked awful bright.

"If someone takes an interest, I'll pretend I'm digging a stone out of the horse's shoe," she said. "Just get going and get back."

Riding away, I knew what to do about hungry. As for worried, I wondered if that hair color Maude used didn't come in some other color but red so she might not be quite so much of a beacon in daylight.

We were in a hurry, but I took time to breathe in the smell of that store, the inky cotton odor of bales of overalls, the fresh paint on farm tools, the dried-tobacco scent of new rope mixing together with kerosene and coffee and the tart stink of open pickle barrels.

These same smells were so ordinary in a day-to-day life I didn't take notice of them. But on the trail again, they made my blood rush a little. I didn't know what to make of it.

I spied a slate with a bill of fare written on it. Meat and gravy or greens with salt pork could be had for a high price.

The greens were gray and coated with grease. The biscuits looked dried out. I passed them by.

I knew stew meat could just as easy mean prairie dog as chicken. I didn't care if I couldn't tell them apart in gravy. Due to past experience, I wasn't partial to prairie dog and would not eat it.

I bought canned peaches and beans for the trail. A purchase of ten cans got us the can opener for free. A huge slab of corn bread and a mound of soft cheese could be eaten right away. I got hard cheese and crackers. Spoons came tied together, six in a bunch for the penny.

Next to the spoons were bright blue bowls speckled with white. They looked cheerful, and I was ever a fool for what looked cheerful, so I picked up three. The third bowl would feed Marion; that was how I planned for it.

I thought long and hard on the subject of coffee, which would need a pot and a cup, and for that matter, a fire. I had the pot and the cup, but I wasn't sure we were going to have a fire. Coffee didn't make a wise choice.

I chose a metal comb, feeling for the one with the smoothest teeth. Standing in front of the shelves, I couldn't find hair color. I settled for boot black. The stuff was cheap; worth the try.

Hats were pricey. I picked up a neck kerchief to be tied over Maude's hair like the day cook at George Ray's wore. I didn't know if Maude would consent to looking like the day cook, but our bellies were worse off than our heads, was how I looked at it.

During this time, I'd kept my ears open to the talk going on around me.

"Long time since we've had a rain," a farmer said.

"We're overdue for one," the man behind the counter said, as dry as sand. Likely this was the main conversation he had over the course of a day and it got old.

"I don't believe my crops are going to hang on long enough to collect what's due," the farmer said on his way out the door.

A fellow mentioned an empty house in the neighborhood, abandoned since the war. It was up for sale.

Last, not least, the jailbreak was mentioned.

"Some fellows rode through last night, told me three gangs got together and took a whole passel a bad guys outta jail in Independence. The one they were going to hang today was one of them, and that gal that causes so much trouble."

The storekeeper gave me my change. "What gal is that?"

I waited just as interestedly for the reply.

"Mad Martha."

"Don't say," the storekeeper said. "Big gunfight?"

The bell rang over the door, and a man came in, holding the door for a woman behind him.

"Heard there was. But then I also heard tell those fellows rassled them lawmen down to their skins so they couldn't give chase."

I could see the facts of this story were already being twisted every which way.

"I expect we'll see a newspaper delivery today, then."

"What's happened?" the newly arrived man wanted to know.

"Mad Martha and that crowd is raising a ruckus," the storekeeper answered.

I took my purchases outside and struggled to tie a sack of cans to the saddle horn. Mad Martha, I thought, and laughed.

Sixteen

I WAS JUST FINISHING WITH THE TYING UP OF SACKS when I heard the jolly tinkling of piano notes playing over the air. It struck me as something unusual to hear music at such an early hour, especially such a lively tune. I looked at the two buildings across the street. One advertised itself as an inn, and as I watched, an elderly couple came out, headed for a waiting buggy.

The other called itself the Prairie Queen Restaurant. It looked out over the plains through two wide glass windows at the front. I could smell eggs on the fry.

A young woman came out on the upstairs porch while I was looking that way and leaned against the wall as if to take the sun. Something about this struck me as odd—most females were busy in the kitchen at this hour.

This one in particular was sort of fluffy-looking to my eye. Her hair was loose, her dress was light-colored and had ruffles at the wrists.

A man came out the front door as I was heading for the building. He hurried down the steps, and as he did, his coat flapped open and I saw the flash of a badge on his chest. I didn't stare. He climbed on his horse and rode off.

I went around to the back door of the restaurant and knocked. The piano music was coming from inside. The smell of eggs wasn't.

After a good deal of knocking, the door was answered by a fellow who wasn't in the least fluffy. He looked like he'd been sleeping; his face still held creases from the pillow.

"Wot's witchu?" he said.

I stared. He said, "Whaddya want?"

"Hair color," I said. "My ma doesn't want the church ladies to know she's coloring it, so she sent me."

"Waytcheer," he said, and I waited.

He went into the house, where I heard him call somebody, and then the papery slap of their leather slippers as they came downstairs. He said something more, and then a small, pretty woman came to the door, not the same one I'd seen on the upstairs porch.

"Neville says you want some henna. We only have brown."

"Can you sell me just a little of it?" I said. "I don't have but a dime."

"Come on inside." When I hesitated, she said, "Come on, I'm not going to bite you."

I stepped inside and followed her to a tiny room with a washstand and a good-sized tub, heavyweight, the very sort Aunt Ruthie was always saving up for. Unlike most tubs that had to be lugged outside to dump the dirty water, this one drained out the bottom. More, they'd fixed it to drain out through a hole in the floor.

While I was looking at this wonder and then admiring the

yellow wallpaper with small red dots, she put some of that coloring powder in a small jar with a lid. I thought this a good idea, as it would keep the stuff dry. She said, "Ten cents' worth or thereabouts."

"Thank you," I said, making the trade.

"You've made yourself into a nice-looking boy," she said, "but you're going to be a pretty girl someday."

There was no accounting for the bleak feeling this gave me. I said to her, "I didn't understand that fellow. What's your name?"

"He's talking the King's English. Nobody can understand a word he says," she said with a grin. She put out a hand. "Geranium, that's me. What's yours?"

"Sallie." I shook her hand.

SEVENTEEN

I DIDN'T SPEND ANOTHER MINUTE IN TOWN, BUT RODE right back to Maude.

She took the potato sack, saying, "Any news?"

"They know about the jailbreak," I said as I slid off my horse. "Not much more than that."

"There's talk?" She began to go through the sack.

"Some," I said. "Mad Martha is a whole lot more interesting than the lack of rain. Less worrying, too."

"Mad Martha?" She grinned as I sat down. I reached for the corn bread packet, which was some flattened.

Maude held up the boot black. "What's this for?"

"Your hair."

Maude sat back from rummaging around in the sack. "I would sooner cut it off again."

"Never mind, I found the right stuff. Brown. I got a kerchief so you can cover up meantime."

"Oh! Peppermints." Maude set the packet aside. "You're forgiven for the boot black."

"Let's eat and talk later," I said.

We first tried to spread the cheese, then tried spooning it

onto the crumbling corn bread. Finally we ate the cheese with spoons and followed it up with a bite of corn bread.

As my belly filled, I began to think. "You're going to need pants."

Maude hadn't turned away from the problem of her hair. "I guess you're right about the color," she said. "Only I've come to like it as it is."

I glanced at her and saw she'd licked her spoon clean and was using it for a mirror. "There's the kerchief."

"A kerchief is never a waste of a penny," she said. "I'll tie it around my neck and pull it up if things get dusty."

"I can still get you a hat," I said, "if you give me another two dollar."

"I can't spare it," she said in a way that got my back up.

"There's a new wrinkle on penny wise and pound foolish."

She put the spoon down, but not to argue with me.

Four riders on the trail had caught her eye—they weren't riding all in a bunch, but they could be a posse. I sat still, figuring we looked less interesting just sitting there than getting up and riding off in a hurry. One of those riders looked our way.

"I think we might have company." The words were no sooner out of my mouth than that rider slowed.

Maude looked up. "Just sit quiet," she said. "I'm not up to shooting him."

From this I knew she didn't see anything to worry about, but it wasn't until he turned his horse toward us that I recognized him. It's a funny thing to know someone by the way they sit their horse.

It was only the relief of a moment, for in the back of my

mind was the worry over Uncle Arlen. But for that moment, I could breathe deep and easy.

"If you girls ain't a sight for sore eyes," Marion said as he drew near.

"We heard shots as we rode off," I said as he swung down from his horse. He had my shotgun and I was glad of it.

"Things got a mite excitable," he said mildly.

"Tell us what happened," Maude said.

"You were barely out the door and Black Hankie was on his way down the stairs. The sheriff took on with one of those fellows," he said in that tone he uses for a good story. "Things went wild. I scooted out the back door, laid in with a heel and rid this reluctant son of a mule—" He stopped, fixed in Maude's stare.

She can be daunting in a way Aunt Ruthie had been, and his reaction wasn't surprising. "They got out," he said. "That's the long and the short of it."

His gaze shifted to look meaningfully at the corn bread and cheese. I pushed Marion's bowl over to Maude, for she was sitting closer to the cheese.

"What did the others do?" I asked him.

"Aw, they knew enough to scatter," he said. "'Course, the bullet hole in Black Hankie slowed them up some."

"Bullet hole?" Maude said. She stopped with the cheese poised in midair. "You thought that wasn't important enough to mention earlier?"

"I did tell you," Marion said. "One of those fellows went for a gun, and when the sheriff jumped him, it went off."

"Was he killed?" I asked.

"I don't believe so," Marion said.

Maude set a piece of corn bread on top of the cheese and passed it over to Marion with a spoon. "Lucky thing I spotted you," he said around his first mouthful.

"Two posses passed us by while we sat it out here," I said. "I saw a badge passing through whilst I was over there to the store."

I got up to pull the saddlebags off his horse.

"Find some pants in there for your sister," he said. "One of those deputies was a smallish fellow."

I let out a whoop of laughter loud enough to startle his horse. "You kept their pants?"

"I had them as an armful when the shooting started," Marion said. His tone was grave, but there was a glint in his eye. "I didn't take time to lay them down anywheres."

Maude gave us both the benefit of her Aunt Ruthie look.

However, she stretched the four pairs of pants out on the ground to see the size of them while I wiped down Marion's horse. It didn't look overtired, but the saddle blanket was damp, so I knew it had done some running.

"What about this shirt?" Maude said.

"I took it off a clothesline," Marion said. "I pinned a two-dollar bill in its place."

"It has a hole in one sleeve."

"You telling me I paid too much for it?" Marion said, and winked at me.

"It'll do," she said.

Marion said, "We ought to find a place to dig in for a

piece, let them run themselves ragged. They'll give up soon enough."

Maude said, "We have to get to Uncle Arlen."

"Getting arrested again will slow us down a whole sight more," Marion argued. "By tomorrow they'll have a handful of false leads to follow."

"I heard there's an empty house near here," I said, "when I was in the store buying supplies."

Marion scraped up a final spoonful of cheese with corn bread crumbled over it. "I'll go on in there and ask after it like I'm in the market."

He got up slowly, looking a little the worse for wear.

I figured he didn't get as much rest as we had during the night. I said, "Which way did you light out after you left the jail?"

"The wrong way, son. The wrong way."

"Take my horse," I said. "Give yours a little more graze."

The corner of his mouth twitched in half a smile. "You are all heart."

Maude made use of the time he was gone, and the far side of the horses, to change into a pair of those pants. "I never thought I would change my clothes out in full view of a mercantile like this."

"Nobody looking over this way can tell what you're doing. Not unless their eyesight is a match for yours."

Maude came out from behind the horse.

The pants weren't snug on her, but there was no danger of them falling off. Marion was right to find her a loose shirt to wear with them, but she wouldn't easily pass for a boy again.

A few minutes later, Marion came back with another bulging potato sack. "I've got the whereabouts of that place," he said.

It was nearly an hour's ride from where we sat. The good thing was, we were mostly still headed in the right direction.

EIGHTEEN

THE WAGON RUTS LEADING UP TO THE HOUSE HAD been washed smooth. We walked alongside the horses, taking care not to leave stones or fresh chunks of overturned earth. Marion swept a leafy branch behind us to erase any tracks in the loose dirt.

The house, built of weathered gray stone and half hidden by a mass of fir trees, had a general unlived-in air about it. The barn behind the house had been burned. Only part of one wall still stood.

"Here's a lamp with oil left in it," Marion told us after he'd walked through. That made us all feel welcome somehow.

A fenced-in area at the back had once been the vegetable garden, from the looks of things, but nothing worthwhile to anyone but a horse grew there presently. We set them loose to graze.

The well water was clear, and cold enough to make our teeth hurt. Marion hung a leaky bucket down in the well, hoping the wood might swell and seal the leak.

Maude came up with an old cook pot the horses might drink from, though the bottom was more rounded than not.

Marion set chunks of stone on all sides of the pot so it wouldn't roll; horses could get right picky over such things. Once we filled it with water, it all depended on if the mood was right.

Maude's horse stepped right up for a drink. The others crowded in to get the next turn at it.

Inside, the place had been stripped nearly bare. But there was a bathtub under a curtained shelf, and the enamel was chipped only a little bit.

Me and Maude walked around in the house for a time. She came across a worn quilt in a window box. Once the mouse droppings were shaken out, she pronounced it good enough to sleep on.

I found half a dimer. I'd seen it before, but Aunt Ruthie would have said to me, don't look a gift horse in the mouth. It might could be said I was lucky I had seen it before, since some of the pages were missing.

Maude put a toe into some mattress stuffing piled in the corner of a wardrobe, where it might once have served as a nest.

We used a worn-down broom to scrape a piece of floor clear of dried leaves and such. This uncovered a broken mirror.

Small piles of butternuts littered the corners of the rooms, but we left them untouched. We couldn't get into them anyway, butternuts being hard enough to bust a nutcracker.

It was an old house, comfortable with the company of mice and squirrels and with the smell of damp. And yet it lent itself to the notion of someone living there again.

Late in the afternoon, Maude went through Marion's sack. It yielded eggs and fatback, some of those dried-out biscuits, and some coffee and sugar. I did like that he remembered sugar.

"No matches," Maude said in a despairing tone.

I said, "In my sack." This gave me a feeling of uncommon good cheer, to offer up something I'd kept stashed in the loft.

Marion made a fire. The chimney was good; it didn't smoke. "Here," he said, "I'll cook up that fatback, then we can fry some eggs in the fat." I carved off some thin chunks while the pot heated. The first meat to hit the pot gave off a sweet smell that made my stomach growl.

At the bottom of Marion's sack, Maude found a newspaper. The light from the windows was fading, but standing right next to them, we could read. Right off, I saw the picture they drew of Maude came not even close. The headline read:

MAD MAUDE APPREHENDED AND ON THE LOOSE AGAIN

"Read it to me, why don't you?" Marion said.

Maude read, "'After laying low in an undiscovered hideout, Maude March was apprehended while serving soup and spuds in a lowly dining room.'—Oh, George Ray is going to appreciate that—'Her rough-and-ready gang of eleven men'"— Maude bristled at the mention of eleven men. "Who is writing these accounts, anyway?"

"Someone who is seeing double," Marion said.

I looked over Maude's shoulder and finished the article:

—broke the now-flaming-haired female out of jail late in the same day. They were not satisfied with this feat but freed the Black Hankie Bandit, too.

I was right off glad I'd bought some hair color.

Maude had since begun to read again, and when she finished, I said, "Black Hankie's gang did all the waving guns around. Where's the story about them, anyway?"

Maude flipped the sheets over with a smart crackle of paper. "Here it is. Why didn't they put him on the front page? He's the one they meant to hang."

BLACK HANKIE CHEATS THE HANGMAN

Those folks who look on a hanging as the next best thing to a barn dance were sorley disappointed today. The Black Hankie Bandit, who was shot off his horse while attempting to escape the jailhouse the night before he was to die, expired of his wounds while resting in a bed with a fether mattress and a goose down pilloe. It is for the reader to decide if justice was done.

"If the story won't make you cry," Maude said, "the spelling will."

I read the whole of it aloud and the spelling didn't hamper me. "What do you make of it, Marion?"

He was sitting near the fire, keeping an eye on the fatback so it wouldn't burn. "My guess is, the law is trying to make it sound like Maude's the reason they lost their grip on a fellow everybody was looking forward to hanging."

"I can't believe he's dead," Maude said, throwing the paper down. She was up and out of the house like something yanked her across the room.

I started up off the floor to follow her, but Marion said, "Let her go. She needs to take it in."

"It's not like we knew him personal," I said. I didn't need the look he gave me to know it was a matter of luck that Black Hankie wasn't sitting around reading about Maude.

"She's just thinking," Marion said. "She'll be in here again in a minute. Eat your supper."

When Maude came inside, she said, "Maybe we should start out now. We would have the advantage of riding under cover of darkness."

Marion said, "You're right about night-riding, but we should wait till tomorrow night to start out again. It will give those posses time enough to start wanting to quit and go home."

"I'm anxious to reach Uncle Arlen," Maude said.

"To be any help to him at all, we must keep you out of jail."

A quiet did stretch. Maude decided to eat. Marion went out to check on the horses. I took up the paper to read it for myself, but I watched Maude over the top of the damp pages.

She settled down to study the map, sucking noisily on a peppermint. The firelight was barely enough for me to read by; it wasn't sufficient for Maude, who couldn't see things close up so well. After a minute, she was only ignoring me.

"Don't be so hard on Marion," I said. "He wants to get to Uncle Arlen as bad as we do."

"Bad*ly*."

I scanned the stories again, trying to figure in all those fellows they let loose and see if the numbers added up. Nothing about me, of course. I never got used to being ignored in these news reports.

"It's the unfairness of it all that gets to me," I said.

"Well, you're lucky if that's all that does," Maude said.

I looked my question at her.

"If they're not locking the door on you, you're fine," she said.

NINETEEN

MARION STAYED GONE LONG ENOUGH TO TAKE A turn around the property. He found a garden claw we could use to poke the fire, and a glove. Only the one glove, big for Maude and small for him, but the leather was thick enough for handling a hot pot. He threw it on top of our sacks.

"All the comforts of home," Marion said as he sat down with us. We were all sleeping in the front room around the fire.

"I was just thinking the same thing," Maude said to him. A roof over her head and a fire to warm her feet, along with a surfeit of peppermints, had put her in a mellow frame of mind, considering her earlier mood.

Over our heads a butternut rolled across the floor. There was some scrabbling around up there that meant the current owners of this house had come home to dinner.

"Squirrels," I said.

"All the comforts," Marion said, and grinned.

"There are not enough marks on this map," Maude complained.

"It looked fine to me," I said.

"I believe I can add to it," Marion said. He went at it with a pencil, making Uncle Arlen's lines darker and the print a little larger. Before he was done, he was entirely back in her good graces.

She said, "How far do you think Uncle Arlen has gotten?"

"He's been gone four days," Marion said. "He ought to be right about here if he's making a change of horses every so often."

I watched and saw his pencil point did not come anywhere near halfway. "That's all?"

"The man has to sleep sometime," Marion said, as if he himself stood accused of slowpoking. "He can't ride hard all the time, no matter how fresh his horse. His old bones won't like to take such a pounding."

This was no doubt true. Uncle Arlen was a sturdy fellow, but he had passed the quarter-century mark last year.

We had dried out the horse blankets as best we could, and Maude folded that quilt for a pallet. She didn't offer to share it with me. We were no sooner settled and watching the fire die down than a bat glided over our heads, silent, and went on to the next room.

"Holy Mulroney," Marion said, flattening himself to the floor as it swooped back toward us.

Maude's eyelids flickered, taking in the uninvited company. She wasn't in the least bothered by bats and could have taken care of it, but she didn't look inclined. Her eyes were half closed.

Bats bothered me only a little. I got up to open a window to get rid of it—that is, I hoped it would take the opportunity to leave. It made another pass just as I leaned out to throw the shutters wide open.

Marion yelled, "Get down, Sallie!"

More startled than frightened, I ducked, but the bat veered away from the open window and disappeared into the next room again. It could circle around all night, and I made up my mind to let it.

"Quick, run back here," Marion said, still rather loudly.

Maude shushed him.

"Those things will suck your blood," he told her.

"They do not," Maude said.

"Then what do they eat exactly?" Marion said. "Just tell me that."

She couldn't tell him, and neither could I. We only had Aunt Ruthie's word for it that they didn't suck blood. A creepy crawling feeling down my back chased me to my horse blanket.

"I think it's time we went to sleep," Maude said.

"She's just eager to enjoy the extra padding that quilt puts between her old bones and the floor," I said to cheer Marion.

Like she was the momma, we all got into our sleep positions and waited for it. Ten minutes later, only Maude was breathing in the way of someone sleeping.

Another butternut rolled, upstairs.

"Believe I can live with those," Marion said. "Although they are some noisier."

That was when the bat skimmed overhead again. Marion pulled his blanket over his head, then folded it down like he wouldn't be caught hiding.

"Give it some time," I said, feeling confident a bat could find its way out.

Then another bat flitted across the room, and to state matters honestly, they flew quite a bit lower than before.

Marion drew in a breath so loudly Maude flipped over to give him a hard stare.

She noticed the one bat was now two and said, "Dang and blast! Sallie, get up and shut that window." She was throwing her blanket off as she spoke.

I scurried over to shut the window, but wouldn't you know it, another one made it in before I yanked the shutters closed. Marion pulled his head down between his shoulders.

Maude rooted around in a potato sack for that glove, then stood and watched the bats circle. "Sit down, Sallie," she said in the tone that said she didn't know what I was up and around for anyway.

I sat. Those bats went on circling the room for some time.

Then, like they'd all heard a whistle somewhere outside, they flew one by one to land on the shutters. They hooked their toes over a slat and hung upside down.

Maude didn't waste any time.

She pulled on the glove, walked over, and clapped her hand over one of those resting bats. It started in right away on that rusty-hinge screaming they make.

The other two bats spread their wings but didn't lift off, as Maude opened one shutter and let that first bat free. She closed the shutter gently before she laid her glove over the next bat.

Maude wasn't in the least bothered, but those critters were, shrieking in scratchy voices until she set them loose. A last slam of the shutters and we were bat-free.

With a glance at Marion, Maude said, "I hope nobody is afraid of squirrels. They're a whole lot harder to catch."

She came back to her pallet, dropped the glove on the floor, and covered herself again.

TWENTY

MAUDE FELL ASLEEP LIKE SHE WAS A CANDLE DOUSED. Marion was still staring into the firelight. "She's afraid the sheriff of Cedar Rapids threw our letter away," I said in a low voice.

"This has been a niggling worry to me all along," he said.

"She hasn't mentioned the money, exactly, but I expect she has her doubts about it getting all the way back to Des Moines."

"Now that was the chance we were taking," Marion said. "Wearing a badge hasn't never been a guarantee of an honorable man. Honesty is more of a personal decision."

I said, "What about Uncle Arlen? Independence is his home. Me and Maude lived there for five months and he didn't turn her in."

He met this question in silence. Marion didn't come to a speedy judgment of someone or something newly met. Which is not to say his conclusion was usually right, only reasonably well considered.

"It has me worried," I said. How could Uncle Arlen go back to the little house he'd built and his business? Besides that, I couldn't imagine where me and Maude would end up if we couldn't go back there with him.

Oh, I could see us landing somewhere and taking jobs, but it could be nothing like the same as we had just left behind. We had come to be part of a home again. Part of a family.

Marion commenced to deep breathing like he might be gone to sleep. In the stillness of the room, another bat swooped overhead. I watched Marion, but he didn't move a muscle.

I turned over on my side to watch the fire die. Times like this changed a man, and I figured I was in the midst of such a change. I reckoned it didn't come without wringing the heart like a sponge.

We woke late the next morning to find the leaky bucket still dripped but nowhere nearly as fast. Maude decided she could have a tepid bath if she heated enough water to mix with cold.

This turned out to be a slow process, but we had all day to wait for nightfall. Before we threw away the water, I combed in the hair color for Maude. She didn't look happy about putting dark color in. For that matter, it didn't look awful different than the boot black to me, but I didn't say so. There weren't many ways to change the look of her.

Maude had to wait for a time for the color to set. She stared out a back window, biting her thumbnail until it bled. She wrapped her shirttail around it.

"Maude."

"It helps me think. I have to plan."

"Plan what?"

"I need a rifle," she said. "We can't get by with only a shotgun and Marion's pistol."

"Are we going to have a fire?" I said. "If we can't have a fire, we might could stop worrying about a rifle."

"Birds aren't the only critters we might need to pop," she said.

"Are we planning now for what we don't want?" I said to her.

She dropped the matter as she rinsed out a little bit of the color to see the results. I saw her hair had taken the color real well.

She looked into the mirror fragment with a doubtful expression. In the next moment, Maude cried out, ran to the tub, and dunked her whole head, shaking it to loosen the color.

"Maude," I said in surprise.

Then the water turned pure dark. It did give me pause.

"You'd better come up for air," I said.

She reared up with a sploosh. "I might just as well have used the boot polish," she said tearfully, and dunked her head again.

I started thinking up things to say right off. "It's supposed to be darker," I said when she came up for air again.

"Not black," she said.

"It's just wet."

Maude grabbed the soap and lathered up and rinsed. I handed her the shirt we were using for a towel. She rough-dried her hair, or as near as she could come, considering the shirt was already quite damp.

She held up the piece of mirror. She was wearing the look of a tantrum. "It'll dry lighter," I said in some desperation.

"Sallie, why don't you go on outside for a while?"

"They only had brown, Maude. She didn't tell me—"

"I just need to get used to it," Maude said. "Alone."

"It ain't that bad," I said. "Besides which, if it don't wash out, it'll grow out."

"Just go on outside."

"You ain't going to cry, I hope."

"If you say 'ain't' to me once more in the next hour, I'm going to slather *you* with boot black."

I went out to where Marion was sitting on the front step. "How'd it go?"

"Her hair's dark," I said in the tone of dire news being given.

"What she needed," Marion said, as if that had anything to do with it.

"She ain't exactly happy about it."

"Well, it's just temporary," he said.

I decided not to go over that territory again.

The horses had eaten everything they liked out of the fenced-in place. Marion had picketed them outside the fencing to graze. He was reading the slice of a dimer I had left on the floor. That is, he held it upside down.

This surprised me. "Why, you never said you couldn't read." Though now I thought about it, he'd several times done a fair job of getting me and Maude to read for him.

He went pink. "I don't care to let on to Maude," he said. "Your aunt having been a teacher and all, Maude thinks everybody reads."

"She shoots better than me," I said, "but she doesn't look down on me for it."

He looked away.

"How'd you read the map last night?" I said. "How did you do the lettering?"

"For the letters, I followed the lines," he said. "I don't have to read letters to read a map."

"Here, if you're going to make a secret of it," I said, turning the dimer right-side, "you have to know the top from the bottom. See this letter like a pointed hat? That's an A. And this here is T. Look for them and make sure they look right to you."

"Thank you."

"I can teach you to read when Maude isn't listening in," I said.

"I'll help you work on your aim," he said. "We should have plenty of time to practice out there in Colorado Territory."

I showed him a few more letters and had him find them on the page, sounding them out. He picked out a couple of words all by himself. He was getting it in no time at all. Don't believe what they say, that you cannot teach an old dog new tricks.

As for my aim, it was better than I let on. I'd discovered I only had to look and shoot, the way Marion had once told Maude to do. It was just I didn't like to hit birds and such.

Maude came out of the house ten minutes later, ready to ride. Her hair wasn't pulled up to the top of her head but hung straight at the sides of her face.

"Well, now," Marion said at the sight of her. "That is some darker all right."

Maude didn't reply.

Once her hair was darkened, I should have been satisfied.

But I wasn't. The stuff didn't give her a natural brown color but one with a strange purplish cast. She suddenly looked to me more like those wanted posters than ever she had. Like she was drawn in dark pencil. This didn't strike me as a good idea, although I didn't have a better one. Not just yet.

I reached into the sack for the kerchief.

Marion was thinking along the same lines, for he handed his hat to her. "Keep the sun off," he said, and Maude took it without a thank-you. It came down over her ears, which was an advantage. We didn't mention this.

We rode into a sunset made up of pearly pink clouds and a burning sun, prepared to stay on our horses through the night.

TWENTY-ONE

AT FIRST MARION FELT WE SHOULDN'T RIDE BY DAY, and don't get close to any encampments by night. In this way, we saw no one on the trail. We didn't see trouble, which counted for a great deal.

At the end of one night's travel, we couldn't feel comfortable sleeping in daylight. After the horses had a good feed, we pushed on, staying off-trail and following the water.

Maude began to complain once more she lacked a rifle.

"We shouldn't shoot game," Marion said. "Nor do much cooking, unless we run out of store-bought. The smoke and the smell of it may draw unwanted attention."

"Then we'll need more canned beans," Maude said.

Not much later, we came upon the remains of a small mule train. Arrows scatter-marked the sides of the wagons. It wasn't a recent event; the animals had dried and shrunk to a thin stretch of leather over the skeletons.

"I still need a rifle," Maude said. "'Should not' is a sight different than 'cannot.'"

The next break in this landscape was a small town called by a woman's name, Eudora. Marion said I should ride in to get Maude a gun. This was no sooner suggested than she worried aloud if this was a good idea after all.

"If a posse comes across us," Marion said to her, "put your hands in the air. But you can't protect Sallie by being defenseless."

I went into the store looking to get her the selfsame kind of rifle we had left hanging on the kitchen wall in Independence. As it happened, the fellow had a Springfield carbine up for sale.

I hefted a few likely ones, shut one eye, and squinted through the sights of two of these. When I picked up the Springfield, it was with the air of a man convinced he would find nothing at all that interested him.

Right out, he named me a reasonable price.

When I tried to talk him around to more reasonable yet, he threw in a box of cartridges, and we called it a deal.

I got hats to fit me and Maude and better bedrolls for all of us. I got corn bread and soft cheese for two days. Marion was partial to it. We had some beans left, which would have to do, for their cans were dented and I would not buy them.

I got a dimer, *Olen Rushforth, Texas Ranger*. I considered this a wise purchase, since we were on the run from the law. I learned practically every useful thing I knew from dimers.

I rode away feeling I had better enjoyed wanting to ride into a town than being there. At this, I was more fortunate than Maude, who didn't get to see that much.

"Lawrence is ahead of us," she said, consulting the map. "It's a big enough city for me to ride through unnoticed."

Marion said, "It's a big enough place to have its own newspaper."

Maude gave him the look of, So what?

"A place with a paper has newspaper*men*," he said, "who are by their nature the nosiest of people."

"I just thought of something," Maude said. "Uncle Arlen could see a paper before we reach him."

"It didn't sound to me like he has time for newspapers," Marion said. This didn't make us feel any easier, so we picked up the pace some. We rode around the outskirts of Lawrence. There was enough traffic on the road to scratch Maude's itch to see the inside of someplace. One woman looking at her with curiosity was all it took.

Not long past it, we didn't have a river beside us anymore. No river. No trees. No clouds.

No hope of a town in the next few miles.

"These horses need to rest," I said as the afternoon wore into evening. Uncle Arlen didn't think much of pushing horses hard, and I didn't care for it, either. "They're getting too tired to grab a mouthful of grass."

"We've done nearly thirty miles since I found you," Marion said. "They've earned a good feed and a fair rest."

Thirty miles was a drop in the bucket, but I didn't say so.

Not long after, we stopped for the night. I pulled Uncle Arlen's map out of my pocket and tried to measure out three weeks of travel on it. We ate from our supplies and tried out our new bedrolls. I suspected they were fine, as Maude fell asleep before I could ask.

We passed three days in this manner, uneventful. Then Maude ran out of peppermints. She started to complain. We passed a place too small to boast of township but likely to have candy to sell.

Marion wouldn't agree to go in for something we didn't need. We needed beans, but I kept quiet.

"I don't see how it looks safer to you that Sallie can go into town to buy dimers, but I can't get a twist of peppermints."

"You *had* peppermints," I said. "You ate them."

Maude showed her teeth at me, saying, "I had help."

I said, "Not that awful much," for she had been eating them quietly for a time before me and Marion asked for any.

"Here now, let's have an end to the bickering," Marion said.

"We aren't bickering," Maude said with some venom.

Marion did not give in to the peppermint argument, but Maude did not leave off wanting to go into town.

At first I felt some satisfaction in this, for I'd always thought I ought to be the better range rider, what with everything I learned reading dimers and all.

I had to admit, Maude had unexpectedly turned out to have more grit and gumption than I had credited her for. But I saw now that she didn't have the pluck to make it over the plains. She was probably going to turn out to be like one of those pioneers who finished the trip with glassy eyes and dull expressions, who had lost touch with something of themselves they needed.

The moment this thought was finished, I said, "Maude has to get into a town now and again. This range-riding is not for everybody."

Maude shot me a look, but let the remark stand.

Marion said, "If we were to ride a little off-trail, and come across some small burg, we might could send your uncle a telegram. Have it waiting for him at Fort Dodge."

"I'll do that," Maude said.

Marion said, "I can wire him. Tell me what you want to say."

"You can't leave me to stand out here in the grassland by myself," Maude said in a more reasonable tone than she had used in some hours. "Something might get me."

"It would have to be something with great big teeth," Marion said.

Maude looked a little flattered by this.

Not long after, we stopped beside a creek for the night. We planned the telegram over and over.

"We have to tell him we're coming along behind him," I said.

"That's my worry," Maude said. "I can't feel it's right to slow him down."

Marion said, "We have to warn him Macdougal's one man down. That'll keep him on the move."

It may have been we all slept badly for we were up early the next morning. We weren't long on the trail before Maude took up whining about going into town. She wanted to send that telegram. She wanted peppermints. She wanted to see a paper.

I wanted to buy beans and potato hash.

We didn't see another town until mid-afternoon. Maude said, "There are a few small houses in the distance." My stomach stood up to take a look, was how it felt to me.

"All right, then," Marion said at last. "I need to trade my horse in. It's looking a little fagged and we can't favor it."

"We're low on water," Maude said, not wanting to let the thing go.

After a time, I saw these houses stood on the fringe of a larger town. We didn't stop at any of the homesteads, not even to fill our canteens. Our faces had gone unwashed, and we couldn't be certain of the reception we would get.

We let the horses slow to an ambling walk so they could nibble on dandelions as they found them. In this way, we gave ourselves time to sort out the kind of town it was.

Industrious, since people had gone to the trouble of putting up little whitewashed fences with roses tumbling over them. There was corn, beans, and squash growing tepee-style in another yard.

Prosperous, because the sow in a nearby pigpen had half a dozen little ones rooting around. As we passed another such house, Maude pointed out a sign on the gate. It read, B. GOOD & KIND. "Somebody's name, do you think?"

I said, "Maybe the preacher lives there."

An older lady popped up from behind the fence. "Nope, not the preacher," she said.

TWENTY-TWO

SHE'D BEEN WORKING AT SOMETHING IN THE DIRT; SHE wore gloves and held a trowel. The woman said, "I'm Beatrice Good. Bee, to my friends. My husband is Borden Kind."

"Oh, I'm sorry," Maude said. "We weren't making fun. Just the sign caught my eye."

"It's supposed to," Miz Good said. "It's the law this town lives by. You look hot and dusty. You want to come in and freshen up at the well?"

"It would be a kindness," Marion said.

"Come in, come in," she said. "Help yourself to the water, and you'll find a washbowl right there on a rock table. I keep a bucket with a ladle in the kitchen; I'll bring it out."

When she came back outside, she was followed by a man I guessed to be Borden Kind, who carried the bucket for her. He was a jolly-looking fellow, which suited his name.

"I see Mother here has herself a couple of customers. Watch out now, or she'll have you weeding the garden while you wait for dinner."

"That wouldn't be a bad trade, if we had a little more time," Maude said.

"Can I give you good people directions to anyplace in particular?" Borden Kind said.

"Just passing through," Marion said.

Maude added, "We'll be stopping to wire news of our progress to family and then moving on."

Borden Kind said, "Telegraph office is at the other end of town."

I thought he looked unusual close at Maude, but only for a moment, and he was still smiling.

Marion didn't appear to be bothered by that look. He asked, "Seen any Indian activity in these parts?"

"Well, now, you got Custer pushing them north, you're going to see activity," Borden Kind said. "Before that, we didn't see much."

Miz Good turned Maude's attention to the many buds on a lilac bush she was proud of. Neither of them took Maude for a fellow.

"The trail ahead generally safe?" Marion asked Borden Kind.

"No guarantees," he said. "I wish you folks the best of luck."

We spent a few minutes more admiring the garden, then got on our way. We found the crossroads in the middle of town unusual cluttered for such a small place.

A medicine wagon had set up to do business on one side of the street. I'd seen it in Independence a month or so before, being driven by a silver-haired gent, finely dressed, his hair parted in the center and swept back from his face like wings.

Stained barn red and built like a little house on wheels, it had a wooden door on the backside and a black chimney pipe sticking out of the peaked green roof. This wagon was pulled by matched white horses, heavy as oxen, with harnesses dyed red. I would have traded off all my dimers to ride behind those horses.

On one side of the wagon, I read:

DR. BARNABAS ALDORADONDO'S MIRACULOUS RESTORATIVE ELIXIR
This Most Potent Panacea Is a Centuries-Old Family Secret That Cures All Ills

As we rode past now, I read around the bottom edge a printed list of ailments: "biliousness, the headake, ague, the punies, diarea, gout, dropsy, rheumatiz, warts, rash, fleas, the shakes, consum—"

Maude brought her horse to a stop as a woman with two children in tow stepped off the boardwalk. One side of the wagon let down to make a shelf, and that shelf was filled with bottles of every color and shape.

Me and Marion pulled up to wait for Maude as people moved into the street as a crowd. A fellow I guessed to be Dr. Aldoradondo stood inside the wagon, behind the shelf, talking fast and smooth.

"Ladies, do you wake up each morning feeling weary and dispirited?" he said in a voice deep and rich and just a touch bitter. "Do you fall into bed at night, your mind filled with the cares of the day, your body too weary to sleep?"

He gave them a moment to think on their misery, then added, "Here you have before you certain relief from your aches and pains, the cure of your ills. Yours for only one silver dollar." His fingers were spread across the bottle tops.

From my horse, I could see the bottles themselves were a wonder. Many were colored like jewels, and others were shaped like tigers or lilies, some were twisted or dimpled.

"What condition do you need to treat, madam?" he was saying. "I have just the thing here, take one spoonful in the morning, one in the evening, and none in between."

Ruby red for rheumatism. Cobalt blue for the ague. A weak green if the person suffered loose bowels. A dark brown if they were trying to encourage loose bowels.

Maude rode over to us at a slow walk. "Let's split up here," Marion said to her, "where no one is taking any notice. Then meet out the other side of town." He turned down an alley, following a sign to the livery.

Maude rode on, to send a wire off to Uncle Arlen.

I tied my horse to the rail in front of the general store.

I couldn't help the nagging feeling I had that we ought to be in a hurry, and I made my choices quickly. Pickled eggs and biscuits and chicken in gravy. I trusted this last because I could see the chopped-off chicken feet right there in the waste box.

I bought cornmeal and fatback as well, and added peppermints to the order at the last. I bought a second twist, but I wouldn't tell Maude I had them until she needed them, for she could go through them at a good rate.

The headline that made me pick up the paper was this:

MAUDE MARCH KILLS AGAIN

Wormwood, Texas, is a dusty little town that sees little excitement. Until this morning, when Mad Maude and her gang of Fearless Marauders hit the First Community Bank of Wormwood.

The teller didn't hand over the money Quickly Enough and was shot dead with greater ease than most of us swat a mosquito. After many months of laying low Mad Maude is back and she is Mad as a Hornet.

I couldn't understand why the newspaper people didn't wonder how Maude had got to Texas in only a few days; there wasn't a word about that. Not that I wanted them hot on our tails here in Kansas. But it wasn't good news that Maude was being blamed for another murder.

I turned over a sheet to look at the smaller headlines on the other side. I saw this: RANGE WAR RAGES, and in the small print the words "Colorado Territory" stood out.

At this point the storekeep walked over and said to me, "If you ain't buying it, fold it up the way you found it. This ain't no reading room, and I'm not in the business of selling used items."

I did as he said, but as I eased the crease in the page, I spotted another headline that made me grin: WYOMING TERR. TO GIVE WOMEN THE VOTE. Now, Aunt Ruthie would love to have lived to see that.

The storekeep cleared his throat noisily, and over the edge

of the page, I saw him glaring at me. I thought about buying the paper outright, for he could have nothing to say then.

But the Aunt Ruthie in me rose up and said to me, why buy the paper if it doesn't have the news I'm looking for? I set the paper aside.

I headed out of the store, lugging our provisions and thinking fond thoughts of chicken in gravy. It struck me Maude had something when she said my stomach ran my brain.

TWENTY-THREE

As I STEPPED OUTSIDE, A BIG BOY RAN PAST ME, NEARLY knocking me flat. I gave a shout after him and then regretted it, for I didn't mean to draw attention to myself.

But it didn't matter, for he kept on running fast, carrying a fluttering sheet of paper in his hand. He ran across the street and into a doorway further along the boardwalk.

I noticed that medicine wagon moving on. It went past me down the street, heading out of town in the same direction I would go. I told myself when I passed it I would ride to the side of it I hadn't yet read, for the ailments held a kind of fascination for me.

I had nearly done with tying my purchases to the saddle when the boy came back outside. Borden Kind put his head out of the same doorway. He took no notice of me. He called the boy, then walked out to meet him halfway. I saw a star on Kind's vest catch the light.

He was a lawman. The weight of it near took my breath away. Another fellow came from two doors down to stand with them. I could hear none of what Borden Kind said at this distance, but the two men went back inside, and the boy went running along the boardwalk on that side of the street.

I looked all around for Maude or Marion. We were agreed to meet outside of town, but that didn't rule out one of them might be nearby.

I didn't see them, nor Maude's horse, and I rode for the alley where Marion had turned. I didn't like to see lawmen in a hurry.

I reminded myself there could be a dozen things happening to stir them up. Only I couldn't stop thinking of the look Borden Kind gave Maude. I had allowed myself to be fooled into thinking it was nothing because it was gone in a moment.

Marion came out of the alley at a good clip, scattering like chickens three women who were crossing the street. He wasn't on a fresh horse.

When he pulled up alongside me, I said, "Borden Kind is the law."

"He and a deputy grabbed her," Marion said. "This is going to work the same way as before. You go in crying."

"He won't believe me," I said. "He knows who Maude is."

"I'm not interested in changing his mind," Marion said. "I want to get the drop on him."

"Do we know there's a back door?"

"They'll have some way of getting to the outhouse without the whole town knowing when."

"Okay," I said. "But we aren't going to shoot anybody, are we?"

"I'd rather not," Marion said, and lifted slightly the coil of rope over his saddle horn.

"Let's all stick together when we ride out of here," I said. "Where's Maude's horse?"

"Hard telling," Marion said in the tone of one more piece of bad luck.

"What about your horse? Why didn't you trade it?"

"I couldn't find a piece of horseflesh to match him. From where I stood at the corral I had a good view of your sister's mishap."

"You might could try again," I said. He would be better off on a fresh horse if we had to outrun a posse.

He shook his head. "This is it. What we're on. I have to round up your sister's horse right quick."

"I'll go to the jail, and you come in when you're ready."

"Naw, you wait outside somewhere till you see me with the horse," he said. "What we don't need is for me to get arrested, and there you'll be right inside the jailhouse, and we don't have another card up our sleeve."

He was right, and I did as he said. I didn't know what I would do as the last card up our sleeve. I began to plan for it, though, and what I planned was to ring the church bell. If the entire town turned out to see what was the matter, maybe I could double around and open up the jailhouse doors.

I didn't want to bet on such a middling plan.

I hid in the alley across the street and some down from the jailhouse. It gave me a view, but like as not, I wouldn't be seen if someone looked out the window.

Here sat the smallest jailhouse I'd ever taken notice of. The good side of this was to think it might be that much easier to get Maude out. I tied my potato sack more securely. I didn't want to lose it during the gallop.

This might could be a second chance at making Maude's side of this story known. But a lot of things would have to be working in Maude's favor to see things come out right at the end; that bothered me. For it did also occur to me we might have gotten in and out of this town without incident.

I might could have said to myself, If only we hadn't stopped to read a sign at just the hour when the sheriff had gone home for a spell. But we had stopped, and Maude herself had pointed that sign out to me. I'd come to think of this as something Maude and Aunt Ruthie had in common, a gift for being in the right place at the wrong time.

I could see little traffic in and out of the sheriff's office, and no fuss at all. Surprising, considering they had just captured Mad Maude. Fortunate, since me and Marion were about to test our jail-breaking skills again.

I rode out to meet him when I saw him coming down the street with Maude's sorrel reined in behind him. "Good. She likes that horse," I said. "She wouldn't be happy to lose it."

He said, "How many have gone inside?"

"None that I saw. Two came out at different minutes and went off someplace, that's all."

We tied all three horses to a post. "We'll all be coming out the front door if everything goes all right," Marion said.

"Give me a minute to work up some tears," I said as he headed into the space between two buildings. He raised a hand to show me he'd heard.

I stood there for a minute, but tears weren't what rose up in me. It was the need to have Maude's story known. I walked into that sheriff's office dry-eyed and determined.

TWENTY-FOUR

Borden Kind was sitting there at a desk, in a chair on little wheels, and he was alone. "My sister is innocent," I said, taking note of a closed door behind him.

Another such door stood open, and inside I could see a room not much larger than the cot inside it. A window high on the wall was too small to allow anything larger than a cat to crawl out of it. It did look clean, I'll say that for it.

Maude could likely sit down while she waited for whatever happened next. I worried for a moment she might not mind being in there enough to overcome her feeling of wrongdoing and leave.

This being my second go at it, I knew better than some that jail-breaking was largely a matter of chance. Maude could ruin everything if we caught her in a fractious mood.

I said, "I have written to the sheriff of Cedar Rapids about the matter, and sent the money back, but I didn't know if he believed me."

"What money is that?" Borden Kind said.

"The money from the bank robbery in Des Moines. We didn't rob the bank"—and here I had to think about what

I'd written, for Marion was supposed to have breathed his last—"but got the money when the true robber died of his wounds."

"I have a nose for lies," Borden Kind said.

"Then you should take a look at today's paper and smell one. Or better yet, have Maude tell you her story, and you will smell the truth."

"I have heard nothing of money being received in Cedar Rapids."

"Perhaps the sheriff is crooked."

"That's an interesting story you tell," he said. "But you aren't saying anything different than what a guilty person says: 'I didn't do it.'"

"It's what the innocent person says, too," said I. In some deep corner of my heart, I was enjoying this conversation. "For what innocent ever comes to you to say he's guilty?"

"That's not my point," he said. "The guilty don't claim to be guilty; they claim to be innocent. What fool of a lawman believes such a claim?"

I said, "If this is how you think, how can you ever believe anything?"

He gave me a long look of the resigned sort.

"Can you ask about that money?" I said, and I saw on his face the look of not wanting to be fooled. "Can you find out if any money was returned to the bank?"

When finally he answered me, he said, "It ain't that easy, son. The sheriff you're talking about is in another state, taking the whole matter out of my jurisdiction."

"Then you don't have to hold Maude, either."

"If what you say is true, and he has money he didn't return

to its rightful place, it's your sister's word against his. That's a hard fight to win."

He didn't see any good coming out of this conversation, and for a fact, neither did I. I took a firmer tone and said, "My sister has done nothing wrong. She shouldn't be sitting in jail."

"I can't help you, boy. I have a job to do."

Marion opened the back door and came in, a pistol in his hand. I was struck by how quiet he was, compared to the kicked-in door of the last jailbreak. But Borden Kind heard him coming and broke off sounding impatient with me.

"Well, now, I should have realized you weren't alone," Borden Kind said to me.

"You don't leave us any choice," Marion said, and I figured he must have been listening the whole time. He threw the rope to me and I commenced wrapping it around Borden Kind and the chair he sat in.

"This will not help your sister's case," Borden Kind said right before Marion stuffed a rolled-up sock into his mouth and tied it over with a kerchief. Marion had come ready to do justice to the job.

"We're sorry to do this," I said to him, "but according to you, nothing will help Maude's case. We can't leave her fate to the kind of justice that considers the truth too hard a fight to win."

Between us, Marion and me tied the chair to the leg of the desk so he couldn't roll around in it, banging against the wall. Something about doing this together with Marion, or maybe that so far we hadn't run into trouble, began to lift my mood.

More than that, I was entirely happy in the way of working at something I liked. Trading horses, for instance. I wasn't grinning foolishly, just noticing jail-breaking, when it went well, had its good points.

This was our second jailbreak, and while we had done well enough at the first one, we were much better at this one. There was a piece of Aunt Ruthie at work in me, for I did like a job well done.

While Marion tightened a few last knots, I looked in the desk drawer and found a key. Maude was standing right inside, at the ready, when I unlocked the door.

"You don't look much the worse for wear," I told her as she brushed past me. Marion held out Maude's hat, which had been on the sheriff's desk.

He said, "I hope you aren't going to get arrested again. It's hard work, breaking you out. Never had such a hard time breaking myself out."

Maude took her hat from him fast, almost as if she would slap him with it. "I guess I don't need you totting up how many times I've been arrested," she said, "like it's something I do for sport. Like I bellied up to the local watering hole and broke all the mirrors and drilled holes in the floor."

"She has a mouth on her like a drover," Marion said to me.

Since working at George Ray's, Maude's language *had* gotten a little ripe. "Getting arrested puts her in a bad mood," I said cheerfully. I was right in the midst of one of the best times of my life.

Marion gave me a meaningful look and said to her, "I don't know what you have to be mad about. You got yourself arrested again and here I am in the nick of time. But I can't continue riding with you. I want the boy to come along with me. I'll leave him with his grammaw in Wichita."

"We don't have time to fight about it," I said. Maude could just have her conniption fit later, was how I saw it. "We don't have enough rope left over to tie up someone else if they happen in now."

Maude walked out of there, bold enough she didn't peek outside first. We went straight to our horses and rode away at the same walk other riders were using, without ever looking back.

"I hope you don't think you've fooled him with that sorry attempt to steer him south," Maude said to Marion.

"I doubt that I have," Marion said. "But it means he'll have to consider more than the single possibility of following three sets of tracks westward."

TWENTY-FIVE

I DIDN'T NOTICE ANYONE LOOKING AT US AS IF THEY thought us unusual. The peddler's wagon had moved on and the town had gone back to its usual business, and I was glad of it.

Maude rode well ahead of us. Though she did drop back as we got to the outskirts of town. She said, "I hope we didn't lose the eats."

I passed her a twist of candy to hold her.

"Let's us ride faster for a time," Marion said, and so we did. We rode south, which might have lost us some time but for the fact we turned west soon enough.

Within an hour we had run back onto the trail. We had horses and all of our supplies, and we weren't riding hamper-scamper in all directions, hoping to meet up later.

There was no one chasing us, but it had been a thing to get the blood moving. A feeling like laughter kept rising in me. I wished I had a way to share it all with Aunt Ruthie. Lately I felt I'd come to know certain things about her, and I believed she would have enjoyed a good jailbreak.

I didn't know which was more surprising, the twists of fate

that got Maude arrested, or the stroke of luck that made it possible to free her again.

After several minutes we slowed down again. It was tempting to make some distance. Yet we couldn't keep our horses running full-out, or they wouldn't have the speed if we needed it worse later on.

"Have a peppermint," Maude said. "That usually makes you feel better."

That usually made *her* feel better, but I didn't say so.

"Did you get the wire off to Uncle Arlen?" I said.

"I was still figuring out what to say when they grabbed me," she said. "But I hadn't yet said who I wanted to send it to, so that's all right."

"We might could try again," I said. "I saw a newspaper that reported a sighting of you in Texas."

"Texas!"

"That's where they're looking for you today," I said, deciding that was enough for her to know just then. I had on my mind that newspaper story and had made up my mind to wait until Maude fell asleep. Then I would tell Marion the whole of it. "If we're quick enough to reach the next town, we can send a message before Borden Kind sounds the alarm."

"She has something there," Marion said. "Right after that sheriff gets loose, they're going to be watching for you in these parts."

"I'll wait for you at the edge of town this time," she said with a glance that included Marion. "You mustn't be long enough to worry me."

Marion didn't give any hint he'd heard this near apology.

"I'll leave one of my dimers with you, and you can pretend you're caught up in reading," I said to Maude.

To this she made a small huffing sound.

"Powder Keg McCarthy makes good reading," I said. "He has fought Indians in Kansas, brought a murderer to justice in the Dakotas, and tracked a rogue bear in the mountains of Colorado."

"I would rather have the dime you spent," Maude said in a lively tone.

"Keg is often in some kind of trouble, but is seen to do the right thing in the end," I said. "I think you'd like these stories."

"How many dimers do you figure you've bought?"

"I might could've bought a horse if I'd saved the dimes," I said.

This got her. She pushed her horse for a little speed and rode ahead, as if to say she hoped I wouldn't bother her.

"You're awful quiet," I said to Marion.

"I'm thinking we'll send you into the next town." He looked at me. "If word is being passed along, they aren't looking for a boy alone."

"All right."

He said, "Unless you don't care to do it."

"I'll do it." I didn't care to think a great deal about it, but I would do it.

Then Maude rode back to us and said, "What did we agree to say in that telegram?"

Marion joined in on planning the words as we rode. *Macdougal is ailing, but we will arrive in a timely fashion,* we finally decided. I would sign it with the initials SAM.

Some might guess it came from someone named Sam, going to meet someone they didn't know, but it would mean "Sallie and Maude" and let him know we were coming his way.

Maude didn't like the idea of waiting around for me on the edge of a place. She still might be recognized.

I said, "You can pull your hair to the back of your head, and it will not matter so much then the color is dark."

"At least I wouldn't look so much like the posters," Maude agreed. "But I've lost my hairpins."

I said, "Can you tear a strip off that petticoat?"

"What boy do you know who uses bits of petticoat to tie his hair?"

"If it's dirty enough, they will not know what it is," I said. "For right now, it's all we have."

We ate from the pickled eggs and biscuits as we rode. We didn't reach another town for two hours. Heavy on my mind was the worry the sheriff would have been found and he'd've telegraphed all the surrounding towns to be on the lookout for us.

This place was some larger, some rowdier, and nowhere near so prosperous-looking as Sheriff Kind's town. I saw that medicine peddler's wagon again, just closing up shop. I might could have gone for the closer look I wanted earlier, but the mood for idle curiosity had flown.

The telegraph office was hung with wanted posters, three and five in a sheaf. I riffled the pages of some and didn't see Maude's poster anywhere. I couldn't look like I was interested in anyone specific, but like I was doing it to pass the time as I waited my turn.

I came across a picture of the Black Hankie Bandit. He

didn't look awful much like a man with a bad reputation. This picture was taken before he had a bullet hole in him.

My turn came up. I waited as the telegrapher tapped our message out. Aunt Ruthie had taken the trouble to teach this alphabet of dots and dashes to her students one year, and I remembered enough of it to know he sent the message I paid for.

I said all of what we agreed to and then added something I thought of at the last. I told Uncle Arlen he was to leave us a message at Fort Dodge. He should send it to Sam Waters, and we would pick it up when we arrived there.

I stopped for a minute as I came to a newspaper office. Some of the recent pages were stuck up on the window, and I looked to see what stories they had run lately.

I would have missed it if I'd been going by the pictures alone. They showed a woman with her hair pulled into broomtails at each side of her face. I had never known Maude to wear her hair in such a manner, and she wouldn't be flattered.

The headline wasn't awful large, which was something.

MAUDE MARCH RIDES AGAIN

As Edgy as Ever She Was

About nine o'clock last night the city was thrown into considerable excitement by a fire in the Hotel Flynn dinette.

I stopped reading and looked right away to see where this paper came from—Wichita. I thought, Well, that's good; due south of us, and right where Marion claimed we were going to anyway. I went on reading.

> It is reported that Maude March and her gang of four burlies ordered eggs and grits with sausage gravy. Following a complaint there was not enough sausage in the gravy, shots were fired. A busted lantern spilled oil and flames onto the table below. A stack of paper menus blazed up. Mad Maude walked out of the place looking unruffled.
>
> Hotel employees were able to douse the fire, but the dinette will be Closed today.

I didn't think it made a bad story. There wasn't nothing but rough behavior being complained of. Worse happened on many a Saturday night.

I almost felt it was too bad we couldn't tell the right side of today's events and read of them later.

I'd more and more come to realize that a story as reported in the newspaper could be so far removed from what really happened that the tale might just as well have come over the clothesline.

I went inside with every intention of asking for a copy of this paper. I thought it might ease Maude's mind. I noticed a smaller article to run on the back of that page.

Dang. Something more about Maude. I stood long enough to read it.

A MAD MAUDE MYSTERY

Unknown Facts Come to Light

This curious reporter has learned that the notorious Maude March has been living in Independence for some months with a younger brother.

Investigation reveals this young troublemaker is known for having a short fuse and fast fists. One of his classmates says of him, "He does not fight fair. He hits too hard."

Although it did not seem to be an important detail at the time, the sheriff did tell of a young boy being in the jailhouse just before Mad Maude's breakout was begun. Could her younger brother have gone in as a distraction as the jail was surrounded?

This fellow who bragged about being curious hadn't looked hard for the truth, if no one told him Maude didn't have a younger brother, but a sister.

Still, it lifted my heart to see a mention made of me, and then sank it, as the full meaning of this came home to me. Maude, whether she was dressed as man or woman, wasn't in the least disguised by traveling with a boy.

I was made to think how often it happened in life something appeared before my eyes for no other apparent reason than as a message meant especially for me. I was noticing how I never appreciated this fact unless the news was good.

I didn't want to ask for the paper anymore, even one more than a week old. I figured, who would buy an old paper, except someone who had an unusual interest?

TWENTY-SIX

I HAD THE BROOMTAIL MAUDE ON MY MIND AS I RODE out of town, and the fresh knowledge we were a hot topic—somewhere.

Not only that, I was afraid Maude was right; these newspaper articles about her—us—might move west faster than we could. What we needed was a big bank robbery to bump us off the page. Where was Jesse James when we needed him?

Lost in these thoughts, it came as something of a shock to me to see Maude stood talking in a friendly manner to the two people in front of that medicine peddler's wagon.

I rode halfway past them before Maude waved a "come here." So I let my horse saunter on over, much like I didn't know her any better than I knew them. Like my heart wasn't beating faster.

Maude said, "This is my sister, Sallie."

I didn't know what to say to this. It amazed me to hear Maude introduce me as a girl; we had let people think I was a boy for so many months, I just naturally thought she'd expect me to go on being one.

"Sallie, I've taken a job with Dr. Aldoradondo and his

missus—Rebecca, she says to call her that. They're going west to Fort Dodge. We'll have a few dollars in our pocket when we get *home*."

I heard the way she said "home," she was letting me know she had told them a story I was to fit into. My heart was beating fast; I couldn't think about a story right then.

"My wife has been my right arm in this business," the doctor said, the same silver-haired gent I'd seen before. He used that hearty voice he'd used for selling the elixir—he sounded like he was talking with the help of a bellows. "But we're getting on in years."

His wife beside him wasn't so showy. She looked older in a way that he didn't. Her hair was pure white, and her cheeks were softly wrinkled. She smiled at me, and from somewhere inside myself, I mustered up one of my own.

"Thanking you for your offer, Dr. Aldoradondo," I said. "I'd like to talk to my sister alone for a minute, if you don't mind."

I didn't wait for a reply but rode past the horse end of that wagon and then some. Any minute now there would be a new story to hit the papers, one that would truly place Maude right about here. Maude and her little brother.

"I know what you're going to say, Sallie," Maude said in a fierce whisper as she came to stand beside my horse. "But don't take it up with me. Marion overheard the missus, Rebecca, say she was looking for a hand and told her he knew of four."

"You stood still for that?"

"He told her it was unseemly for me to be traveling unchaperoned with the likes of him."

"You should have whomped him," I said. "Made it clear to the missus there was a good case of unseemly going around."

"I wish I'd thought of it," Maude said. "I just stood there with my mouth hanging open."

"Where is he?"

Maude said, "He'll ride ahead of us at some distance until he's sure it's working out. Then he'll wait for us at the Cotton-wood River crossing."

"But why?"

"I'll be disguised," Maude said with that impatience all big sisters master. "I must get out of boy clothes, now that sheriff has seen me dressed this way. You said yourself my hair is long enough to pull back, and I can hide its color entirely with the right hat."

"You make it sound like you've thought it through," I said, meaning I could see she'd made up her mind.

"It's only for a few days," Maude said. "Soon the towns will be few and far between, and we'll be able to make good time on the open prairie."

"Why'd you go and tell them I'm a girl?"

"I don't know why I told them, Sallie. I just felt like it would be good to have one truthful thing to say."

I understood that feeling and felt more inclined to forgive her. But I wasn't yet ready to give in. I said, "If you're selling elixirs, what am I doing?"

Maude looked bewildered and said, "What do you want to do?"

"Ride shotgun," I said.

"I've lost a dress size; my hair is falling out and may never see its true color again," Maude said, and the scariest part was, she wasn't yelling. "I don't want to go back to anyplace where the mattress is wet and the soles of my boots crickle as I walk over the sticky floor. I have only a shred of sanity left. Do you think you could just do what I ask of you, at least when they're within earshot?"

"I guess so," I said, but Maude would not settle at that.

"I want to look like we're just ordinary girls."

"You want a great deal," I said to her.

TWENTY-SEVEN

MAUDE SHOWED HER WORKING DRESS TO THE MISSUS, who promptly started looking for a dress she considered more suitable. I figured she meant cleaner. She did have a trunk with a great many dresses in it.

Also, Maude carried water inside to take a spit bath.

While they were busy with this, Dr. Aldoradondo stripped off his fancy jacket and shiny red vest. I helped him see to watering the horses and putting a little hay in front of them.

I'd hung the sack of foodstuffs from Maude's saddle before coming into town, and it was gone now. Maude must've given it to Marion. He would eat well tonight, I knew that much.

"Where'd you get such big horses?" I asked the doctor. The broad backs of these animals outsized Uncle Arlen's big bay.

"They're a special breed for working, better than oxen for speed, but equal to oxen for pulling strength."

A simple question didn't need so much of a voice to answer it. He didn't notice his manner put me off a little. He checked the felts on the team's harnesses and made sure nothing was rubbing them any which way.

I didn't want to look any less careful, so I pulled the

saddles off our horses and rubbed them down. The doctor put a little back into this, which I appreciated, seeing he didn't have to do anything for my horse, by rights.

I had not mentioned to Maude the worry that we would find less water ahead of us. The lack of rain lately didn't appear to trouble the doctor. The rain barrels were nearly empty, and I pointed this out.

"We'll get water from the town well before we go," Dr. Aldoradondo said in an offhand way.

Where we stood, tracks made deep marks in shifting powdery dust. Maybe he hadn't noticed this because he wasn't striking out on any great stretch of land that didn't promise a well. But the creeks were low.

"I'll get the water," I said, for I was sure the well would be covered after dark. It made me feel a sight better to pour a couple of buckets of water into those rain barrels.

"I see you're a hard worker," he said. "Hard workers make a success of themselves in this world."

"Not always," I said. "Or my Aunt Ruthie wouldn't have been behind in her house payments when she died."

"Ah," he said to this. And after a moment, "You have the right of it. Luck plays a hand in most endeavors."

"Endeavors?"

"The effort we make," he said. "Some efforts don't play out well if the luck isn't with us."

"That's it exactly," I said. He wasn't so bad, after all.

But he had meant for this talk to lead up to something, and after another sashay or two, he got his point in. "You could be working alongside your sister, if you care to."

"How's that?"

He showed me a basket with a neck strap affixed to it so it could be worn, leaving a person's hands free. When he talked up his goods to the ladies, he wanted me outside in the street hawking small items that could be sold for a nickel or a dime.

"Why do you sell sundries if your business is medicine?" I asked him outright.

"Some customers are just naturally leery of buying something for the first time," he said. "A first small purchase of something they trust can change their minds."

I nodded. I would do it. I didn't care to be eating for free.

In the evening, when the customers were men, I would have an assortment of envelopes of tobacco for chewing or smoking, rolling paper, and the like. The pricing, he told me, was set so there was little need to make change, just shove the coins or bills in my apron pocket.

I ignored the mention of an apron pocket.

Truth to tell, there was some excitement in this for me.

I liked the feel of money in my hands. It never mattered to me that I would hand it over to Uncle Arlen or, now, to the Aldoradondos. It was the doings of business I liked, the question of how much to pay or to sell for, not the keeping.

I knew someone had come across Borden Kind by now and heard the story he had to tell. While me and the doctor talked, and then as we waited for Maude and the missus to finish the work they were about, I watched for any sign of the law, or anyone else hurrying about. I saw nothing to alarm me.

Maude came out of that wagon and, under the sunburn, her cheeks were lit up like Christmas. She wore a dark blue dress that rustled when she moved. The skirt spilled ruffles down the back and had some spangles besides.

"Sequins," the missus called them. Her tone had a bit of Aunt Ruthie in it, giving me to know there was nothing wrong with them.

I don't suppose there was anything wrong with them except I'd never seen my sister wearing them. I'd had half an idea Maude might get to work inside the wagon. I saw now they wanted her to stand in the street and do her best to attract attention. That was the business they were in.

"She has to cover her hair," I said, giving in on the spangles and going to what really mattered.

Maude said, "I believe a hat makes a lady respectable."

The missus turned back into the wagon, using the little step at the back, and Maude went in behind her. I followed them with great curiosity. On one side—the home side, you might say—a long bunk ran along the wall from corner to corner, only wide enough for one person to sleep.

On the business side, where part of the wall let down to become a shelf, bottles were lined up on narrow shelves with railings so they couldn't fall off. A rocker occupied the floor behind the wagon seat.

"Look over your head, Sallie," Maude said. And there I saw two chairs and a table with folding legs were fitted into wood angles so they hung out of the way till they were to be used.

Lanterns hung there as well. "I've never seen anything like it," I said, and the missus was pleased. I sat on the bunk to watch her work.

She pulled Maude's hair back extremely tight and pinned a hairpiece in the wrong color over the short ends. A deep purple scarf was wrapped around Maude's head so it couldn't be seen that the hair didn't match, and an ostrich plume was added to that.

The effect transformed Maude entirely. I was satisfied that, if she didn't look like my Maude, she didn't look like that Maude in the newspaper, either. I doubted Uncle Arlen or Marion would know her right off.

The missus turned to me and said, "You'd look real nice in a dress. We can buy you a bonnet."

Only the week before I would have fought this idea tooth and nail. But I was bothered to think people might watch out for Maude riding with a younger brother, especially now that Borden Kind could back up that story.

I didn't say no precisely, but I didn't say yes just yet.

Come time to work, small square bottles were set out on the shelf in a box. The bottom of the box slid out, and when the bottles stopped jiggling, the sides were lifted, leaving the bottles lined up for purchase. It made for fast work, done easily.

These weren't the pretty bottles I remembered. They were filled with liquid dark brown and strong-smelling. This discouraged no one, apparently.

Maude took the money and made change as needed, doing a brisk business. At first I watched to see if anyone looked at her with special interest. Maybe it was the cover of near darkness or the come-to-me tone in the doctor's voice, but men hardly looked at Maude once they got next to her. They almost acted like they were in a hurry to get away.

I figured it had to do with a night on the town. The pianos

in the halls played lively music. Laughter and loud voices could be heard from inside the saloons and, once in a while, the crash of glass.

The doctor sounded like a cross between a preacher and a gun-toting sheriff. "Gentlemen, your valleys shall be raised and your mountains ironed flat, your crookeds made straight as a corpse in December, and your rough places smooth as a mule's coat."

This sounded like a big promise. I figured the doctor was going to need some help from on high to make good on it. One fellow asked him what he had in those bottles and was given this answer: "These good soldiers hold the cure for the disease of royalty."

For most, this was proof enough we were selling the very thing they were looking for. I thought Dr. Aldoradondo was smart to have found a way to compliment them into buying his wares.

Three men rode past us at one point, and I realized they were lawmen. I didn't stand there like a tent pole, but strolled among the customers, saying, "Finest pipe tobacco, sweet cherry smoke, thin paper for rolling," like it read on the packages.

These riders looked us over and moved on.

Maude's horse and mine were tied at a trough a little distance from the wagon. So were several others, but it struck me as a good thing that ours were. Looking at us, our disguise was helped by the fact the peddler's wagon didn't have two more horses tied to it.

I resolved to do this again if we continued on to another town with the Aldoradondos.

In fact, but for the neck strap did rub a little, I didn't find the work unpleasant. The tobacco smelled of cherry, one kind, and another tobacco smelled like honey.

It reminded me of the stuff Aunt Ruthie never would buy at church socials, little sachets with dried flower bits inside. There was an odd comfort in this and in thoughts of Aunt Ruthie.

I kept an eye open for Marion, but he was nowhere to be seen. He liked to play down the stories that were told about him, but he had his talents. Blending in was one of them.

TWENTY-EIGHT

Just as I began to wonder when the pianos would stop playing, the doctor pulled in three unsold bottles and shut the wagon up. I saw Maude's shoulders relax. I was growing oddly impatient by then, wanting to ride further, and faster, wanting to make more distance.

Equally, I wanted a glimpse of Marion. I hadn't had a share in the making of this plan, and I didn't feel quite resigned to it. I was growing tired, and that helped me through this.

We rode outside of town and camped for the night.

Once we had put the horses to bed, that was how the doctor put it, I was ready to take to a bed as well. We sat for a few minutes inside the wagon, me and Maude on the two chairs the doctor took down from the hooks in the ceiling, the missus and him on the long bunk they slept on, the bottoms of their feet touching. She laughed as she told us this, and sliced apples for us, and made us feel quite at home.

I began to warm to them.

To the doctor, I said, "You closed down right smartly once you made up your mind you were finished. Don't you lose a few customers that way?"

"I shut down the minute I see no one is looking for a loose coin," he said. "The hesitant come to the table quicker next time."

"I guess that's wise," I said. "What's your elixir made of, anyway?"

"I start with a base of brandy or whiskey," he said. "Both of these have medicinal properties. I add amounts of cascara and horseradish, goldenseal or turpentine, depending on the desired effect."

"People swallow turpentine?"

"People swallow most anything," he said. "A few drops of oil of peppermint or wintergreen will disguise any unpleasant odors."

"Sounds not altogether bad," I said.

He said, "Tastes terrible," and made a face.

I didn't reply to this, nor did Maude.

A look passed over his face in an instant, as had happened with Borden Kind, but after a minute I realized it only meant he'd hoped to make me and Maude giggle.

"We're some tired," I said, for I didn't care to hurt his feelings.

The missus stood to clear away the bowl of apples, saying, "Well, of course you must be. It's been a day of change for you."

"Yes, ma'am," I said.

We slept that night on the floor of the wagon. Dr. Aldoradondo took a pallet under the wagon "to make a ladies' space." I thought it right good of him.

The only odd thing, he insisted we all wash our hands with strong soap. He kept a pail of water in the wagon for the sole purpose of hand-washing, and he didn't stop talking about the need for it while the four of us took turns at the basin.

"We bathe as often as circumstance allows us," the missus said.

They didn't look uncommonly clean to me, but I took this to mean me and Maude looked dirtier yet, at any rate not clean enough to be working for them. This was undoubtedly true after several days on the trail, and I felt some apologetic for it.

He was *real* finicky about his fingernails. I asked him about it and regretted it ten minutes later, when he was still telling me how important it was to have clean hands in every task from household cooking to putting balm on a scratch.

I could have spared myself this lecture if I'd told him I rarely found a scratch worth bothering about, I felt sure, but there was something kindly in his manner that made me listen equally politely. Probably he couldn't help it he still sounded like he spoke through a horn.

In the morning, me and Maude hitched our horses to the wagon rail and rode into the next town sitting on the back step of the wagon. It was a rocky ride, but we couldn't be overheard.

I said, "Have you told Dr. Aldoradondo or the missus what we're running from?"

"Let's keep our story to ourselves," Maude said. "We don't yet know what they're running from."

It had not occurred to me they were running from anything.

"I forget," Maude said. "Working at George Ray's, I would

forget how beautiful it is out here. How much there is to feel." She had taken on that look of love again.

I didn't know what to make of this at any time, and I didn't know what to say now. I pulled my compass out of my pocket and watched the needle quiver. "Due west," I said. "We're traveling due west."

"I know that," Maude said in lilting tones.

Aunt Ruthie used to scold her for that manner; Aunt Ruthie thought those tones meant she was teasing and not caring. But that was never so. I never truly understood those tones, but they weren't teasing and Maude was ever caring.

"Do you want to see Uncle Arlen's map?"

Maude gave me a smiling look, like I was a puzzle she couldn't complete. "Don't wear it out," she said, and she was fully my big sister again.

Once in the town of Council Grove, we drew a running herd of children. No one I saw looked twice at Maude or me.

"Run alongside the wagon," the missus said, giving me a handful of candy sticks. "Pass them around."

We did indeed take advantage of the bathhouse, first thing. As she paid for my bath, I told the missus, "Me and Maude are fond of bathing."

I felt the need to say this, although it was truer of Maude than myself. Her rule was twice a week, and at that I thought the practice overdone. What was accomplished in two baths that couldn't be done with one?

By the time we were ready to do business, the children's mommas were collected in the street around the wagon. My basket was filled with packages of needles and pins, thimbles, nail brushes, and hair combs.

I had the chance to see how useful that basket could be. Even those ladies who wanted such favors as packets broken up for the sale of one needle put down a coin for one of those colored bottles, or maybe for the cure inside it.

I didn't waste twenty minutes deciding my daylight customers were those ladies who stood on the outside of the circle, the shy ones. And right after that, the ones who hung about in doorways, unwilling to mix with the "nicer" ladies of the town, but every bit as much in need of relief from their ills.

To the sundry items in my basket, I added a few well-chosen bottles.

"Are you worn up and worn down?" I said in a low voice that didn't interfere with the doctor's. "Is your sleep fitful; are you full of worry and woe, aches and pains? One spoonful of this panacea will bring you sure recovery."

I sold twelve bottles the first time out. My pocket was heavy with change each time I worked my way over to the back door of the wagon, and after the first time, the missus, Rebecca, was waiting to hand me more bottles.

When the last of my customers drifted over to hear what more was being said by Dr. Aldoradondo, I stepped inside the wagon. The money was counted, and Maude put two dollars in her pouch.

There was hand-washing to follow touching the money. I got first turn at the basin. The doctor said, "I think we could have another round of sales in an hour's time."

"I'm ready for it," I said.

I chose a different set of bottles to sell. I liked a clear, square bottle that was plain but for the bird etched in the glass. The doctor took it out of my basket without saying a word.

For a moment I thought he meant I shouldn't sell bottles. But he didn't look angry. When I reached for a different bottle, he nodded. I made up my basket.

When we went back to work, I noticed the doctor sometimes sold that clear bottle, but he didn't set it out on the shelf with the others.

Later in the day, as they treated us to a meal at the hotel, I said, "Why won't everybody sell medicine, if it makes so much money?"

"Not everyone trusts medicine," Dr. Aldoradondo said. "Many times I've paid the price of someone else's shoddy practices."

"What does that mean?" Maude asked with a sharp look at him. "You got run out of town?"

"Those were the old days," the missus said, her frown telling me they were also days she remembered.

"That kind of thing doesn't happen anymore, does it?" Maude asked, passing the bowl of stewed meat and potatoes to me. I'd put my suspicion of stew meat aside in favor of good manners. "I can't let Sallie get hurt."

"You need have no fear," Dr. Aldoradondo said, the way he'd told his customers his medicines were surefire. Most people were reassured by his manner, I'd give him that, but Maude was not most people.

"I can't let Sallie get hurt," she said again.

He looked at his wife and said, "Isn't there a bit of shopping you mean to do, my dear, before we ride on?"

"I could use a twist of peppermints," Maude said to me. "Run to the store for me, won't you?"

I went over to a sweet shop and bought the candy. I was tempted into buying a dozen oatmeal cookies dotted with raisins.

I knew she meant for me to look for news. I looked for Marion. No one on the street looked the slightest familiar. I didn't see a newspaper. I wasn't eager to see the paper, truth be told, but I did feel I had to look for it.

A worn copy of *Ulee Derouen, Explorer of the Alaskan Territories* lay beside the register in one place I stepped into. I said, "Can I look at it?"

The fellow behind the counter said, "You can buy it, like four people before you. I'll buy it back for two cents." I riffled through it to make sure all the pages were there before I paid half the original price.

I was halfway thinking it didn't interest me, for I wasn't one to read happily of cold toes and noses, unless I was to find a Wild Woolly. I'd had my share of breaking through snow to get a morsel of food, and it was my feeling that Wild Woolly knew the truth of such situations.

But then I thought of being without a book entire, and I gave in. I could read fast through any parts I didn't care for. I congratulated myself on retaining the better part of the dollar.

"Did you find a paper?" Maude asked me the minute I got back to the wagon.

"Nope." It bothered me more we hadn't seen hide nor hair of Marion. "He could pass us right by," I said to Maude. I didn't have to mention names.

"He told me he would ride ahead of us," Maude said. "We aren't to meet up again until we have run through this string of towns. A week, maybe."

A lot could happen in a week. These little towns didn't all of them sit square on the beaten trail, either. I had a sudden picture of Marion and Uncle Arlen and me and Maude all missing each other by scant miles, each going our own way and never coming together again.

Maude said, "Quit worrying. He's waiting for us at a point west of here."

I felt for the map, the way I did several times a day, and said, "I hope that's the way we're heading."

TWENTY-NINE

Rebecca called to me from the wagon. "Sallie, come help me with these bottles, please."

This was only an excuse to get me inside, where she presented me with a store-bought dress; a fine gingham, deep blue, the tiniest checks I'd ever seen. I'd had that bath recent enough I was still reasonable clean. It would have been too poor of me to refuse to try it on.

She'd matched up the dress with a bonnet of white eyelet. It was probably in the nature of a bribe she had also purchased bloomers with a white eyelet ruffle at the hems.

"You knew about this," I said to Maude, who had come in right behind me. Her eyes were all a-sparkle with a good joke on me.

"Let me help you with the buttons," Maude said.

I turned so she could get at them. "I didn't think I wanted a dress," I said, enjoying the particular crispness of the cotton. "But I think I like this one."

"If you come with me when I go shopping," the missus said, blushing as if she were the one wearing the new dress, "we'll look for button-up shoes. Those boots you wear are fine for riding, but not at all pretty."

I said, "These boots were never meant to be pretty," giving in to the idea of button shoes as well. I pulled my hair into a short stiff braid behind each ear. I didn't look half bad when I put on the bonnet.

"Thank you, Rebecca."

It was only too bad to think of getting my whites dirtied by riding the trail. I couldn't bring myself to soil the bonnet, so I wrapped it in my sack and went on wearing my hat over the braids.

I thought our disguise couldn't have been improved much if we had been wrapped in rugs and smuggled away on camels like Poor Lula in the Perilous Fortunes line. I didn't know until the next day something else was happening that helped keep Maude's identity a secret.

THIRTY

AT MIDDAY, BETWEEN ONE TOWN AND THE NEXT, I noticed a sizable dust cloud coming from behind us. It wasn't much of a dust cloud, which probably ruled out a posse, and maybe it ruled out Indians.

This didn't make it good news.

"Someone's coming," I said.

We couldn't hide here in this flat spread of low scrub and half-tall grass. Even if we roughed up the horses in a dead run we couldn't be sure of escape.

"It's almost certainly trouble," Rebecca said. She put her parasol away.

We didn't stop our progress, which suddenly felt to me awful agonizing slow, but looked on that dust cloud as if it were an oncoming storm we could do nothing about.

Maude had ridden ahead, watching for game. She came back to us. "There are four of them," she said. "We can make a stand of it, if it comes to that."

Dr. Aldoradondo's answer was to pull his rifle up to lay over his lap.

Not only did the doctor have a gun, but so did Rebecca. I'd always believed that little reticule of hers to be heavy with coins.

Certainly there were some, because I heard them jingle as she pulled out a tiny pistol meant to shoot at close range. No bigger than her hand, it looked ready to do a damage.

"Do you know how to use that?" I asked her.

She replied, "What a silly question that is," which surprised me more than a little. She carefully placed one of the folds of her skirt over her hand.

We stood at the ready, for that dust cloud was drawing near.

"No one shoot unless I do," Dr. Aldoradondo said. "If they want money, I'll give it to them."

The riders came a-hooting and hollering in our direction. They were a sight and sound to take the breath from the bravest man; not only loud and filthy, but reckless with their horses and ours, jostling us in a practiced manner.

They drew their guns as they pulled in tight around us, bringing us to a halt.

I got so scared I yelled for Maude. If not for the weight of the shotgun in my hand, I would have reached for her as if I were still truly a little sister.

One of the wild riders tried to take Maude's rifle, but she turned her horse away from them, which put the rifle out of reach. I'd been holding my shotgun pointing down my leg, so they may not have seen it at all in the crush.

"Reach for the sky," one of them shouted in the midst of all the dust and yelling. "I am Mad Maude!"

"You?" Maude said to this pretender. Maude's voice shook, but only on that first word. "You're the one with her face on all the wanted posters?"

The woman met this with a horrible grin. "That's me."

"You can't be," I said, because one of her gang had stilled his horse, taking an interest in my Maude's willingness to answer back. "Maude March is a girl, and you are some years past that."

She was a woman as old as Aunt Ruthie had been, if she was a day. She was missing a front tooth.

Her cohorts ceased their mindless caterwauling, since no one was bothering with them much. One of them said to the other, "What's she saying?"

I added, "You haven't the neighbor of a resemblance to Maude March," and my Maude promptly swatted me to hush me up.

"How do you know that?" the pretender said.

"I have seen posters."

"You can't make no never mind of those posters," she said. "The people drawing them haven't seen me."

"Her name is Maude," one of her fellow riders added. "I've knowed her my whole life."

"Then what has she done that's so terrible?" I asked him.

"She has been chased by two posses this week alone," he said. "She has outrun them once and outwitted them the other."

His Maude was far off the mark, but his manner was that of one friend standing by another, and I liked him for it.

"Stand and deliver!" another of them yelled, trying to get them back on track.

One of them reached for Rebecca's reticule, which was looped over her wrist under that fold of skirt. He reached for it roughly, which was no doubt how he believed these things ought to be done.

I couldn't be sure how the next event came about.

Maybe Rebecca shot him on purpose. But maybe the outlaw jerked her so hard she couldn't help it, and he shot off his own earlobe.

This happened quickly, and without any chance of Rebecca taking aim, so it was lucky for him the bullet did not land somewhere more likely to kill him.

But an earlobe is a surprisingly messy place to get shot.

All of us got sprayed a bit with blood as his horse startled and turned away from the sudden shouting and jostling and brandishing of guns. No more shots were fired, probably because we were all afraid of hitting one of our own in such close quarters.

Right in the midst of this, the one who claimed to have known this Maude pretender all his life groaned and slid from his horse. It brought us all to a standstill.

Although his shirt was sprayed with blood, it wasn't his own blood. There were some glances all around.

"Winslow!" The pretender holstered her pistol and slid off her horse to get to him. He was clearly a favorite with her. She delivered to him a swift kick. Nevertheless, he lay on the ground, his eyes open and glassy, like a dead fish.

"He cain't take the sight of blood," she said sadly. "It's his weakness." At this reminder, the actually injured man commenced to howling.

The "stand and deliver" fellow grabbed the pretender's

151

horse's bridle and kept it from running off. Horses don't care for yelling, which is why a person does it to get them to run faster. In fact, all of our horses needed handling as the smell of blood reached their nostrils.

The earlobe was bleeding something ruinous. As a sight, that fellow was enough to turn the stomach. Despite this I breathed a sigh of relief. Better mortally injured than already dead.

"The tip end of his ear is gone," the pretender said.

A voice rose over the new confusion of voices that sprang up. "I'm a doctor. Let me tend to his wound before he bleeds to death."

Mad as this Maude claimed to be, she knew a generous offer when she heard it. She waved a hand in a "come over," and Rebecca took the reins while the doctor climbed to the ground.

"Hold your hand down tight over that ear," the doctor said. He took a moment to wash his hands, dipping into the rain barrel.

While he was about this, I took Rebecca's place so she could do more important things. Under the eagle eye of one of those fellows, she rummaged through a leather bag to find a needle and thread.

She found other things there, too. She gripped Maude by the chin and passed a bottle under her nose. My sister wasn't easy with the sight of blood, and looked pale.

Then Rebecca took a bracing whiff of the stuff herself.

The pretender pressed against the ear as the doctor made ready to sew that fellow up. He didn't stop howling, but he didn't flinch, either.

I flinched. It didn't seem to me to be a natural thing to take stitches where earlobes used to be.

While this was being done, the pretender looked around at us and said, "I guess we cain't rightly rob you after you fixed up Heck thisaway."

"I wouldn't need fixing if it weren't for one a them shooting at me," Heck said. Whined, more like. I wanted to kick him.

"Nobody would've shot you if you were doing us a good turn," Maude said. Our Maude, that is. "I could do with a cup of coffee."

"Now there's an idea," the pretender said.

Thirty-One

"I'LL GET THE MAKINGS FOR A FIRE," I SAID.

Winslow, the fainter, stayed flat to the ground beside Heck, the one with stitches in his ear.

The third fellow, the eagle eye, followed me as if there was a chance I might escape them. I broke dry grass and twisted it into cats. I tolerated his standing around doing nothing for about two minutes.

"If you want coffee, you'd better make yourself useful," I said.

I didn't expect him to do anything, but he surprised me. He helped me pull grass until we had a good-sized pile. Enough to burn for a time, even considering how brown the grass was.

Maude had meanwhile dug a little pit for the fire and had it going well in no time. "Your horses need water," I said to that fellow, and pointed out to him the bucket we used for the horses.

The pretender asked where were we folks traveling to, nice as you please. Like she had made up her mind to act like she'd forgotten why we were all gathered there.

"Fort Dodge," Dr. Aldoradondo answered her. "We're well known in these parts."

"And welcome, I reckon," she said. "Doctors are scarce hereabouts."

"And no wonder," I muttered, listening in as I filled the coffee pot.

"We're a little peckish, if you have anything to eat," said that eagle-eyed fellow who had been helping me as he took his place in the circle of his fellows and the doctor.

"There's a round metal box on a shelf," Maude said to me. "There are lemon cookies to serve with the coffee." She gave my foot a little kick as she turned to put the coffeepot on the fire. I took this as my go-ahead and hopped into the wagon just as Rebecca was coming out.

She had let down the shelf and made ready the coffee ingredients. Along with her good china cups, she'd set out my tin cup and the blue bowls. Also, sugar lumps. Of greatest interest to me was that mysterious medicine the doctor guarded so closely. It stood apart from the other things, but it was there on the shelf.

No one was looking right at me. Like I was doing something ordinary, and with not a tremble, I uncorked the bottle and squirted a dropperful into each of Rebecca's four china cups.

If someone had said to me, How much is too much, my answer to them would have been, We are about to find out. I reached for the tin box with the cookies.

I walked the cookies around like I was waiting on tables. Heck looked a sight. His ear had swelled up like a bladder. His shirt was still bright with his blood, but then so was nearly everyone else's. The ear, with its dark stitching, was more troublesome to look at.

The pretender told him to put his hat on over the injured part so the rest of us wouldn't have to think on it. Not knowing he was about to receive strong medication, she gave him a flask of something that made him cough so hard some of it shot out through his nose. He complained with a wordless groan, but she just clapped him on the back in a friendly fashion.

I didn't blink when she took a fistful of the cookies. "Will we have read of your exploits in the paper?" I asked her. I made it sound like she ought to be proud to tell.

"Possible," she said to me in a coy fashion.

"Personally, I don't take the word of newspapers for much," I said. "They have reported you in three districts at once, just lately."

Maude said, "The coffee's ready," and I set the cookies down, in a hurry to make sure these rowdies got the cups.

Rebecca was already doing that. Maude stood ready to give them sugar. Both of them acted as if they tended to invited guests in their parlor.

The pretender said she could do with more sweetening, and Maude gave it to her without a word. "Good coffee," she said on her first sip. She was a polite one, she was.

The shaky Winslow held his cup carefully, keeping his pinky finger crooked. Heck wasn't so dainty and sloshed his first coffee about. Rebecca poured him some more. She gave him another two lumps of sugar. He downed it in one swallow. He made a face like he found it bitter.

"You think that's bad," the pretender said, "wait till you can feel the stitches in your ear."

Rebecca poured a swallow of coffee to the doctor and to me and to Maude, each of us drinking from a bowl. We weren't offered sugar. I did reach for it but was met with a sharp look from Rebecca and changed my mind.

She poured a little more coffee in their cups and offered around the sugar. The pretender and her fellows helped themselves to the bottom of the bowl. Heck just popped his sugar lump into his mouth. I had no idea what the medicine tasted like, but I had no doubt that much sugar could cover it.

Heck said he was feeling a little poorly, he thought he'd lie down for a minute. The pretender and her crew didn't think a thing of it.

Winslow said in a faintly slurred voice he wondered if he was truly cut out for this kind of work himself. Stand-and-deliver sneered at him.

This caused the pretender to send a slap in his direction, but it never got that far. Her hand fell into her lap as if it was too heavy to hold up. Stand-and-deliver fell into her lap, too. It dawned on her then something was wrong.

Maybe it occurred to that eagle-eyed fellow as well, but they both of them at the same time let their eyeballs roll up, and passed out.

Rebecca and Maude were quick, reaching for the cups before they hit the ground. Winslow looked at all of them in confusion and then fell over on his side.

"It worked faster than I'd hoped," Rebecca said, looking a little a-wonder about it. "I do think sugar speeds it up somehow."

I said, "You put it in the sugar?"

"I was afraid I couldn't give them enough without melting the sugar lumps," she said.

"I put it in the cups."

The doctor said, "How much?"

I shrugged. "A dropperful."

Rebecca gave a little laugh. "I guess I needn't have worried."

Maude said, "Could it kill them?"

The doctor said, "It could."

I looked down at them, and just as I wondered if I'd killed another man, Winslow began to snore. The pretender followed suit a moment later.

"Then again," the doctor said, "they're likely to sleep it off."

I picked up the cups and bowls and washed them out. There was a little discussion over what to do with them. We couldn't leave their guns. We didn't want to make it easy for them to catch up to us, either.

"In a dimer I read, some fellows left Hardweather his horse but dropped his saddle a ways off. They dropped the other gear further off, to slow him down."

It didn't take long to agree to this course of action. We took the saddles off the horses but left them hobbled so they couldn't wander away.

Maude pinned a note to the other one's chest. It read: *This is not Maude March.*

THIRTY-TWO

W E RODE ON TO THE OUTSKIRTS OF THE NEXT TOWN, which was Diamond Springs, and camped for the night. The place had a fast, rough way about it that wore on the nerves.

Partly I didn't like to hear the cattle bawling. They didn't get quiet as the sun went down but sounded ever more mournful. Partly it was the traffic on the road, which got worse, even as the night wore on.

With so many wagons trundling past, sleep was a fitful thing. In waking moments, I wondered if Marion was here in town or if he had pulled much further ahead of us.

Things could have gone badly with the pretender and left him with a good deal of explaining to do when finally he reached Uncle Arlen.

Unless something befell Marion along the way.

A person could disappear out here entire and no one ever know what happened to them. I didn't know what Uncle Arlen would make of it if something happened that the three of us never turned up.

That led to wondering what accidents of fate Marion might have. It bothered me more to think of getting to C.T. and finding he hadn't made it. For that matter, we didn't know how Uncle Arlen fared, making the entire journey alone.

"Stop rolling around so much," Maude whispered to me.

"I can't settle."

"Then don't," she said. "But be still."

"When did I become such a worrier?"

"You're not a worrier," Maude said. "You aren't stupid, either. There are times when things are more left to chance than we like to think about."

I turned my thoughts to guessing where on his map Uncle Arlen was by now. We were about a week and a half on the trail. So he ought to be halfway.

We were up and about uncommon early the next day. No one had troubled us, however. It might have been due to the fact that with so many people around, trouble couldn't go unseen.

What finally came to mind were the words I'd read in many a dimer, *Wild West*, and hadn't always felt it to be so hard upon me in Independence. It was some tamed by the time me and Maude arrived.

But once through the wide border state of Kansas, we would be outside the bounds of the law as we knew it. It did appear to me such bounds had some frayed edges.

As I tied Maude's horse and mine to the wagon rail, I heard a gunshot from town. Together with the feel of the place, this decided me to keep the horses close to hand.

It didn't bother me to wear the dress with my brown boots, for I'd worn something like them most of my life. Aunt Ruthie thought the expense of shoe buttons was a waste on children. But Rebecca couldn't abide it.

First thing, when she judged the stores would be open for business, she took me out to find the button-top shoes. I wore my new bonnet.

Maude came with us and busied herself with looking at ribbons and enameled hand mirrors and padded silk boxes. It appeared the people who came to Diamond Springs were uncommon fond of expensive trinkets.

"Now I have a use for that boot black," I said to Maude of my new shoes.

"You have a lot of Aunt Ruthie in you."

"I have no quarrel with that."

We bought the shoes, and then Rebecca had some business at the bank. While she was there, Maude and me were on our own. "There's a newspaper office," Maude said, after a look up and down the street.

The newspaper office was strangely dark. Maude opened the door and stuck her head inside, as if she had doubts about the place.

"Have you come about the job?" a man said to her. He sat at a desk just inside the doorway.

"I came looking for a paper," she said, stepping inside.

The man wore a visor that jutted over his face like a porch roof and a cloth vest of dark gray that didn't hide the ink smudges on it. He was narrow through the shoulders and hunched over the lettering of an envelope.

Perhaps because I had grown accustomed to the exceeding clean hands of the doctor, I was struck by the black line under his fingernails. I remembered seeing this before.

However, that fellow had been some dapper sort, was my impression. He'd looked sharp. This clerk looked like he couldn't pay for a meal, let alone rent a horse and rig.

"People want to write letters," he said. "But it's more than knowing how to write a good hand."

His glasses sat on the tip of his nose. They were the kind of half-circle glasses that Maude had worn until she broke enough pairs that Aunt Ruthie wouldn't buy her another.

"They don't know what to say," he went on. "They want you to know what to say. Can you do that?"

"She knows what to say," I told him, "but she isn't looking for a job."

He finished the *ia* of Pennsylvania before he looked over the top of his glasses. I saw then his eyes were blue. Not cool and watery, but a deep blue that could speak right to you.

I wondered if I wouldn't remember seeing those eyes before. For I didn't think I could be sure of him by his fingernails. I let it go. There were men with ink under their nails wherever there was a newspaper to be run, after all.

He ran a blotter over the envelope and set it aside. "Twenty-five cents for two pages," he said. "Ten cents is yours."

Maude said, "That's a high price."

He said, "It's cheap, if it buys them a story as well."

Maude said, "What kind of story?"

We stood in a building that was something larger than a shed but not much better outfitted. There was a cot on one side of the room, neatly made up. A table held a bowl and jug and several other items to suggest someone lived there.

The back of the place was taken up with a jumble of wooden pieces, as if something had come off the wagon but had never been put back together. These reminded me of a loom but were just different enough to interest me in putting them together in my mind.

"Any story must be somehow true to them," he was saying. "Do you have the truth in you?"

"I'm living a long way from the truth lately," Maude said.

I didn't think Maude needed to start thinking about this. I said, "Is that a printing press back there?"

"It is," he answered. "People hereabouts aren't steady readers. They have other things on their minds. Business and cattle, among them."

"Why are you here if there are no readers?" I asked him.

"I'll move further west when the time is right," he said. "When I know of a place that is hungry for the truth."

"That's a far thing from the stories I have seen in the papers."

He pushed his visor back. "She likes to read," Maude said, as if she were apologizing for me. "But she's always looking for true stories."

"What true story would you have me tell?" he said, still looking at me.

"There are stories all around," I said. "It's only the lack of recognizing them that keeps them a secret from you."

There was a silence while he digested the fact he didn't get the whole of what there was to know, but he didn't get a lie, either.

"That's the right spirit," he said finally. "Out here, a man with the right spirit is his own boss. He only needs a printing press."

"He needs more than that," I said. "He needs readers."

This got a short laugh. "My name is John Kirby," he said. "I'm easy to work for."

"Why is that?" Maude said.

"Because I'm a poor man of business."

For reasons I can't explain, this made Maude smile. "It's too bad, then, that we aren't looking for a job. Only a newspaper."

I saw Rebecca outside and nudged Maude. We said a speedy good-bye that brought John Kirby to the door to see us off.

"You haven't told me your name," he said to Maude, holding out his hand to be shaken.

"Maude Waters," she said, after a moment. "This is my sister, Sallie."

I didn't care for the sudden light in his eyes.

We went with Rebecca to the store. Standing by the window, I saw John Kirby didn't make a hurried trip to any other office, such as the sheriff's. In fact, I could see him at his window, bent over pen and paper.

Rebecca bought ham and potatoes and stewed dried corn, ready to eat, and some greens that hadn't been boiled quite gray. I couldn't fault her choices, though I couldn't cheer the last.

But then she turned to me and said, "Greens are not my preference, but the doctor insists on them." We smiled in the way of having a secret to share.

She asked then for a dried apple pie. I had already seen she hardly considered the price of a thing. She considered first the wanting of it, which was a thing I wasn't used to but was most prepared to admire.

Me and Maude carried the purchases on the way back to the wagon. We trailed behind Rebecca like ducklings on the busy boardwalk.

We were coming up on a glass-fronted barbershop. Maude pulled at my sleeve and whispered, "Sallie. If there's a newspaper to be found, it'll be in there."

"It would've been easier to get in there whilst I was dressed like a boy," I said. We had come to a stop, and so did Rebecca, although I didn't think she could hear much of what we said.

"Just dawdle past," Maude said.

I would, of course, but I couldn't resist saying, "That isn't much of a plan." Maude pinched me, though Rebecca was looking on. The terrible thing about being orphaned is big sisters do not have to worry about being caught at picking on the younger.

I slowed as I passed a fellow sitting outside, waiting on a haircut. He was cleaning his fingernails with a pocketknife. At the back side of him, in the shop, another fellow held a St. Louis paper. I was able to read it through the thinly soaped window.

The article interested me.

I read as fast as I could, stepping to one side where the window was too cloudy to see through. Then his turn came up, and he folded the paper away.

Maude and Rebecca were some three or four shops distant, waiting to go inside. Rebecca went inside when I looked that way.

I hurried over to Maude. "They've shot her," I whispered.

"Who?" But I could see on her face she did know.

I said, "They tried to arrest her, but then she was killed in the shootout." By my lights, this was cause for dancing.

Maude looked confused. "There, where we left them?"

"Not that one," I said. "There's another. This one was over St. Louis way."

Maude didn't look overjoyed. "That's awful."

"It's awful for her," I said. "But it's fine by us."

"Sallie, I don't like it you're so cavalier about that girl's death."

"Cavalier?" I said. I could see Maude was not in her dancing mood. Maybe I ought to care about that other girl; I could see Maude's point of view. But I didn't know that girl. She wasn't my sister. And she may not have been a nice person, either.

"I don't want to see that article," Maude said. "It's up to you what you read, but I don't want to read of my death."

I had not thought of it in this light.

THIRTY-THREE

WE STUCK CLOSE TO THE ALDORADONDOS THE REST of that day. I looked over my shoulder once or twice, worried about the light John Kirby had in his eyes.

"Sallie." Maude called me away from *Digger McGee, Gold Miner, Forty-niner.* I snatched up my basket and stopped at the doorway as I threw the strap over. I caught a glimpse of John Kirby, standing on the boardwalk. He was watching Maude.

"Come on, Sallie," she called, and I climbed down.

I had lost interest in the selling of tobacco. I may have given a packet or two away without collecting the funds. Each time I looked again, I couldn't see him, but I didn't doubt he was there in the shadows.

I hoped Marion was somewhere about as well.

My fingers trembled over taking money, and I chided myself for the nerves. I rode on the wagon seat as we left town and glared into every dark corner. I kept my shotgun beside me as I slept, but it was no help with the bad dreams.

I rolled the gun up in my bedroll the next morning, ready to hand, as I stared out the back door of the wagon. I didn't see a telltale billow of dust following us, and I was glad of it. I didn't mention the matter to Maude.

I had this to say for the doctor, he made good time. This was as much due to the horses' strength and willingness to move that wagon as it was to grease on the wheels, but I credited the man.

Still, I had a place I needed to be. To Maude, I said, "Have you seen Marion and forgot to mention it?"

"No."

"When do you expect him to show himself?" I said.

Maude said, "It won't be much longer."

"Does that mean tomorrow? The next day?" I said this because I had grown fond of Rebecca. "Maybe we should tell them they have to look for another helper."

"Don't pester me," Maude said.

From this I knew she was troubled about it.

We made a stop at midday. Wandering Creek looked much the same as any other town, except smaller than most we had stopped in so far. "It looks too small a place to bother with," I said.

"No stop is too short to make a dollar," Dr. Aldoradondo said.

I shrugged, putting my basket together. I tended to pick from the bottles I liked best. I went outside to stand near Maude, who was in her dress with the spangles. Her hair was mostly hidden by the daytime bonnet Rebecca gave to her.

Dr. Aldoradondo threw open the side of the wagon and started talking. "Ladies, I bring you sure relief from all your ills and a rapid recovery!"

For a town so minor, we drew quite a crowd over the

course of the afternoon. Once finished, we turned right around and began the evening business.

For such a small place, Wandering Creek was lively after dark. It had only the one saloon proper. On the other hand, any number of establishments stayed open after regular business hours, pouring from gallon jugs. I had a clear view from where I stood.

I had only to see the grimace on the face of a man who swallowed it down, and see how he shook his head, to know how fierce was the stuff he was drinking. I figured he was soon to be a customer.

At the boot maker's place, they had a piano, and a woman with a loose gray bun of hair on the top of her head bounced around on the piano seat rather vigorously as she played. Despite the odor of glue and boot polish, they had a fair turnout.

We worked late into the evening and then readied ourselves to go. I'd just brought my horse away from the water trough when we heard a commotion coming from the end of the street.

The flickering torchlight showed us there was a tight group of people coming our way.

THIRTY-FOUR

THINGS COULD LOOK STRANGE IN THAT LIGHT. SHADOWS could turn the kindest face into a fearful mask, but even weighing that in, these didn't look like a friendly bunch.

To Maude, I said, "We can ride away from this whole mess," but I wasn't surprised to read in the look she gave me that this trouble was our trouble. "Get in the wagon," I said. "I'll ride my horse till we're out of here."

Maude said, "Don't let anyone stop you."

The team had begun to stamp and snort. Dr. Aldoradondo climbed into the wagon seat. My horse turned in place nervously; I fought to get my foot in the stirrup. I was still in my gingham.

I flung my leg over. I couldn't be bothered to be ladylike.

There was a woman at the center of maybe a dozen people. "He called it a sure cure," she yelled. I remembered her from the early crowd, for her eyes were wild then, too.

There were men coming out of the saloons and greeting the noise with wild hoots of their own. I urged my horse forward, thinking Dr. Aldoradondo was likely to make a run for it any second.

"Here now, what's all this about," he said over the noise.

Mostly women made up this angry crowd, but a few men stood bunched in front of the horses. They were shouting things like, "Here, don't you be going anywhere," and, "Catch 'ose hosses, don't let 'em run."

Voices rose, calling Dr. Aldoradondo a quack, a fake, a death monger. This last was a new word but sounded to me like a serious accusation to throw around.

A man yelled to someone else to come on out and catch the show and was answered with the clomp of boots and a swing of bat-wing doors.

"I paid my money, and I fed it to my mother," that woman shouted. "Warn't ten minutes later she rolled over and give up the ghost."

"Hang 'im," someone on the edge of the crowd shouted.

Matters were getting out of hand. A gunshot into the air could have a quieting effect if it came at the right moment. But our cache of pistols was in the wagon with Maude's rifle.

"How old was this woman in question?" Dr. Aldoradondo said. "How ill? Perhaps she was simply too far gone to expect medication to do anything for her."

The woman shouted, "She warn't taking your potion for illness, just her back hurt." And then she broke down and sobbed loud sobs.

I would've liked to say these were what Aunt Ruthie used to call crocodile tears, but they looked and sounded genuine to me.

"It poisoned her," another woman called out.

"There is nothing in my elixir that could do any harm," Dr. Aldoradondo said.

His voice overshadowed those raised in question and in anger, but now something else was at work besides the actual grievance. Some of the men gathered there had come away from drinking, and they had come away in the mood to look for trouble. They would find it. Or cause it, either one.

I could see I had the right of it. Others of the men who had lately joined in were deciding it was just good sense to back out of the tide of anger and resentment, rather than try to fight it.

At least I figured that might be why a few of them were going back to the saloons. However, this left several people in the street who would never listen to reason.

In the next instant, the noise rose suddenly to sound as if twice as many men were shouting. Three fellows jumped the wagon and pulled Dr. Aldoradondo to the ground.

One of those men hit his own head on the wagon seat.

It started in to bleed, real fast. It wasn't Dr. Aldoradondo's blood, but the sight of it running down that man's face made my heart thump all the harder. I was yelling at the top of my lungs. I tried to ride into this fray, but my horse sidled off to one side, away from the racket.

One of the wagon horses had begun to fight the traces by lifting off his front feet. He couldn't buck, but he jigged the other horse into more frantic snorting and blowing and stamping around. Their jostling knocked a man into the horse trough.

The team shied and danced at the splash, flinging their heads up and down, unnerved by the racket of so many voices raised to shout, and maybe the smell of blood.

They were hemmed in by the crowd and, in yanking the wagon around, did step on two or three people and knocked another fellow clean over. The worst of these cases was a young man I'd seen swatting at the horses with his hat like he didn't have good sense. He rolled out of range and wasn't stomped. It was an additional piece of good luck he lost his taste for trouble and crawled back to the boardwalk.

All of this was the happenings of less than a minute, probably less than half a minute, and at the same time there was some yelling and fists a-flying. The noise was such that I couldn't hear if anyone called for help. I couldn't tell how Maude or Rebecca were faring inside the wagon.

Dr. Aldoradondo tried to hold his own against the men who'd grabbed him. He was taking a beating. When someone struck him from behind with the butt of their gun, it was probably a kindness.

The doctor sank to the ground.

I fought my horse into riding forward again, with an intention of riding into the midst of things and trampling on the bulliest of them. Maude clambered over the wagon seat. She didn't grab the reins but looked like she might climb down into the fray.

"Maude," I shouted at her.

The horses pulled forward, traces jangling, and another man fell with an injury. Someone dealt the lead horse a blow to the nose. The horses pulled back, then gave another try.

It happened that jerking the wagon kept Maude clinging to the seat long enough to know I was part of the noise. I thought it a wonder she could hear me at all, the shouting around us had reached such a pitch.

"Maude, you can't get down there in that ruckus," I yelled. "You ain't dressed for it."

I heard this last thing I said more clearly because the men

began to move off, carrying Dr. Aldoradondo with them. "Get in the wagon, Maude," I said, and I was near to crying. There were several men against the one, and as far as I could tell, there wasn't a blamed thing we could do about it.

Maude pulled the brake on the wagon, although once the crowd moved off, the horses didn't appear to be ready to go anywhere. They shivered all over like bugs were biting at them, and flashed their tails and manes about.

"Tie your horse and come inside," Maude said.

She was staring down the street at that pack of ruffians. Their womenfolk had come together in a clump at one point and let the men move on. That one woman still shouted her accusations.

I looped the reins on the hook at the back door and swung myself inside the wagon. Rebecca's shape could be made out in the light from the torches. Her hands shook as she held the long dropper of that clear bottle that I couldn't put in my basket. She put a measure of the cure in a cup, sloshed in a little water, and drank it down fast.

"Rebecca, what is it they mean to do?" Maude was asking. She was shedding herself of that dress. "Surely they won't hang him."

"More likely tar and feathers," Rebecca said in a weak way. She settled into her rocker, somehow older than ever I'd noticed her to be.

Maude tore off that feather headdress hard enough to make me cringe; hairpins flew. She tossed stuff out of a drawer and came up with her rough pants and shirt.

THIRTY-FIVE

I'D HEARD OF TAR AND FEATHERS BUT HAD NEVER KNOWN the thing to be done. "What can we do?"

"It's a worse end than hanging," Rebecca said, and her face crumpled for a moment. But then she gained control of herself. "Some live through it."

"Has this happened to you before?" Maude asked her.

"To my brother," she said, her voice coming on a little stronger now. "The burns are a slow and painful way to die."

Rebecca acted as if now it had come to this, she could sit back, almost peaceful. I couldn't leave her be while the doctor was being carried down the street by his four limbs. "Rebecca." I jogged her rocker. "Should we go for the sheriff?"

"I have no doubt the sheriff has just been called out of town," Rebecca said in a voice now firm and full of knowledge. She reached for her knitting and began to rock gently. "It takes time for the tar to boil," she said. "We'll be here awhile."

I stood back. It chilled me the way she had settled into knowing disaster had fallen on her doorstep and would do nothing to try to stop it.

"I'm going to need both our horses, Sallie," Maude said. "Get them ready for me." I did what she asked. I wished I had put on my boy clothes.

When Maude jumped out of the back of the wagon, she carried her rifle and the doctor's. I said, "What are you about?"

"I'm going to take him from them, Sallie," she said. "You take the wagon back the way we came. Fast. I want you out of this town before I am. I'll circle around with him and meet you back where we camped last night."

"I can't let you go on your own, Maude."

"You saw her," Maude said, nodding toward Rebecca. "She can't drive this wagon. Besides, I don't want you there. Do just what I'm telling you and nothing else."

I said, "But there's hardly any cover. It's all grass."

"Just ride," Maude said, getting on my horse. She took the reins to the sorrel she'd been riding. He was larger than my horse and the better one for a man to ride. Maude surprised me with how clear-thinking she could be at times like this.

She slid one rifle into the boot, clearly meaning to ride with the other rifle in hand. I might have argued some more, but she said, "Get up there, Sallie, and move this wagon," and rode off.

I soon took up the reins. I'd never driven a team before, and I was counting on them knowing more about it than I did. I loosed the brake and yelled, "Yah!" They broke into a run, all right, and nearly yanked me off that wagon.

I dug my heels into the corners of the foot well and sat back, leaned on the reins, but I couldn't turn those horses or slow them down. They pulled on my one arm and then the other, and I had all I could do to keep to the seat.

I could see the dark outline of Maude riding away ahead of me, well past the edge of town. I saw the crowd of men beyond her, their figures lit up by a good-sized fire as they threw tree limbs onto it.

As Maude rode into them, startling a few men into rearing back, she shot her rifle into the air. I saw the flicker of movement that was a man drawing on her, but before he could shoot, his gun was shot out of his hand.

Another fellow screamed and pitched to the ground, as if hit by the same bullet.

There were three more shots, spitting into the dirt at the mob's feet and breaking up the wall of them. None of these shots came from Maude's rifle, by my guess, although my guesses were hampered by the jerky movement of our onrushing wagon.

I tried mightily to slow the horses, but I was doing no good at all. The shots didn't give those animals pause but may have added fuel to the charge.

I was bearing down on the scene with a racketing wagon. I sawed at the reins, trying to turn the horses, but I had no control over them. The mob scattered, yelling, and Maude pulled her horse to one side, giving me just about enough room to pass her by.

I was moving like I had a steam engine pushing from behind. I had only the moment to register the sight of Dr. Aldoradondo trying to pick himself up from the road, and then I was past them and charging like a freight train into the full darkness of the night.

I still didn't know who had been doing the shooting.

If I was scared for myself, I was also scared for Maude. She was still back there behind me, and I didn't know what was likely to happen to her.

I fought the horses, trying to make them know I meant to take charge, but they ran on as if the weight of that wagon was nothing. Maybe that was the case of it, for we had only the day before greased the axles. The wagon didn't feel like a dead weight behind them.

Although they hadn't been called upon for any great speed during the time we had traveled with the Aldoradon-dos, the horses were used to the idea of leaving a town in the dead of night and going on for an hour or two. If I couldn't bring the wagon to a halt soon, I would be knocking on the door at Fort Dodge before Maude caught up to me.

I didn't really believe the horses could run for that long, but I wasn't able to stop them—stopping was an idea that had to dawn on them.

It hadn't dawned on them as yet.

I leaned my weight to one side and the other, trying to hold them to the middle of the trail. It felt like riding a butter churn, the reins yanked at me all the time, and when I leaned, it must have been felt only slightly by those horses.

I'd been lucky so far to have a smooth trail before me, the dried-out ruts had crumbled into dust. Yet there remained the risk of hitting something I couldn't see in the dark and damaging the undercarriage. Or worse, the horses. Or worse yet, me.

What it came down to, fighting the horses meant only to stay braced against the wagon seat and pull back on the reins for all I was worth. It was some time before I saw signs of reason in them.

By then, spit foamed out of their mouths and sweat shone on their hides, and some of this splashed back in the wind of them to land on me. But as they slowed to a trot, I started to watch the ground at each side of the trail. I looked for a place to stop.

THIRTY-SIX

I DIDN'T HAVE TO WORRY ABOUT BOGGY GROUND; WE hadn't seen rain in some time. But the horses were weary, the moonlight was unreliable, and I couldn't be considered an experienced wagon handler.

It was simple good luck the horses slowed just as I spied a roll in the land. I snapped the reins and coaxed them to walk through the prairie grass.

The night was quiet here, like all else had been a bad dream. Only the rush of my blood and the heaving breath of the horses told the real story.

I climbed over the seat to look in on Rebecca. Glass crunched underfoot when I stepped inside. An overhead cupboard had opened and spilled its contents on the floor.

"Rebecca?"

I'd hardly given her a thought once that wagon was on the move. I could only just see her.

She lay on the bunk with an arm threaded through a strap nailed to the wall for that purpose, so she hadn't been thrown around.

"Is it over yet?" she asked me.

I reached for her hand in the dark, and she clung on to me. Her hands were damp and cool, which surprised me, the cool part anyway. Mine were so hot.

"Is he suffering?" She meant the doctor, of course.

"I don't rightly believe it happened," I said, speaking of the tar-and-feathers part. I didn't care to mention the broken look of him. I felt a welling of tears rising, and I brushed all thoughts of him and even of Maude from my mind.

Rebecca was holding my hand and didn't let go. "I don't feel well, Sallie."

"You just stay here, Rebecca," I said, "and I'll come back as soon as I see to the horses. I can't leave them to stand wet."

"I think I may sleep," she said, and appeared to me to swoon away. Likely it was just the darkness lent that look to her when she shut her eyes.

The horses were lathered up and nervous. It was a time before they let me put the feed bags on them. I gave them small rations, having it in mind only to calm them. I hoped when I took the feed bags off, the horses would graze.

If I stayed out of range of getting kicked, we could manage all right together. I wasn't large enough to move all the hardware off them but could do a fair enough job of wiping them down.

During this time, Rebecca called out to me twice, and I answered that I would be inside shortly. Maybe I should have gone right away, but there was a part of me that didn't know what to do with her and didn't want to try to figure it out. It was a kind of fear took hold of me, I knew this well enough to be ashamed. I knew how to take care of the horses, and that is what I did.

While running my fingers around the horseshoes to check for stones, I heard horses coming. My hopes rose at the sight of two horses in the moonlight, then slid when I saw only one rider.

I waited, praying for it to be Maude. I was sure I'd know her. But they were some distance off yet, and I couldn't be sure.

"Sallie," Maude called. She hadn't yet seen us.

"Over here," I called, but remained where I stood. I was still in the grip of cowardly fear—when I heard the worst, I didn't want it to be more than I could take.

Then I saw Maude had Dr. Aldoradondo with her; he had fallen forward over the horse's neck. "Is he dead?" I cried, running to him. I hadn't realized I'd gotten so fond of that old man in the short time we'd been riding together. But he and Rebecca had treated us as kindly as anyone could hope, and paid us for working alongside them.

"Sallie, he's alive," Maude said, "and look who turned up to help me."

He rode out of the darkness. Likely he'd been riding a little apart so three horses wouldn't leave much of a trail, the way I'd read of in dimers. It was John Kirby. I knew his horse, too.

There was a great deal to take in all at once. "Silver Dollar," I said. "You're the one who rented Silver Dollar? Where's Uncle Arlen's rig?"

"A little the worse for wear," he said. "I traded it in some miles earlier."

I was for a moment torn between arguing the loss to Uncle Arlen's business and wanting to know what he traded it for and knowing it really only mattered that he'd come to

Maude's aid, even though at the back of my mind I questioned the why of it.

I said, "Have you followed us from Independence?"

"I didn't follow you," he said. "I got there a few days ahead of you, if you remember."

We couldn't spend time arguing. The doctor needed help. Maude and John Kirby each took an arm over their shoulders as he slid off the horse and helped him walk. I was glad to see his feet weren't dragging.

"Let's get him on the cot," Maude said. John Kirby took most of the doctor's weight over his shoulder as Maude scrambled inside the wagon. Then he pushed the doctor through the door to her and followed them both inside.

Rebecca had slipped to the floor.

Maude said, "Are you hurt, Rebecca?"

Her eyelids fluttered, and when Maude lit the lantern, she tried to sit up. She put her hand down on a piece of glass. She didn't appear to notice.

"Wait," Maude said, and helped her up.

The glass hadn't caused but a tiny cut that hardly bled. I helped Maude to prop her in a corner at the end of the bunk, and John Kirby was able to put his burden on the greater length of it.

I was still not sure why this fellow had taken such a risk to help us. Barring ink smudges, he looked like he'd never been this dirty before in his life, let alone interfered with a crazed mob.

Maude sent me outside, saying, "See to the horses, Sallie."

I reached for the lathered-up reins on Maude's horse and mine, wanting to get them under cover. As for Silver Dollar, I only needed to whistle for him. He was ever expectant of good things, such as pieces of apple or carrot, or a nose bag, and he answered readily enough by following me to the far side of the wagon.

While I pulled the saddles off our horses, Maude yanked the door shut on the wagon. That was how I knew there might be men to follow. She didn't want a light to lead them straight to us. By a stroke of good luck, the part of the wall that came down as a shelf was turned away from the trail, so any light leaking through the seam wouldn't be seen.

I kept the horses well behind the wagon, and as I rubbed them down, I listened for men coming along the trail. I'd lost track of how far we might have traveled when the horses were running wild. It could have been two miles, it could have been twelve.

The more I didn't hear anyone coming, the better I felt.

Dr. Aldoradondo had escaped the tar and feathers and, in Maude's estimation, wasn't dying.

We had added one more to our band, was how I decided to look at it, and maybe we could trust him. At any rate, he had proven himself helpful when we needed help most.

I couldn't help feeling things were looking up.

I'd brushed the horses down and moved the nose bags over to feed them the same light rations I'd given the others before the back door swung open again.

Maude came outside carrying her rifle and the doctor's. She handed me the weight of her kit bag so she could load. I said, "What happened back there?"

"Their taste for mayhem has been satisfied. Only one of

them came back after you scattered them," Maude said as she loaded her rifle. "We left that one trussed up like a chicken for his persistence."

"I couldn't manage the horses," I said. "I couldn't stay in the wagon with her, Maude."

I didn't like to think I hadn't done entirely right by Rebecca. She had turned scary, but I should have found the nerve to face our situation.

"There's nothing you could have done for her," Maude said. "She isn't hurt, don't worry."

Silently, I resolved to do better the next time I was needed to do the right thing.

"Everything will turn out all right," Maude said, but not with a great deal of assurance.

"It looked like gunfire took a few of them down," I said. "You'd have mentioned it if any of them died, wouldn't you?"

"Two are bullet-nicked, but it isn't more than a scratch on either of them." She raked her fingers over the open box. She had to load without any light, just feeling her way along. "I tied up the worst with a kerchief."

"A clean kerchief?" I said. Since traveling with Dr. Aldoradondo, I'd learned more than I ever cared to know about infection. "It ain't a good idea to keep racking up accidental killings."

"It was his own kerchief," Maude said, her voice coming on stronger. "And quit saying 'ain't.' How many times do I have to tell you?"

"What about the woman who died?"

"None of them knew who she was," Maude said in a bitter

tone. She set down the rifle she'd finished with and picked up the other. "Thanks to the drink in them, they were only half the men they ever were."

I said, "I'm proud of you, Maude."

"You don't know what a close thing it was, Sallie," she said. "I'm glad you didn't take off in the other direction, after all. We're just that much further west."

"I didn't have any say in the matter," I told her. "Those horses had a mind of their own."

Maude said, "How are they holding up? We have a ways to go."

"They're as tireless as Aunt Ruthie's rocking chair." It was true, they had the grit to go a distance. I only hoped they had some speed left in them after the run we'd made.

THIRTY-SEVEN

INSIDE THE WAGON, REBECCA HAD RALLIED ENOUGH TO put out a basin of water for John Kirby to wash his hands. However, she looked some wobbly as she passed a wrung-out cloth over the doctor's face.

"Cleanliness is most important," she said for maybe the third time. But I wasn't sure she had noticed a stranger sat beside her.

The doctor had come around enough to say which balm was needed for his cuts. His face had a couple of lumpy swellings, but he didn't appear to have been broken anywhere. I was glad of this, but also satisfied I could move on to my next concern.

"You have a nerve to trade away Uncle Arlen's buggy," I said to John Kirby as he touched the paste to the doctor's face and ears.

"Sallie," Maude said in that way she had when my manners were lacking. In fact, this hadn't been foremost in my thoughts until I'd laid eyes on him again.

"Who is he, anyway?" I said to Maude before I turned

back to him. "And don't think you can put me off with word-play. You had a reason to follow us from Diamond Springs."

As I neared him, he reached for me and dabbed a bit of that paste on my scraped knuckles. I dropped the feed sack, reacting as if I expected it to sting, and for a moment it did want to, but then the hurt went numb.

I said, "What's your interest in us?"

"I know who your sister is," he said, and when I didn't say more, he did. "Not Maude Waters, but Maude March."

"Maude March?" Rebecca said as if a fresh weakness had come upon her. "You're Maude March?"

Maude did look like the worst of the posters under the lantern light.

"I have been following your story in the papers," he said. "It interests me."

"She *is* innocent," I said, without inquiring of his interest. "We'll clear her name."

Always quick to read a man, or a woman, Dr. Aldoradondo saw right away how things stood. "It won't make it any easier, now you've broken up a mob with gunfire," he said.

I looked at John Kirby. "You did the shooting."

"No one is dead of it," he said.

"What I'm saying is this, Maude will be blamed for it, unless you stand up." My feelings for him were mixed; I couldn't get the measure of the man.

Maude made the more timely argument. "They didn't have any business taking the law into their own hands. Is it possible they never gave chase?"

"Any reasonable mind might think this way," John Kirby said. "But these are not reasonable minds we're dealing with."

"Then we must save the talk for later," Maude said. "The sheriff might yet make a showing."

I left the wagon, and John Kirby was right behind me. We hitched the horses to the wagon rail in a tight silence. The doctor remained on the bunk, and I heard Maude settling Rebecca next to him in her rocker.

I took to the wagon seat, and after a moment John Kirby decided to ride up there. He took over handling the team, and I didn't mind it. Those horses took to the trail again as if they were starting fresh, and set a brisk pace.

In the tone of making sure he knew what he was doing, I said, "Are you not worried about someone following us down this trail?"

"If we don't hear from that mob in the next few minutes, we don't have to worry till morning," he said. "If anyone comes after us in the morning, it'll be the sheriff, and he won't be in a mood to listen to our side of things. Either way, it's a matter of getting as far from here as we can by the middle of tomorrow."

He was a planner, I had to give him that. And there was no better way to make speed than to follow the trail.

Maude rode watchful at the back door for a time. It was still full dark, and all was quiet. I loosened my jaw just enough to say to John Kirby, "I haven't thanked you for stepping in to help my sister."

He said, "No need."

"I don't have a generous supply of sisters," I said. "This one means a great deal to me. I saw that fellow drawing on her."

"He might have missed, being jostled by the crowd. But I couldn't take the chance," he said. "His aim might be bad and he could hit her accidentally. People die both ways."

I said, "I'm just glad you did not kill him. Maude already stands wrongly accused for a death."

"You have a point," he said. "But I wasn't thinking of Maude's reputation. Only my own. As you already know, reputations are easier to pick up than to put down."

I said to him, "How is it you came to be in Independence to rent Silver Dollar and were in Diamond Springs when we got there?"

"There's a good question," Maude said, coming to stand behind the wagon seat.

"I was staying for a time in Independence. I got news of my cousin's death in Diamond Springs," John Kirby said. "He was the newspaperman. The letter-writing business was his as well."

"So you found yourself set up in business," Maude said.

"I thought about it," he said. "But business isn't my game."

Me and Maude spoke up together. "What game is that?"

"I write books," he said.

I said, "What kind of books?"

"True stories, when there's a call for it. I could write your sister's story."

"You were planning to write about my sister." I felt the beginnings of excitement in my belly. "That's why you followed us. Admit it."

John Kirby said, "Don't you want your sister's story told?"

"I don't want another lie told." A truthful account did matter to me, for what use was it otherwise? But it wasn't only the thought of truth made my heart beat harder. I was ever a fool for an interesting story.

Maude wasn't decided; I could see it in the set of her mouth.

John Kirby said, "You are, what? Ten years old? Who has the last word here?"

"I do, and I'm thirteen."

"She's twelve," Maude said, "and she makes an excellent point. Do you have the truth in you?"

"You don't trust me?" he said.

Maude turned from him a little, impatience partly, but also, she didn't trust him entire. "We have a great deal more than a twenty-five-cent letter riding on your answer," I said.

"Think of it this way," he said, talking direct to Maude. "I'll make you the hero of your story. People are near to admiring you for your boldness; it won't take much to make them love you."

Maude said, "What people are you talking about? The law wants to hang me."

"Public sentiment hangs more men than the law," John Kirby said.

I said, "Would such a book clear my sister's name?"

"It will go a long way toward swaying public opinion," John Kirby said.

Rebecca piped up from inside the wagon. "Public sentiment won't want to punish her for any misdeeds that occurred while she was trying to save herself. And she did indeed act the hero tonight."

"Public sentiment does not always carry the day," the doctor said. "She will have to prove her innocence."

This had the makings of a lively debate.

John Kirby said, "People will read a book longer than they'll stand still and listen. You need to publish your story. You need me to write it."

"Why you?" Maude said to him.

"I have been an eyewitness to all that you've done since being broken out of jail, including saving this man's life."

"That isn't precisely true," Maude said.

"It's close enough," he said.

I took his point. If there was more than one crazy woman going around pretending to be my sister, the one thing we needed was someone who could claim they knew the truth. Better he was not a friend of ours, or a relative, like me.

Maude said, "Would you have returned Silver Dollar to Independence and paid us for the buggy?" She took matters of business very seriously.

"I would," he said, his teeth flashing in the moonlight. "It would be horse thievery if I did not."

We let the matter drop. It was a long night ahead of us, and tempers shortened by disagreement would not make it easier.

THIRTY-EIGHT

"**A**T LEAST WE DON'T HAVE TO WORRY ABOUT WATER for the horses," Maude said sometime later. The trail had come to a point where it followed the river again, and the water looked like a bright ribbon shining in the moonlight.

"We need water for us," John Kirby said.

"I've been refilling the rain barrels from the wells we passed," I said. "We haven't seen one day of rain since we started out."

"It's a drought," John Kirby said. "It's in all the newspapers."

I didn't remember reading about it. "That's not what I watch the newspapers for, I guess."

Rebecca said, "Is anyone hungry?"

I climbed back into the wagon, where me and Maude dished up ham and potatoes and greens. In a low voice, I said, "We've both found ourselves in a situation of having horses that didn't belong to us and no clear idea how we might return them. We were lucky enough circumstances did the hard part for us."

"I haven't forgotten," Maude said.

Rebecca listened in as she moved shakily around the

table, poking forks and knives into the meat on the plates. This didn't worry me. It was John Kirby I didn't want to make part of this conversation.

She made up a dish for the doctor, choosing stewed corn and then fully half of the dried apple pie, mashed with a fork, for he wasn't up to chewing hard.

She meant to feed him like a child but was hardly able to handle the fork. I took this task on; it was not so distasteful as it sounds. He was grateful for the help and admired the apple pie so outrageously that Rebecca laughed.

By then, Maude had eaten and made up a plate for John Kirby. I stood near her and said, "I'm contented that circumstances have put Silver Dollar on the road to Uncle Arlen."

I didn't need more than that. I hoped that same was true for Maude.

She made no sign of how she felt, only clambered over the wagon seat. "Let me spell you," she said to him.

"Greens are for horses," Rebecca said to me quietly when I got around to making up our plates. I agreed with her complete and didn't put them on our plates.

Hoping to be forgiven for having been leery of her earlier on, I said, "I'm sorry. I can't think what got into me."

She said, "Let us admit we were both badly frightened and call that the end of it." She patted the place beside herself on the bunk. Together we finished off the ham and potatoes and corn in a companionable way. We were quiet, though, for the doctor had fallen asleep and we didn't want to disturb him.

Much of the night was taken up with Maude telling bits and pieces of our story in answer to John Kirby's questions. He had a way of turning a story that could polish coal to a gloss. I had to admire the man, and more, I came to realize that he might make the doubtiest parts of Maude's story believable.

Maude didn't admire this entirely. She didn't care for his method nor trust him complete. "This book-writing business has turned your head around," she said. "These are dimers you are writing, not stone tablets."

"What you are most in need of is a stone tablet," he said back to her.

I thought dimers good enough, and one that explained Maude's circumstances would be useful. I climbed out onto the wagon seat to sit between them. I didn't offer an opinion.

Although we traveled westward, the sunrise in the east did paint the sky in a wash of color and shadow. Rebecca had become more like herself as the night wore on, and she was steady enough on her feet to stand behind the wagon seat with me to watch the show.

For Maude missed it entire. It was blue-dark when she fell asleep, leaning back, Rebecca's arms wrapped around her. The last streak of pink was fading when she jerked awake with a sudden sit-up.

"Oh," she said, looking about us in some relief. "I had a bad dream."

"I had a good one," I said, wanting her to forget hers as quick as she could. I told her the one about dancing ring-around-the-rosy with Aunt Ruthie.

Maude's face lit right up. "Why, Sallie, that was Momma. You confuse them sometimes."

"No, it was Aunt Ruthie."

"I remember that day, I do," Maude said. "I wore the green

195

calico in your dream, didn't I, and you were in my old rose-figured cotton. Those ones you cut the patches out of."

"I remember the dresses," I said. "I do think you were wearing the green one in the dream."

"You remember Momma," Maude said. She put one arm around me and squeezed.

"You are such good girls," Rebecca said.

John Kirby snapped the reins a little. Those horses didn't change pace. But I saw the end of his nose was pink, and it struck me he was a sentimental man.

Maude woke me midmorning by standing on the wagon seat. She looked around and didn't see a worrisome cloud of dust being raised in any direction. On her worst day, and maybe this was one of them, she could see further than most people did on their best.

"I don't see any kind of cloud," she said. "The sky is un-broken by any feature, save the sun."

This news of more dry weather did not cheer me much.

We weren't stopped for but a moment before all of the horses busied themselves with getting a meal off the grass. My stomach growled at the sound of their teeth grinding.

To take my mind off it, I said to Maude, "You might go back to wearing your work dress and wrap your hair in that dark blue scarf."

"Only a few days ago, you thought I should wear pants," she said.

"I've changed my mind," I said, turning to get my sack. "You look too girly to make anyone believe you are a boy. The same isn't true for me."

"Just go on being a girl for a time," Maude said, catching me by the arm. "It will not hamper your grip on a shotgun, but you will surprise the heck out of someone if you need to use it."

"Don't swear," I said to Maude, but only to have something to say. "It ain't becoming." I picked up a blanket and went out the back door.

Maude met me on the ground. "Now that you're a girl again, don't say 'ain't,'" she said in that lofty manner of she could boss me around. "It will ruin your disguise."

"Girls can't go everywhere," I said. While I sometimes gave in to pleadings, she'd pushed me too far with her big-sister ways. "It may prove useful for one of us to be a boy."

"Now don't go getting rankled," Maude said as I dragged my boy clothes out of my sack.

"Too late."

I figured us for doomed if we do and doomed if we don't. Having been a girl and a boy, the only way left to disguise me for sure was to dress me up like Maude's poll parrot, in bright feathers.

The doctor came out of the wagon to walk a bit, leaning a little on Rebecca. John Kirby rushed to take the weight of him. When Rebecca walked toward us, I saw the medicine had worn off. She was pretty much her old self.

The doctor didn't look well, but then he had bruises. Maybe he'd begun to know he would live. There's something to be said for that at most times, but not when the body hurts.

I threw the blanket over my horse and started to unbutton, calling out the rest of my argument, which was mostly for Rebecca's sake. "Besides, this is the prettiest dress I've had since outgrowing the ones Momma made for you, and I don't care to ruin it by riding it to death."

Whether she agreed with me or not, Maude came to the other side of my horse to hold the blanket from falling. I stripped my braids and finger-combed my hair, then carefully packed my dress into a saddlebag. For what I'd said was true, it was the nicest dress I'd had in some time.

"Remind me to buy you a hat," Maude said. "You'll get sunburned if you're giving up that bonnet."

I figured this for her way of making up with me. Maude burned and peeled, over and over, like Aunt Ruthie. But I'd never been one to do worse than burn one day and turn brown the next, like Uncle Arlen.

By the next day, I was feeling some impatient.

"What about Marion? I don't know what to make of it he has not shown up," I said when I had a moment with Maude.

She said, "We haven't reached the river crossing yet."

I dug the map out of my sack and flattened it on the wagon step.

"We've got a town dead ahead of us," I said. "I'm going in there for things we need, and I'll look around. If there's a telegraph office, I'll send a message on to the crossing."

"We're low on water," John Kirby said, overhearing.

"I'll take the canteens," I said.

John Kirby passed me a coin. "Buy a newspaper, if you come across one."

I put away the map and set out to make a list of everyone's wants. Peppermints I put at the top.

"No soup," the doctor said, "but something soft enough to chew only a little."

"Don't stint," Rebecca said.

"On what?"

"On anything tasty," she said, fattening my wad of bills.

"We could all go in," Maude said.

"No, we can't," I said. "We don't have the look of being well matched and the doctor is not in good shape. We'll be talked about."

Further, the Aldoradondos' horses were unusual, to say nothing of the wagon. Maybe the law would be on the lookout for the wagon.

"How far do you judge us to be from there?" I asked the doctor, showing him the map. He'd done this route before.

"Be careful," Maude said. "That last place looked rough around the edges before we ran into trouble."

"Every place out here is rough around the edges," I said. "I know how to stay out of trouble."

"I'll go with her," John Kirby said.

"I'm going alone," I said. "You should be getting the details of Maude's several misunderstandings with the law."

"If you're going in," John Kirby said, "ride my horse. The shoe on his left hind hoof is slipping."

"He is Uncle Arlen's horse," I said.

I was rewarded with a look of exasperation. But he was right; we had no time to let Silver Dollar rest up from a sore. That hoof wasn't used to walking bare.

"We can't go on sitting here like ducks on a lake," Maude said. "Let's ride."

THIRTY-NINE

"Y OU'LL LEAVE US WHEN YOU MEET UP WITH YOUR friend," Rebecca said. Her voice was oddly toneless.

I said, "I'm sorry for it, but me and Maude have to ride hard to reach our uncle Arlen."

Maude said, "There will soon come a town that boasts of a hotel where you and the doctor can be comfortable."

"We would lay over with you until the doctor can travel," I said, "but we can't."

"As for riding hard," Rebecca said, "you'll be striking out across a terribly dry stretch of the Kansas plains. We know how to make it across."

I looked at Uncle Arlen's map.

"She's right," I said. "Once we cross the Cottonwood, the next decent-sized creek is four days' ride at the least. It's hard to pack fifty miles' worth of water."

Maude squinted over my shoulder. "What's this one? What does it say?"

"The Little Arkansas."

The doctor said, "You must hook up with other riders who have done the trip before."

Me and Maude glanced at each other. We expected Marion to know the way.

"There's a town up ahead," John Kirby said.

"Keep going," I said to Maude as I boarded Silver Dollar. "I'll catch up to you before long."

"A lot of things could catch up to us," Maude said. "Do not take long."

Apart from half a dozen cabins, the town was only an old stage station turned livery, a whiskey bar, and a general store. But there was enough brisk business being done that I didn't stand out as a matter of curiosity.

I rode in with the intention to buy an evening meal and the makings for breakfast while Silver Dollar was being shoed. A sign in front of the store read:

BUY HERE OR WE'LL BOTH CROAK

This inspired me to think of getting more of everything.

The well had a fence around it, which made me glad of my fat purse.

The fellow at the general store knew his business was canteens, and he sold them cheap enough. I paid a few cents extra to have them filled. I'd never heard of such a thing as paying for water but couldn't chance an argument.

The candy, two apple pies, and a sack of dried fruit and nuts would have to hold us in the sweets department. I found egg custard for the doctor and was glad of Rebecca's reminder not to stint, for I had to buy the dish in order to take the whole thing with me.

Chicken and ham and potatoes were all cold but didn't

look greasy. It had looked good to everyone who had come before me. I bought all that was left, which might last us the day.

I added enough cheese and hard-boiled eggs and biscuits to last a week, I figured. Because I didn't like to think of a week of cheese and eggs, I bought a bucketful of last season's apples.

I saw the newspaper first thing on going in, but I did as most shoppers did, picked it up while they totted up my bill. I didn't look at it especially, but the headline was impossible to miss:

$400 REWARD
OFFERED ON MAD MAUDE

I was given a box to carry on one shoulder and held the bucket in my other hand. I couldn't set these down anywhere until I got back to the livery. There, I read through the article.

BUT WHO IS THE REAL
MAUDE MARCH?

An article from the Able, Kansas Civic claims Maude was shooting out windows in Able earlier in the same day that she is said to have broke jail in Independence. We see a mention in the Fast Pony Gazette, a Louisville rag, which locates Mad Maude dancing at a foxhunt ball while she, or someone very like her, rode away from the jail at breakneck speed.

So it is up to the man on the street to know whether it was Mad Maude serving him his soup in Mr. George Ray's establishment, or if, in the same hour, she was several days away raising Cain, or miles in another direction, the soles of her shoes smoking as she skimmed across the dance floor. Could any of these gals be the same gal reportedly laid to rest in Missouri, seven ruthless men lowering her box into the ground?

I looked up to find some fellow noticing my interest in the story. I hadn't seen him standing in the shadows of the livery, until he lit a cigar. He didn't say anything right away, but drew deep on that thing.

A puff of smoke escaped into the air when he said, "She makes good reading, don'tcha think?"

I didn't reply to this.

"Some fella come through here this morning said he heard she was just down the road a piece," he said.

"You don't say."

"Some sheriff got himself tied to a chair," the fellow said. "He claimed Maude and her gang did it."

I said, "How many men?"

"Now, he didn't say," the fellow said. "I didn't think to ask."

I made like I'd lost interest in the matter and ran my eyes over the horseflesh. Silver Dollar was his old plump self. Maude's horse and mine were a question in my mind. A diet of grasses had thinned them out. We had a punishing ride ahead of us, and they could get played out.

I thought of my own horse, the selfsame horse we had picked up at Ben Chaplin's. He was sensitive to the bit and could hit any clip I called for, and he could stay with it until he heard from me again. He didn't mind a long day, and I'd come to know him for a real trail horse.

I believed it far better to leave my horse here where he could rest for a time and eat a little grain with molasses than to drive him across the plains and peter him out entire.

It turned out that talkative fellow worked there, and he threw himself into the pitch with some energy.

He offered a sweet-natured dark buckskin with mane and tail of a cream color. Its spine swayed like a back porch. That one was followed by an offer of a roan with popped knees. All of them otherwise lovely horses, but I wouldn't fall for a pretty face.

He thought I'd go for a pretty gray with bowed tendons. She ought to have been put out to pasture. I felt nothing but sorry for her.

This decided me. If the riding wore on my horse, I would put him out to pasture at Macdougal's, giving him a better finish. I said, "I have a good horse and feet left under me to walk on if he wears out."

"Gonna be a long walk in any direction," the fellow said. Which was a point. I began to like talking to him.

When I didn't bite at these offerings, he showed me a plain horse in better shape overall, but as hard-mouthed as a new boot. The only difference being, a boot can be broke in. This horse was past that.

I said, "I would do better to ride a mule."

"Never a mule, son, they is incurable," he told me. "This horse is fine. Here, just hold him by the ears, see, and you can get by without reins, too."

This brought some snuffled laughter from a few old cronies sitting around a cold woodstove. "You can't expect me to pay top dollar for a bottomed-out horse," I said to him. I sounded more like Aunt Ruthie than I cared to, but it couldn't be helped.

Another fellow came over just then, leading Silver Dollar and handing me some pieces of shriveled carrot, cut up. When Silver Dollar had put away all the pieces of carrot and had his nose rubbed good, I turned to find a man standing behind me.

FORTY

Marion said, "How did you come to have Silver Dollar?"

"It's a long story." I took him in at a glance and saw he looked well.

"I got worried when you and your sister didn't show up," he said. "I started back from the crossing this morning. I couldn't go on to Liberty without the two of you in tow."

"Did you think the coyotes got us?"

"Naw. They might eat you," he said. "But they wouldn't dare mess with the likes of your sister."

"Good to have you back," I said, grinning.

We began walking to his horse where it stood at a corner of the corral. It didn't look nearly as fagged as it had on the day Maude would have traded it in. All it had needed was a good rest. This made me feel a sight better about my own horse.

"We are still with the medicine peddler," I said to him.

"That worked out all right."

I didn't think he needed the whole of the story. Not yet anyway. "Maude's hair was covered and I wore a dress."

His eyebrows rose. "Did the dress suit you?"

"Well enough."

"Do you still have it?"

"In my sack." We mounted our horses and rode out.

"Come Christmas, you will have to wear it so I can see what a girl named Sallie looks like."

"Come Christmas," I agreed. "Did you see the paper hereabouts?"

"Your sister gets around."

"It strikes me the papers are making our case for her innocence."

"Now don't warm to them, son," Marion said. "It's only the story that interests them, and the story could be some different tomorrow."

We came to the edge of the town and dug into those horses for a little speed. We hadn't ridden far before I saw the wagon ahead of us. I signaled to Marion to slow down. "I forgot to say we ran into some trouble."

"What kind of trouble?"

"The unexpected kind," I said. "A fellow helped us out, goes by the name John Kirby."

"John Henry Kirby?"

"He didn't give us his middle name," I said.

"What did he look like?"

"He wears a vest," I said. "And reading glasses."

"Sounds like John Henry," Marion said.

I said, "That John Henry? The one who wrote about your adventures as Joe Harden?" I tried to recall the name of the man who wrote those books. "J. H. somebody."

"J. H. Kirby," Marion said. "The very same."

It'll sound funny, but I liked it that John Kirby might turn out to be J.H. "He was riding Silver Dollar," I said, and filled him in on John Kirby's offer to write Maude's story.

By then, we had picked up our pace. Maude greeted him by walking back to meet us when she saw us coming.

"You girls take your old sweet time," he said, getting off his horse.

"You were just worried we'd beat you to the Colorado Territory," Maude answered him playful-like. I thought she wasn't in the mood to fight with him as she had right after he'd broken her out of jail that last time.

She climbed up behind me, and we rode up to the wagon, which was not moving. John Kirby came away from checking the horses' hooves. Marion was expecting to see him, but John Henry was taken by surprise.

John Henry, that was how I began to think of him the moment I saw color rise in his face. He and Marion greeted each other with a handshake and stiff punches to each other's arms. They started to look glad to see each other.

"We have a lot to talk about," Marion said.

Maude said, "You know each other?"

"Marion was the side gun on the stage coach I rode the first time I came west," John Henry said. "He must've saved my skin twice a day."

We couldn't make more of an explanation then, as we made Marion known to Rebecca and the doctor. The doctor lay in the grass with Rebecca's quilt-stuffed carpetbag at his back.

Maude and Marion set out a little meal of eggs and biscuits. John Henry made the coffee. Over these doings, we each told something of the trip we'd shared in Marion's absence.

Maude told Marion how we had come across John Henry.

John Henry talked about how he had thought Maude a venturesome young woman until she gave her name. He had been reading old newspaper clippings and put the Maude together with the Ruth Waters of the stories.

I thought Maude wasn't yet ready to talk about the scary business of riding into that mob, so I said, "Turned out, the best way to disguise Maude is to trick her up in sequins and feathers."

John Henry reached for her hand, saying, "Feathers are becoming to pretty birds." Maude blushed and pulled her hand away.

Marion stepped between them to hand plates of food to Rebecca and the doctor. He said, "I count myself lucky I got here in time to see Sallie's dealings with that horse trader. He didn't know who he was up against," he said. "She had him agreeing to trade a perfectly fine horse for a broke-down dog she had not even located yet."

I began to feel the adventure of it all once more. For we all had a story. Although Marion didn't have enough of a story to suit Maude. "You can't have enjoyed a trip so uneventful as to have nothing else to tell but finding Sallie," she said.

I wondered if she wanted to brag a little, if she might be sorry she'd taken to wearing her plain dress. She might be wishing she still wore that dress with spangles.

"I got lucky, I guess, eventful-wise," Marion said. "I waited around till I got the feeling something must have gone bad."

"What gave you that feeling?" Maude said in an unusual snippy tone.

"Just nothing," Marion said. "A feeling. Then I got the idea to mosey on back."

She got up suddenly and stalked off through the grass. John Henry made a move to get up, but I was quicker. "Leave this to me," I said.

I ran to catch up to Maude. "What's the matter with you?" I said to her.

"He's a waste of my worry," she said, never slowing down.

"You're a match for Aunt Ruthie yourself," I said. "We're the three of us together again and able to ride on to Uncle Arlen. Why can't you just count our blessings instead of looking for grudge material?"

To this she said nothing.

"We'll soon know everything we ever wondered about the Joe Harden stories," I said. Which was how I put it, though I'd thought a great deal more about them than Maude ever had.

"What are you talking about?"

"John Kirby," I said. "He's the one who writes them."

She gave me a look of surprise. I grinned and started back to the others. She wasn't far behind me.

Marion and John Henry were going back and forth on that issue. The Aldoradondos sat in quiet suspense.

"They're interesting books you've written," Marion said. "I'll say that much for them."

John Henry said, "Good books."

"Sallie likes them," Marion said.

"That isn't a recommendation," Maude said.

"Not true," the doctor said. "It's exactly what we were talking about earlier, public sentiment."

"What everybody wants, isn't it?" John Henry said. "To have a book written about them? It makes people feel important, isn't that so, Marion?"

Maude glanced at Marion, but he didn't answer.

John Henry blinked behind his dusty eyeglasses. He said, "Didn't you want to have a book written about you, Joe—Marion?"

"That's the question you might've asked me earlier on."

"Here's what I would've said to you. Those books aren't about you, particularly. They're about every Joe, the men who are trying to keep skin and bone together out here."

Marion took up a stalk of grass and twisted it. I was fidgeting some myself. There were too many decisions in the air, like biting flies, and I couldn't be still.

"Tell you the truth, John Henry, I don't mind my made-up name being there," Marion said. "Maude's story is different. Don't embroider on it."

"Here, you can't have this conversation without me," Maude said.

"No, we can't." John Henry layered a piece of cheese on a cracker. He ate this, then said to Maude, "I reckon you have a day or two to think it over."

"We won't be traveling with you," Marion said. "We can ride as the crow flies."

"Then I hope to have your answer sooner than that," said J.H. "I hope you decide in my favor. In yours."

For my money, he could have it. We hadn't been through

thick and thin with John Henry the way we had with Marion Hardly. But he'd put himself on the line to help Maude.

I glanced at Maude, and she nodded her head at me ever so slightly, which I took to mean we were in agreement on the matter. As they reached to shake hands, a flutter of small grass birds rose on the air, making high-pitched cries. Silver Dollar was close by, and he high-stepped a few times, tossing his head.

I reached for that bucket of apples while Marion was telling how accidental it happened to Maude that she got mixed up in robbing the bank. I tried one, first cutting away the bad parts. The good parts were sweet, and juice ran down my chin.

Maude told me not to eat the black specks, but they couldn't be tasted at all. The doctor took out a pocketknife, and Rebecca helped me to winnow the apples down to half a bucket's worth, both of us passing pieces of apple to the others.

The parts we judged too poor did meet the horses' lower standards. I don't believe they left a piece on the ground. As we went through those apples, me and Maude told about the snowstorm and finding our way to Ben Chaplin's.

"Just one accident after another," I said, enjoying the telling of it. Before I could tell John Henry it really wasn't my fault I killed Willie, Maude said, "One of those boys tripped over his own feet and shot the other one."

My eyes stretched wide, for I'd never known Maude to tell such a large and deliberate lie, at least not without having planned for it. John Henry didn't notice it.

He said, "Do you know who these other boys were?"

"No idea," Maude said. I thought the matter through, knowing she had lied to protect me. I could see nothing to be gained by telling John Henry a different story than we had given to the sheriff.

"I believe one of them was said to be a cousin to the dead boy," John Henry said.

"There was no family resemblance I could see," Marion said. He went on to tell how we found Uncle Arlen by accident. Maude pinked up some as he told about waiting outside the Lavender Door.

"I guess you know the rest," I said.

Maude gave him an address for Uncle Arlen's friend Macdougal. John Henry promised to bank some of the funds from the book for me and Maude; that was one reason to give him a way to find us. But we were anxious to hear any news of Maude's name being cleared. That was a better reason.

FORTY-ONE

WE PARTED RIGHT THERE ON THE WIDE PRAIRIE, WITH half a day ahead of us to make use of. Me and Maude were taking Silver Dollar out to Uncle Arlen.

John Henry could ride on to the river crossing with Rebecca and the doctor, moving at a slower pace. From there he could get a ride back east, and they could wait in the comfort of a town for the doctor to feel better.

At the last minute, I had an urge to throw my arms around Rebecca's neck. Me and Maude had come back to being a usual part of civilization while living with Uncle Arlen, although we couldn't truly be ourselves.

With Rebecca and the doctor, we stood outside the bounds of usual civilization in a most acceptable way, and we were ourselves entirely. We had Rebecca to thank for that.

"I do like the dress," I said to her.

I looked back and waved to them a few times. Rebecca always waved back. It wasn't sadness made me look back. I felt good, really, like I'd found some extra time with Aunt Ruthie. I knew myself lucky to have had it.

We reached the river before evening. As we filled our canteens in readiness for the journey ahead of us, I noticed the few trees along the bank were wilted.

We didn't have to ride far out of our way to find a place to ford the water. The land changed something fierce on the other side of the river. It felt strange to turn in every direction and see nothing but straw-colored grass and cloudless blue sky.

We rode and rode and never felt like we made a distance.

Worse than that, we might could wander in circles, for once the trees petered out there was nothing to fix the eye on up ahead. I often brought my compass out to be sure we were heading westward.

The sky looked to be lower and heavier than ever I'd seen it before. After a time, Marion urged us to leave the trail, wading our horses through grass grown high enough to brush over our feet in the stirrups.

We came upon another patchy trail. It was nearly invisible, for the ruts in the dry earth had crumbled to dusty hollows. Like the trail had worn away under the flat weight of the sky.

"What's C.T. like?" I thought to ask. "Is it more of the same?"

"It's not so flat," Marion said. "More trees, more hills, more cats."

"Cats?"

"Big ones."

"I like it out here," Maude said, "when I'm not being chased."

I said, "You're more of a range rider than you know."

Riding for hours wore on our backsides, and never seeing another soul anywhere along the trail wore on our nerves. It did nothing to improve the mood, however, to come upon strangers.

We held firm expressions upon our faces, them and us. With sometimes a nod and "Good day" as we passed, since up to then no one had drawn a gun or given us a reason to do so. Our eyes met again as we looked back over our shoulders.

We didn't find water for the horses, so shared the water from the canteens with them. They needed corn, to give them a fresh backbone.

We ran out of hard-boiled eggs and harder biscuits and then went through the canned goods. Me and Maude had thinned down to belting our pants with a rope. She made a joke about it being Beef's style we were copying.

We rode for five days to reach another creek.

Here we could let the horses drink, but a smoke cloud to the north of us made it unwise to stop long enough to boil water for the canteens. We pushed through half of that night and half of the next on knowing the horses had had a drink.

"We have enough water to get us through tomorrow," Marion said. Over three days, the dry weather turned hotter. Our noses had burned and peeled until they were sore to touch.

We walked a good deal of the time, since we couldn't push the horses much for speed. It gave us a chance to get our legs moving, even if it did wring us out. We might have turned back for water to boil after all, but Maude was against it. She would rest only enough to keep the horses going.

"We haven't lost that much time in getting to your uncle," Marion said to her more than once.

I knew this argument was meant to spare the horses.

Wagon travel was slower than horseback by some five or six miles a day. A medicine wagon that was making frequent stops was slower yet. Maude wasn't fooled.

"We're nearly three weeks on the trail and not quite halfway," Maude said. "Uncle Arlen is probably there, if he was able to do it as he planned."

There was a look in her eyes. It scared me.

"I know why they call this land the plains," I said. "It's plain on all sides, nothing of interest for the eye to settle on."

"Except for all those trees," Maude said.

"What trees?" The distance rippled like a sheer curtain.

She lifted a hand to shade her eyes. "Those trees."

Then I knew she was teasing. I yanked off my hat and swatted her. We chased each other a few steps, but the heat and the need for a swallow of water took most of the play out of us.

Our spirits might have slid but for a heavy rustling in the grass a little way from us. I spotted a brown animal, squirrel-like but bigger. "A prairie dog," I said, pointing.

This was the beginning of a big colony. We kept our eyes open and let the horses walk through it. Several of those animals popped out of one burrow and down another; busy fellows, they were, and interesting to see.

We figured we'd gone more than a mile before we didn't have to worry about one of our horses stepping into a hole. Once that danger was past, we had nothing to take our minds off being thirsty and knowing we were tired to the bone.

"We might could have missed that river we were looking for," I said.

"They likelier moved it," Marion said.

In another day, our water was gone and we hadn't come across the river. Our throats burned for water.

"It may only be midday," I said at one point, looking at the sun, still high in the sky. We had all lost the feeling of how long we had been riding since sunup. "Do you want to stop and rest awhile?"

I looked at Maude as I said this, but her face might have been chiseled out of wood. She didn't change her pace.

"Let's keep going until dark," Marion said.

We kept on.

"If these horses get thirsty enough, they might find water on their own," I'd said hopefully early that morning. I had since been watching them for any sign they might smell water but saw not a flicker of interest in any of them.

We spoke not one word in a thousand steps. I couldn't stay alert to signs of danger.

But then, some time later, we passed an area where tepees had once stood. Everything had burned, and from the looks of it, a prairie fire had tried to get going. Likely they threw blankets and skins over the start of it, for the charred remains were still on the ground.

So were the skeletons of several horses.

"They musta been run out," Marion said.

I said, "What makes you say that?"

"The horses don't have shoes. Likely they were shot before the fire started."

"Who shot them?"

"Not Indians, that's for sure."

It was a moment of taking things in before Maude said,

"Are you saying they just came riding in shooting at horses and the Indians, too?"

"That's how it's done."

Maude rubbed at the back of her neck. I felt the same prickle on mine.

"The ones that lived have carried away their dead," Marion said. "That's why there's only horse bones to see."

It might have been an hour later Maude said to me, "Do you see a rider over that way?" I looked but couldn't be sure. So many days of hard sunlight had scalded my eyeballs. They burned even after I shut them at night.

"Let's just drift that way a bit," she said, and put her arm out to change the drag on the reins.

When her horse shifted, we all followed. "It could be an Indian," I said, but not fearfully. An Indian that was but a speck on the horizon didn't scare me awful much.

"It could be," Maude said, craning her neck. She picked up the pace a little, and the horses went along with it, so the rest of us did the same. There was a time without further remarks, until Marion added, "I'll tell you this about an Indian, he'll know where the water is."

From this, I gathered we didn't plan to catch up, precisely, but in this guess I was wrong. I fell back into riding in a benumbed state and didn't rouse until Maude hailed them.

They were three buffalo hunters.

They stopped riding and waited on us to catch up to them. They sat straight and strong-looking on the backs of horses that had the same steely look of power.

Each man had a mule tagging along behind. One of these

animals didn't wear any kind of tether but followed them anyway. Despite the mules, gear hung everywhere off their high-cantled saddles.

Except for those saddles, they might easily have been taken for Indians. One of them rode without a shirt; the other two had fashioned sleeveless coverings with gaping armholes. They wore moccasins. Two were wrinkled and sun-browned and the other was about Maude's age.

He did the talking. Don't think this means he was a willing talker.

"Good day," Maude said to them, and offered the flat smile that was as common out here as a handshake. "We need to find water."

"It's ahead of you," the boy said, and ducked his chin.

"How far?" My tongue felt thick for want of water.

"A day's ride," he said, looking us over in a glance. I had no doubt he was thinking it unlikely we had half a day left in us.

"What will we look for?" I said. Questioning him took a great effort. "A river? A town?"

"Are you a boy or a girl?" he said to me.

"What do you care?" I said to him, for I was in no mood to be thought of as the dirtiest girl he'd ever seen.

"This here is Zeb," he said, not showing us which one he meant, "and this is Micah," which introduction didn't make things any clearer. Neither one of them so much as blinked an eye. "They call me Billy Bat."

I felt this was a trick, so I gave Maude's and Marion's names but not my own. He allowed this to pass, which surprised me.

He said, "If you care to ride with us, we'll see you make it to the old Fort Zarah site at the bend of the Arkansas River. From there you can get anywhere you want to go."

I said, "What about the Little Arkansas?"

"Why, you've crossed it," he said. "This summer is terrible dry and it's down to nothing but a creek. The big one has fared better, and you are nearer to it anyway."

One of the older men hefted a canteen and held it out in Maude's direction. She refused it at first, but Marion took the canteen and asked her to please drink from it.

She took a polite swallow, and then had to be stopped.

"It takes some of them that way," that man said. The boy passed a canteen to me.

We all had a long drink, and I thanked the boy in my deepest voice when I handed the much lighter canteen over to him.

FORTY-TWO

THE WATER REVIVED US.

But if I thought we were quiet before, it was because I didn't know the meaning of the word. When we made the occasional stop or walked a bit, not one of those fellows uttered a sound.

Neither did we. After a time, it felt like a contest. Maude's eyes met mine once, her eyebrows danced up and down, and I felt the beginnings of laughter in my belly.

I looked away with a shake of my head. I didn't care to look foolish to them, at least not more foolish than to be out in the middle of nowhere without enough water.

Surely we were a match for these fellows.

We didn't just ride until dark, but rode until the moon was high, and then we rode some more. The air couldn't be called cool or damp, but I thought it easier to ride at night than with the sun beating down on me. At a certain point I was too numb to feel the pain in my feet or that my sit-down had fallen asleep.

It was still full dark when the horses began to show a little life, with skin twitches and arched tails. "They smell the river," Billy Bat said.

The moon had moved to the place where it flirts with early morning before *we* could smell it, some freshness that rode the air.

"There's the fort," Zeb said to us when the sun was on the rise.

I couldn't see it.

"Why is it flying two flags?" Maude said to him.

He gave her a sharp look of surprise. No doubt he met very few people with eyesight to match his. "That other'n is the flag of Kansas," he said.

Some time passed before I could see the remains of a fort in the distance, let alone the colors flying. The adobe wall was a surprise to me.

Tents had been raised around it, and some shanties built out of scrap wood. The pale covers of a few wagons caught the sunlight.

Dogs barked, warning everyone we were approaching, and a few came out to meet us, hackles standing. Our horses were too tired to be bothered with this and didn't hardly raise their heads.

Only those hunters still sat tall on their horses, riding as fresh as if they were starting out in the morning. "Who goes there?" someone shouted from the protection of those walls.

"Zeb Smith," the boy shouted out. "He's bringing in some new friends."

We rode in and straight over to the well. The horses took

to the trough while we hauled up a bucket to drink our fill. We all used the same tin ladle that hung from a string to serve the purpose.

Those two old buffalo hunters became talkative once we reached the camp and they came across some old friends. They called the boy by both his names, Billy Bat, as the talk moved on to what they had seen out there on the prairie. Buffalo was the main thing. Dry was the other. They didn't mention finding us there.

The boy said nothing, but hung on every word the men said.

These folks had settled here permanent from the looks of things. It had the look of a men's camp, though women and children were among them. Everyone was dressed in a practical way that worked, homespun cloth and leather. Nothing was worn for the look of pretty or fine.

We drank more water, tended the horses, and waited for the place to wake up. Daylight broke with an odd splash of purple on the horizon and the smell of coffee and bacon on the air.

It began to look like a small town sprang up here when the rays of the morning sun hit the dirt inside the broke-down walls of the old fort. There was a kind of dining hall, with a few rough tables set up. We were almost first in line for the eats.

I could say this for the cook at that place: she was good. Her biscuits were tender, her eggs weren't fried but stirred fluffy, her fatback was crisp, and her coffee generously sweetened.

Billy Bat sneaked looks at me as he ate, and I behaved as

boylike as I was able. I wouldn't mind it if I could keep him wondering.

I said, "Is this place still a fort? Where's the cavalry?"

"This is the old fort," he said. "The soldiers moved west to be closer to the Indian fighting."

There were several Abe Lincoln look-alikes loading a wagon. Amish, I thought, remembering a picture in a textbook.

"Quaker," Maude said.

"Mormon," Billy Bat said as the men brought their filled plates to the table.

"Makes me feel like I could use a shave," Marion whispered, though he wore only a dark stubble on his face.

Something in this simple talk pleased me more than I could say and I laughed, making all but Maude stare at me. "There's a sound I haven't heard in too long," she said.

"You could stay here for a piece," Zeb said to us.

"We can't," Maude said.

We went over Uncle Arlen's map, which was some tattered by now. We knew we had another two weeks of hard riding to go, but we did keep wanting to measure the distance every few days.

Just as he had done, I'd marked Fort Larned as a place to lay over for a day. "We'll ride on," Maude said.

I didn't argue this. We were still forty miles off. Beyond that lay a likely five-day ride to Fort Dodge. From there it would be another hundred miles to the western border of Kansas.

"How much further to Liberty?" Maude said.

"Hard to say." I was using the width of my finger as a ruler.

"Maybe two days' ride." She fell backwards into the grass, as if she was giving it up. "This trip is a bear, all right," I said in full agreement.

"A bear?"

I said, "That's what heroes in dimers say. When something tests their mettle, they compare it to the hardest thing to kill, I guess, and that's a bear."

"Are these the dimers written by John Henry Kirby?" she said. "He will have made that up." This caught me by surprise and then struck me funny. I fell back beside her and we had a good laugh over this.

We bought foodstuffs and sweet feed for the horses. We filled our many canteens, though we expected to follow the river the rest of the way.

Billy Bat did an odd thing. He brought to me a paper-wrapped parcel I took to be a pencil. He had about him the air of giving me a present and I thanked him more forcefully than I might have, considering I didn't know what he was about.

"My name is Sallie," I said, and because I was used to saying Uncle Arlen's name now, added, "Salome Waters."

"William Bartholomew Masterson." He held out his hand. We shook. He said, "I didn't think you the least prissy for a boy."

"That is the best compliment of my whole life so far," I told him. He was smiling as he turned away.

"What is that he gave you?" Maude asked of the package. I opened it to find a peppermint stick. This made us both grin as we broke off a piece.

FORTY-THREE

WE PASSED FORT LARNED LATE THE NEXT DAY, STAY-
ing close to the river's edge. Marion called the fort a bump
in the flat, and Maude said it didn't look much different
than the place we had recently left behind.

I said to them it was the most interesting thing I had not
seen all day.

To say we enjoyed uninterrupted travel would be stretch-
ing it.

We had sufficient water, we didn't go hungry, and we saw
no one—which suited us just fine. We talked a good deal, but
not without long, comfortable periods when no one had a
thing to say. We slept reasonable well, and nobody got
snakebit at the water's edge.

We didn't enjoy it because the land had turned into a
thing that got on the nerves. The sky hung flat blue and
cloudless, just too big all around us. There were no cities,
nothing until Fort Dodge to break up the tiresome hours.
Nothing by which to measure our progress.

For another thing, there had been no rain and the land

looked parched. Even at the river's edge there was little enough green to rest the eyes.

We began to feel like we were starting off each morning on the same piece of land we had started from the day before. I put marks on Uncle Arlen's map so I wouldn't lose track of the days.

We sighed from pure relief to come upon a short string of wagons one evening, drawn into a hodgepodge cluster. They were fenced by clotheslines full of billowing linens.

"I think we ought to let our hair loose so it will be plain we're women," Maude said. "You hang back some, Marion. Ride with me, Sallie, so they can see how young you are."

I said, "Why?"

"They have only ladies' things hanging on the line."

"Just ride in slow," Marion said.

I looked at him in a sizing-up way that had not occurred to me in some time. He'd grown a rough stubble after leaving the Aldoradondos, but at Fort Zarah it would have seemed odd to see him clean-shaven among so many whiskered faces. But now he had a short dark beard. To my eye, it made up for the bald spot, but it also made him look like someone to reckon with.

There were several women at work around those wagons. I did notice two men sitting off under a tree on what looked like nail barrels. We aimed ourselves anyway at a big woman wearing a scoop-shovel bonnet and a newly bright print dress.

She was feeding chickens in crates affixed to the sides of a wagon. Two half-sized pink pigs snuffled the ground at her feet. They were mighty clean, for pigs. Maude said to her,

"We'd like to put down our bedrolls near your wagons. We won't be any bother to you."

"It's just the few of you I see?"

"Three of us," Maude said. "No drinking, and none of us plays the piano."

The woman grinned. "Where you headed?"

"Home," Maude said.

Within the circle of those wagons, women worked together in a clump or sat on the end of a wagon in twos and threes. Two of them were folding some of the dried clothes, which were crisp as thick paper. A couple of women were having a friendly squabble over the vegetables they were cutting into a pot. It felt homey.

"Have you got the strength left to peel some potatoes?" one of them said in our direction.

"I am ever fond of peeling potatoes," I said, though it wasn't strictly true. It was eating potatoes I was ever fond of.

"You have a place for the night," the one standing before us said, like she'd taken it upon herself to keep us out of harm's way. "I'm Betsy. This is Lucy, here."

Lucy was older, and if she was more cautious, she was also more curious. She didn't miss a detail of us.

Maude gave Marion a come-on-in wave. She introduced herself, using the name of Waters, and before she could decide for me, I said, "I'm her little brother, Sallie."

Betsy took a long look at me, already sure she knew me for a girl. "Sallie is an odd name for a boy, isn't it?" I said to her.

"That it is," she said as Marion rode near. "If you prefer it, it makes no never mind to me."

"This is our good friend, Marion Hardly," I said.

"Ma'am," he said, and tipped his hat. He hadn't yet gotten down from his horse.

"You all look like some corn bread and buttermilk would go down the right way," Betsy said. "Between the cow and the chickens, we don't go hungry around here."

"Picket your horses over there by my cow," Lucy said.

As me and Marion led our horses away, Maude said, "I hope we'll be good company."

"Don't worry," Betsy said. "After a day's travel we ain't so lively ourselves."

We poured dusty piles of oats into the grass and the horses began to eat. Betsy carried over to us a bowl of horse treats, some dried-out corn bread on the verge of getting musty. If the corn bread was on its last legs, so were the horses, and they greeted this bit of color like pure gold.

Sitting down to the conversation, I heard Maude admire the chicken crates. "We can't let the chickens run loose," Betsy said. "They don't keep up."

Maude said, "But your pigs are safe?"

"Their momma died after they were born, so I had to feed them milk from Lucy's cow," she said. Telling us this brought a smile to her face. "They think I'm their momma, and they don't stray ten feet away."

"How are you going to be able to bring yourself to eat them?" Maude asked her.

"Posie and Petunia?" She laughed. "I could never eat them. I'm going to have to marry up with somebody has a boar hog, that's all."

We were served plates of eggs fried to perfection, with a tasty brown crust on the outside and a tender yolk on the inside. We didn't waste time on polite reluctance. We ate with our fingers, although we were given forks.

Betsy did the talking, telling us they were twenty-eight women from back east hoping to find husbands out west.

"Expecting to find husbands," Lucy said.

"Although we aren't yet promised," another of them said.

"Where you coming from?" Betsy asked us.

"We came from the old Fort Zarah site most recently," I said. "We're headed for Liberty in the Colorado Territory."

"That doesn't sound like a bad place," another woman, name of Miriam, said. "We're going into C.T. ourselves, but I still think we ought to try for Wyoming, where they're giving women the vote."

Betsy said, "I told Miriam it's too far north. The winters are bound to be hard, and there she is, a sparrow of a woman."

Lucy said, "Besides that, it's a territory settled on trying to live with new ideas. I read that someplace."

Maude didn't enter into this conversation. I believe they thought her to be too hungry for talk, and didn't judge her rude. Marion had kept his head down mostly, like a shy fellow.

"New ideas, and a great many men to choose from," another woman said. "How could we go wrong?"

At this, Marion stood to excuse himself. "Think I'll just mosey on over there and sit with those fellows."

Betsy said, "They're friendlies. Just introduce yourself."

"Thanks for the eats," Marion said. "Give a holler if I can do anything for you."

This seemed to kill the mood. Everyone got up, remembering a chore they had to finish. Making good on my word, I took up the bucket of potatoes and started peeling.

Betsy was right, those pigs followed her like dogs. And they had a taste for buttermilk. They stood watching each swallow we took and, when we finished, nuzzled out the bowls.

Having done with the buttermilk, one of the pigs leaned over the cookfire to check what was in the pot. One of the women spotted this and whacked it on the nose with the wooden spoon. The pig set up a noisy squealing and ran to Betsy, who soothed it like a child.

"What made you decide to come west, Betsy?" Maude asked her as she sat beside us at supper.

"Men," Betsy said. "Not the finding of one so much as getting away from a certain kind."

"What kind is that?" I asked her.

Betsy said, "The kind who don't know that being little and delicate isn't the making of a woman. It will be the icing on the cake to find a man who already knows a woman with grit and substance is the equal of any pretty sparrow who graces a ballroom."

"There must be a lot of men who know that," I said.

"I believe there are," Betsy said. "If I find one who loves me for my grit and substance, I'll have my cake and eat it both."

"Yes, but what made you want to go west to find it?" Maude asked her. "Are there more of those men out there?"

Betsy shrugged. "Maybe it's that there are so many men who know what it takes to get there at all. They're sure to appreciate a woman who can do it. Don't you agree?"

"I do," Maude said. "It doesn't take but a few days of riding the trail out here to appreciate it's another thing entirely from a wagon trip to visit with relatives, back east."

A small child kept crawling in our direction, a toothless grin of welcome on his face, or hers, I couldn't tell.

A girl of maybe four years doggedly brought him back to their momma's side over and over again. After one of these efforts, she came back over to tell us, "He's a lot of trouble. I don't know why we had to have him."

I didn't know how to reply to this, but Maude said, "He'll be more useful later. He'll play tea party with you."

The girl gave Maude a look that suggested she'd heard this empty promise before. "Whenever you break something," I said, "you can say he did it."

"Maybe," she said.

"If he leaves his jelly and biscuit lying around, you can eat it and know it for a good joke on him," Maude said, and this made the little girl grin.

FORTY-FOUR

THE FULL MOON HAD RISEN PALE THAT NIGHT, FAINTLY blue, like milk once the cream is skimmed off. I expected everyone to sit down around the campfire once the supper things were put away.

But there was butter to be churned and cheese to be hung in the pantry wagon. The moon had hit its peak and was headed west before that camp settled down for the night.

"You and Sallie could ride on with us if you care to, Maude," Betsy said from the opening at the end of her wagon. She was pretty, in the most billowing nightgown I'd ever seen. "Your friend, too. There's safety in numbers, most times."

Miriam said, "We have several women who are good shots."

"Maude once shot the eye out of a panther," I said, jumping in where I could.

This raised some oohs and aahs. Lucy said admiringly, "You have the makings of a gunslinger."

At this, me and Maude fell silent. We didn't mean to draw attention to ourselves in this way, but we did. These women were ever faithful conversationalists, and falling silent was foreign to them.

It broke up the party, with them wondering who we might be they were laughing with around their fire. But if they were a more solemn group as they turned in for the night, they didn't refuse us the warmth of their circle to sleep in.

Maude soon lay sound asleep, with her hair spread over the saddlebags she used for a pillow. She fought to stay awake, but once she lay down, sleep had been the winner of that battle.

The woman called Young Etta—for they had started out with an older one as well—came to sit with me. She brought two onion crates to sit upon, which did improve the accommodations. I thanked her and went on watching the stars come out.

"You aren't much for talk," she said.

"What do you like to talk about?" I asked her.

"Home," she said.

The very word brought a funny ache to my chest. I'd begun to think of home as the piece of ground I was going to lay on during the night, and just now it already looked familiar to me. I was resigned each morning to leaving it behind.

I didn't ask her why she left home, if she was so happy there. People have their reasons, I had learned that. Reluctant as I was to start out before Maude could travel as a free woman, I didn't regret it now.

I'd had that time with Rebecca, and I'd sold more than a hundred bottles from my basket. We'd never have found John Henry in any other way, and perhaps, in the end, he would be the saving of Maude.

Young Etta said to me, "What about you?"

"I'm right fond of home," I said, "but it isn't so much a place with me. It's Maude. Our uncle Arlen. Marion."

"So you are always on the move? Don't you get tired of that?"

"We stopped for a time in Independence," I said, "and we'll stop again in C.T. Meanwhile, there's something fine about living each day different than the last."

I saw the first sign—the pigs woke and started running among the horses and cow—and I should have known it for trouble.

Minutes later, Maude's horse took to blowing through his nose. Horses don't like having pigs run under their bellies, so I ignored the blowing, and still ignored it when I saw him pointing his ears off into the darkness. That was the second sign, the horse's ears, and I missed it.

The third sign came from the pigs again. They ran out into the darkness, and we could hear the speedy patter of their hooves as they skittered about out there.

Betsy looked out from her wagon and sniffed the air like a dog. She said, "Something's out there," and ducked back inside.

One of the pigs came running back into the circle of firelight squealing to high heaven, cutting up the last vestige of peace. Some of the other women tumbled out of their wagons.

Maude sat up, her quilt still around her.

After a moment, the second pig came through, complaining as loudly as the first. The noise a pig could make was amazing to me.

They raced about the camp. We had just begun to talk loudly of wrestling them to the ground—because talking loudly was the only way to be heard over the racket they were making—when a gnarly crew of troublemakers ran into our midst, yowling and shrieking and shooting in all directions.

They weren't cautious about their firearms and might well have killed someone, but they only killed a chicken in its crate. Out of the corner of my eye, I saw its feathers puff and float to the ground. The pigs ran off to the horses and cow.

The leader of this band was a woman. And she had with her six men who had pulled their kerchiefs up over their noses. Six men, and one of them had a gun in each hand. They stirred up a ruckus worse than the pigs.

"Everybody with your hands in the air," the woman yelled. Her hair was ash gray and her face as weathered as an old board fence.

Everyone's hands went straight up, including mine. And Maude's. Old she may have been, but the gal had a knack for this kind of work.

"I am crazy Maude March, so don't cross me," she shouted.

I saw many a woman holding all manner of useful weapons grabbed up during the shooting, from peeling knife to knitting needles, but no one looked likely to cross her.

It struck me at once that no matter how many of these women could take aim and hit their mark, they were not yet convinced of the need to shoot at anything but what could be turned into dinner.

For their part, our men didn't look any more ready to do something than the women. Their rifles were kicked away before they could decide to reach for them.

The odds were on this old gal's side, I feared, but I started to look for any odds that were left to be on ours. Maude didn't look dangerous in her quilt, but her face had gone from surprised to angry as Aunt Ruthie knowing there was a fox in her chicken coop.

"Where are the rest of your men?" the old gal shouted after realizing she was holding up mostly women.

"They're off hunting," I said, since five men was all we had, counting me and Maude. "They're coming back directly."

"Let's not waste any time, then," she said. "Give me your valuables."

There was not a move made.

Part of it might have been a matter of figuring out what she was asking for, for she said "vowel-you-bulls." This was a mite confusing to me, and may well have been for the others. But few of us, maybe none of us, had anything that fit the description. Also, the pigs kept up a noise.

"We don't have anything," Lucy said, her voice full of genuine confusion.

"We are brides on the trail of grooms," Betsy said. "What do you expect us to have?"

"Dowries," the old gal said promptly, and Betsy laughed.

"I have two pigs," she said, "but I beg you not to take them. They have become my pets."

"I have a cow," Lucy said with a smile. "Even after this long trek, she gives enough milk to earn you twenty dollars a day. But the men will be back before you get twenty yards with her. Cows aren't built for getaways."

"They think we're fooling with them," said the man

with two guns. "I say we shoot one of them and change the mood."

There was something familiar about him, but I didn't think about it as a pig came near knocking that old gal off her feet. She shouted, "Don't make fun of me. I am a dangerous woman."

"I forget, what did you say your name was?" Maude asked her.

"Mad Maude," the other one said. "You heard a me."

I said, "How do we know you are who you say you are?"

She said, "Did you not see my face in the newspapers all this last year?"

"Tell me which of those Maudes you are," Maude said, "or we may not believe you at all. Likelier you're a ninny."

"You look to me like a missy who likes trouble," the other one sneered.

"My middle name is trouble," Maude said in a sure and certain voice. Quick as a snake, she lunged for the rifle under her blanket and loosed a cartridge.

The old gal had just enough time to see it coming, and she let fly a bullet, but her bullet went into the dirt.

Maude hit the pistol dead-on without touching the other Maude, and two things happened because of it. Maude's rifle cartridge ricocheted and hit another bandit in the leg with a sound like *thwap!* A red flower bloomed there in the blink of an eye.

Also, the other one's pistol flew and hit the man standing nearest her, the one with two guns. It spooked him so he swung his pistols toward the old gal as he shot.

A bullet nipped her trigger finger and whizzed so close to my arm it felt like a bee sting, the heat and the noise together.

As I took this in, I saw Betsy leap from her wagon, her nightgown billowing around her, pantaloons ruffling, her rifle held in both hands to do her own battle. She used the rifle butt to put one of the masked men out of order with a swat to his jaw. He fell like a broken doll, and she fell to her knees to check if his heart was still beating, her face writ with regret.

In moments when life hangs in the balance, it feels like time slows down so much you can't miss a thing. I felt certain that this would have been just as true if that bee sting had been a bullet hitting me square in the heart. I would have died instantly, but I would've known all the sides of that instant.

The next moment wasn't slowed down at all; it may have speeded up, for there was all manner of chaos in that camp.

Another bullet hit one of Betsy's pigs.

The pig started squealing and running in circles, and the other pig panicked and followed it, making even more noise, if such a thing were possible.

Betsy stood up and swung her rifle, catching the two-gunner in the midsection. He sat down hard. Betsy swung back the other way, and her rifle butt clipped another of those fellows on the chin, laying him out cold. This time Betsy didn't worry about them.

Our men had been at some disadvantage when the rebellion began, since the guns were mostly trained on them. But they didn't slouch once things went wild. They were helped by the women, all of them eager to get in one good wallop they could brag about.

Guns went off, and dirt spurted up in little fountains. The

pigs went on with that ear-piercing shrill noise that was more alarming than gunshots.

This was not quite matched by the women's shrieks as the last fellow was jumped before he could make up his mind who to shoot—he didn't stand a chance. Two of the women sat on him and another began to bind his wrists tightly with her knitting yarn.

Two men were trying to take down the other Maude, who was turning in a circle, swinging her pistol as if she couldn't decide where to shoot first.

When she stopped circling, her gun was pointing at my Maude. Marion stepped forward and punched her in the nose.

She went over like a felled tree.

FORTY-FIVE

AND STILL IT WAS A SCENE OF UTTER MAYHEM.

The old gal and two of her men and one pig were hurt bad enough to bleed, and I was only barely missed, and of course there was the dead chicken from the start. The uninjured pig raced around in a panic without a care for knocking into people or running them over.

The other one, hurt, lurched about doing nearly as much damage. Betsy followed this piglet, which didn't stop making that shrill squealing noise. Unable to catch it, Betsy wailed like a boat horn, just those kinds of long, deep, repeated blasts, with an indrawn breath in between them.

Betsy was bad, but pig screams are truly a thing to wear on the nerves.

Women were darting about in all directions. They looked ready enough, but I couldn't say whether they were doing any good at all, for I was fighting a strange dizziness.

I went around collecting the outlaws' guns. I moved all the rifles that were lying about to a place where the old gal or one of her henchmen weren't going to get their hands on them if we didn't watch them every second.

Then I had to sit down.

With the help of one of the men who had been leading the wagons, Betsy's injured pig was fought to the ground. And once it lay on its side, shrieking, it took the help of three women to hold it there till a rope could be twisted around its feet. My Maude was among these people who were managing the pig.

Betsy's uninjured pig, still on the move, didn't stop squealing and ran full over the other Maude with its little pointy hooves as she lay helpless in the dirt. Baby pigs they were, but they weren't lightweights. That old gal's internals had to fend for themselves. Everybody looked busy enough without trying to bag a pig.

Lucy had already begun to deal with the other injuries. She was quick to stop the bleeding from that gal's shortened trigger finger and to shout things about caring for the fellow who had been hit in the leg.

And there was more to come.

For when Marion pulled the kerchief off the two-gunner, it turned out to be none other than—

One of those boat rats. The short, smart one.

The injured pig now lay trussed, but not quietly. My Maude bent for her rifle, causing a few others to come to a standstill. But Maude didn't shoot, she clopped that running pig square on the forehead with the butt of her rifle.

The noise was cut by half immediately.

"You're her, aren't you?" the boat rat said to my Maude, and he could be heard. "You're Mad Maude, after all."

"Knot him up tight, ladies," Maude said, as if she hadn't noticed.

"Tie him to the wagon wheels till morning," Young Etta

said. She wasn't in the least timid in the midst of so much going on.

But everyone else, save the injured pig, had gone quiet, as if the boat rat's voice had carried directly to their ears before all other sound. They all looked at Maude.

Betsy's nightgown was dustied up, but she was otherwise none the worse for wear. She said, "Tell us, Maude, if what he says is true. That you are the woman on those posters."

"It's me on the first posters," Maude said, and for the first time she didn't look as if she minded it. "The accusations aren't true. I didn't rob the bank. Well, except we did take the horses, but they were returned."

"They say you shot a man in cold blood," Lucy said.

"*I* shot him," I said. This appeared to flummox even the hurt pig, for it went quiet, and I didn't have to yell to make myself heard when I added, "It wasn't cold-blooded. Only accidental."

There was another moment of pure stone silence, and then Betsy said, "Well, that's going to make an interesting story, one of these evenings." With that, everyone turned back to what they had been doing before.

The boat rat and the other fairly uninjured bandit were tied to the wagon wheels. There was some spirited discussion about the best technique for securing bandits to wagon wheels.

The pig that Maude had knocked cold staggered to its feet. The leg-shot fellow started to do some screaming as the slug was plucked from his thigh. The other Maude's finger was bandaged tightly, and she was tied to the wagon with her arm straight up in the air.

The pigs commenced their noise. This last, because Betsy

went back to digging the bullet out of the one pig's haunch, and when one squealed, they both squealed. But the wobbly one squealed something more quietly, and Maude let it be.

Young Etta tugged at my sleeve and said, "You've been hit."

There was blood staining my shirtsleeve. Now she brought it to my attention, my arm did ache some. Maude saw what we were about, and between them, Maude and Young Etta rolled up my sleeve, decided the bullet just grazed me, and cleaned it up with soap and water.

I couldn't get over it. I was shot, and the soap and water was the worst of it. Stung worse than the bullet. A bit of Maude's petticoat made a bandage for me, and she tore another.

But then Young Etta made Maude put it back into her sack. "It's a pretty thing, too nice for the likes of them. We can bandage them with strips from an old sheet."

I took that piece and put it in my pocket, in case the one I wore got dirty. I still wasn't big on hand washing, but I had learned this much from Dr. Aldoradondo.

By the time I was taken care of, the pigs were quieted. Betsy reported that Posey was going to be fine. The slug had not hit any vitals. By then, that Maude was well recovered enough to air her complaints.

"You shot off my trigger finger," she said to the boat rat with a reasonable degree of resentment. Her nose had swollen some, and she sounded like she had a cold in her head.

"Bad timing," he said with a shrug.

There were the gang's horses to be brought in and wiped down and picketed. The children were read stories and sung lullabies and fed sweets, all in hopes of getting them back to bed.

"It's time we got some sleep around here," Betsy said. "I don't want to hear a peep out of any of you, for I'll use the butt of that rifle to silence you the way Maude did my Petunia."

Maude said, "Sorry, Betsy."

"You're forgiven," Betsy said. "Any rate, what's good enough for Petunia is good enough for these ones."

This proved enough of a threat, for there was not a peep out of any of them. Marion and the two wagon leaders set themselves up under the trees. Me and Maude put our bedrolls outside the circle of the wagons, near the horses and Lucy's cow. The dog came to curl up at Maude's feet.

A momma sang a lullaby from inside one of the wagons, putting most of that camp to sleep. I couldn't lay still; I had a lot to think about. All these Maudes, for one thing.

I parked myself against a wagon wheel directly across from the other Maude. "What's your real name?" I asked her after a time of us staring at each other.

"Mary Rose," she said.

"Very pretty," Aunt Ruthie said. She looked at me. "Isn't that a pretty name for a woman?"

"It'll do," I said, because I didn't want to be won over by a name.

I did realize I had fallen asleep, for that was ever where I came across Aunt Ruthie anymore. Also because she was at the water's edge, a sparkling blue water I hadn't seen anywhere else.

Being asleep, I couldn't be sure I had that answer from the crazy Maude or from a dream of her. But here was Aunt

Ruthie showing me a forgiving heart, and this interested me more. "When did you get so softhearted?"

"I was ever softhearted," Aunt Ruthie said.

"I didn't know that."

"There's a lesson for you."

FORTY-SIX

OVER BREAKFAST, MARION ASKED BETSY WHAT SHE and the others planned to do with our night visitors. "I don't rightly know," she said.

"We might could take them on to Fort Dodge for you," he said in a reluctant tone. He pointed to the rat. "But it wouldn't go well for our Maude over there, because that one knows her."

"Now, I wouldn't ask you to do that," Betsy said. "But what do you think is the best way to manage them? We can't keep them tied to the wheels."

"Here," the other Maude complained. "You can't be planning to hold on to us and let the real Mad Maude ride off scot-free."

"It's not my Maude who came in here and tore up everyone's sleep," I said to her. "It's you and yours, and I'll have you watch how you talk about my sister."

The old gal wasn't easily discouraged. She said, "That sister of yours has ruined my career with that ill-timed shot. I'm too old for most trades, save teaching Sunday school."

"That's a good one, I hear," Lucy said. "You might consider it."

"It don't pay all that well," the other Maude said in a growly voice, "even if I were suited to it, which I'm not."

"The rewards are greater than you think," Young Etta said. "If you were to marry, you might not worry so much about what kind of work suited you. You would be too busy for such thoughts, and sitting down to teach Sunday school would hold more appeal."

"That doesn't sound like much of a recommendation to me," another of the women said.

But the other Maude said, "Who would marry me?"

"There's a good question," the boat rat said, and I realized suddenly he didn't like this gal. I considered this to be a point in his favor. Not that I liked him much. Only I did remember listening to him at George Ray's and knowing him to be a cut above the others.

She gave him back a look of "you'll be sorry," but her one arm was tied upright to the wagon wheel, and her other hand was tied to her leg just to keep her out of trouble. She didn't look to be much of a threat.

Young Etta talked as if she hadn't noticed any of this. "Who would marry me, either? No one, so far. But then, the war has thinned the men's ranks. I'm going west, where there are more of them, and maybe I'll have better luck."

"I would change my ways for that kind of luck," the other Maude said. "This rough life isn't working out, now my trigger finger is gone."

From here, the conversation took a surprising turn, the

women asking each other whether those visitors looked repentant enough to suit all.

"If it's a good man you girls are looking for, I'm a good man," the leg-shot fellow said. "Don't judge me by the company I'm keeping just now."

"It's not your company but your actions I question," Young Etta said.

"You look to be of doubtful quality," Lucy said. "But we have a ways to go. You might could ride alongside the wagon, offering your protection."

"What about her?" one of the women said, pointing to the other Maude. That creature stuck her tongue out at us.

"She's more doubtful yet," Lucy said. "We don't even know what her true name is."

"Mary Rose," I said. I did find in myself a soft spot for her. Not a very large spot, however.

Betsy was much of the same mind. She said, "If the others agree, we could try and see if these ruffians can be turned out good. As for her, I would keep her tied a while longer."

The weak-chinned fellow Betsy had felled with her rifle butt listened more especially to this conversation. "I can be turned out," he said. "I used to be a fine fellow and could be again."

I'd by this time scraped my plate clean and washed it. The Maude question wasn't yet decided, but the men's likely fates interested them all. I heard one woman mention another of them as someone who could straighten a fellow out in no time. It was said she had buried three husbands already, of overwork.

Betsy said, "Don't give her the best one if she's going to run him out that fast anyway."

I suspected they were biting off more than they could chew. I went over to the boat rat. He had a plate on his lap and one hand freed to eat from it. "Where are your other fellows?"

"Scattered, now that Hankie's dead."

"We heard he was shot in the sheriff's office and then read in the paper he was shot off his horse."

"That's right, he was killed twice," he said.

"Maybe the time has come to change your ways," I said, and left him to think on it.

I settled myself near Marion. "What do you make of this?" I asked him. "They're taking these characters to their bosom."

"Those fellows are just down on their luck," he said. "She's another story, she has a rackety temperament. Won't know from one minute to the next what her mood will be."

"Some men like that," our Maude said, overhearing. She crossed her feet and dropped to the ground in one quick motion.

"Maybe," Marion said. "Not me. Me and rackety temperaments just don't mix."

Maude laughed, which struck me odd. But I couldn't question it, for Young Etta made a beeline for me.

"Give me your opinion," she said.

"The boat rat is smart," I said, nodding to show her which of them I meant. "He's a thinker."

This earned me a long look from Maude and Marion both. But Young Etta turned on her heel and whirled back into the fray.

"How's your arm feeling?" Maude wanted to know.

"Like I got a nasty scratch," I said. "I've gotten worse from wood splinters."

Me and Maude were anxious to get a move on, to be safely across the border for one thing, and to see our uncle for another. It was only this last reason we mentioned to Betsy.

Maude said, "When are you starting out again?"

"Not tomorrow," Betsy said. "Probably not the day after. But soon. I know we are out in the wilderness here, but we won't camp for long at Fort Dodge. The chickens are at risk in such places. Too many empty stewpots."

Maude told them we were sorry for riding on and leaving them, but we had to get to our uncle Arlen, who was in some trouble.

Betsy didn't mind these fellows, now she knew her pigs were all right. They hadn't decided just what they might do about that Maude, but there was an amazing air of forgive and forget throughout the camp.

With the wagon drivers listening in, Marion said, "These fellows aren't the worst they could be, but that don't make them marriage material." He told Betsy to keep the whole pack of them tied up till they got to the fort and then leave them off there. I believe he could see as well as me this advice was falling on deaf ears.

FORTY-SEVEN

AFTER SEVERAL HOURS OF LOOKING AT THE UN-changing line of the horizon, I began to look for ways to amuse myself.

I looked at Uncle Arlen's map, now quite soft and faded from so much handling. I took comfort in seeing we were past the halfway point.

We figured him for having arrived, but that only meant he faced the dangers we meant to share in. So far he faced them one man short.

I rode ahead for a time, riding a little one way and then a little the other. Testing my compass. Somewhere along the line it had acquired a dent in the back, and I was worried it might not work aright.

In fact, it did appear to work just fine. I rode back and took up a position between Maude and Marion. My eyes had begun to ache again.

"I have an idea knocking around in my head," I said.

Maude said, "What is it?"

"I think we ought to complain of these Maudes we keep

running into," I said. "When we get to Fort Dodge, I think we should tell what a pestilence they've become."

"Have you lost your mind out here?" Maude said.

"It happens there are quite a few of them running around. It will be like the newspaper reports," I said. "Enough complaints, and you could walk right up and turn yourself in, Maude, and they would turn you away as a pretender."

"The girl has something there," Marion said.

We rode for a time without speaking further of it. I figured them for mulling it over. Myself, I was entertained by thinking of it, enough that I didn't notice the endless sky for some time.

Maude said, "Who would make this complaint?"

"I can do it," Marion said.

"Better yet, we'll do it together," I said.

"I don't care for it," Maude said.

Marion glanced over at me and winked.

We made Fort Dodge two days later.

The fort stood on a slight rise in the land, so we could study up on it before we arrived. Built of mud and stone, it was some larger and more sturdy-looking than Zarah.

Coming in as we did from the quiet of open country—mostly quiet—the hillside looked to be a noisy beehive of activity. Wagons were clustered at one corner, and a few board shanties leaned toward another, looking somehow less permanent than the wagons did.

Tents stood everywhere else, children and dogs ran loose, and cookfires burned between them. The air smelled more of beans than of sweet dry grass—this wasn't a complaint.

We made a stop to let Maude change into her work dress.

I gave her my bonnet, which didn't look quite so white and pretty as it had at the start, to cover her hair.

It was for the best, on the whole, for Maude's work dress was dark and plain. It made perfect sense that a woman might try to relieve the dreary look of it with something that didn't seem right at all. She didn't look awful much like any poster we had seen, having neither a man's hat nor broomtails.

As we rode in, I figured the whole cavalry was out there on the prairie, except for the few that stood in the guardhouses up top. The soldiers were marching in lines, the barrels of their rifles gleaming in the midday sun.

Then we rode through the gates, and I saw soldiers were as thick as termites on the inside. They'd squeezed a small city inside the walls.

This was due to Fort Dodge being a road station for mail coaches, freight wagons, homesteaders, and buffalo hunters to lay over before they headed into Indian Territory.

Marion wanted to put a feed bag on the horses first thing. Maude said to me, "Here is the last of my money. Go find us something to eat while I check whether a telegram has arrived for Sam Waters."

"I'll go to the telegraph office," I said, thinking of all those wanted posters.

"Leave me be, Sallie," Maude said. "If I can't walk around without getting arrested in this bonnet, I might just as well turn myself in."

I couldn't think of what to say to her.

It can happen that you only want to do the right thing, that you try your best, and still nothing works out the way you hoped. I sent up a short prayer this wasn't one of those times.

I pocketed the money and went looking for supplies. On the porch of the general store, I stopped and watched for Maude. She wasn't hard to spot, thanks to that bonnet.

Just because Fort Dodge was a military supply base for an Indian-fighting army didn't mean there were no Indians about. I saw quite a few in the crush of people. Nothing I'd seen of them in Independence had made me ready for the fact of their greatly dour expressions now we were further west.

I felt I'd oftentimes worn a similar expression when I tried to match myself to the person somebody else wanted me to be. This thought made me feel sorry for them.

Then again, there were no really happy faces in sight. All over the outlying camp, people were shouting, children were screaming or crying.

Not that I was expecting to see great joy in the people wearily arriving or impatiently getting on their way, but in this atmosphere they seemed particularly lacking in fortitude. In many cases, badly broken in wasn't an exaggeration.

The noise was overwhelming. The soldiers' voices were steady in the background, singing something to count time. Horses were whinnying. One plunged about as if trying to throw off its saddle. And in all the din, I heard a goat calling, maa-a-aah.

Maude didn't look confused by any of it but headed straight for the building marked Telegraph Office and went inside. I couldn't follow her progress from there, for the windows were small and dark.

The general store stood at my back. I went inside, thinking to finish up quick. This was more likely than I'd hoped. All I had to choose from was salted beef and potatoes that had been boiled so long they were all watery and broken up, or a thin soup with unidentifiable pieces floating in it, or cheese and crackers.

I took the last. The crackers were good and crisp, and we hadn't been disappointed by cheese yet. We'd rely on canned beans and canned peaches in case it continued to be true we couldn't hunt.

With a jingle in my pocket, I wasn't in the mood to rough it more than I had to. Maude got a hoard of peppermints. She always spared the candy out as best she could, but still we'd gone through her peppermints at a good rate.

Never forget some woody carrots and sweet feed for the horses, and I dropped them into my potato sack on top of the cans. I asked for another sack for the cheese and crackers.

While I waited, a woman came from the back and put a sign up on the counter. It read:

HELEN DAVIDSON'S MOLASSES COOKIES

They were set out in a hot pan, straight from the oven. "Pick quick," she said. "They don't last five minutes."

They didn't last two. I bought the whole pan.

She put them into a box, they were so hot; a sack would have broken them to pieces. Outside, I tied my sacks to the saddle. I looked around but didn't see Maude.

I did see Marion. He'd found a soldier of some rank, an officer, and was telling our story of being bothered by rowdies who claimed to be Mad Maude.

Carrying the box that was warm to the touch, I went to listen in.

The conversation was going pretty well, in that Marion's side of the story wasn't being questioned hard. I went over to add my weight to Marion's account of events.

Someone gave a shout, something like "Ho there," and we all looked around.

"There are days it doesn't pay to put on my boots," Marion said.

Which words struck me somehow as a sign something had just gone wrong. If the words hadn't convinced me, there was the look on Marion's face.

There were three men bearing down on us. They weren't soldiers. They didn't look like lawmen. One of them was the clear leader, even though he didn't look a likely choice, being more ragged than the buffalo hunters, and I suspected he wouldn't smell as good.

"Who is he?" I said to Marion.

"A bounty hunter," he said. "The other two I don't know."

By then, they were in front of us.

FORTY-EIGHT

"JOE HARDEN, YOU ARE UNDER ARREST," THE BOUNTY hunter said, loud enough to turn heads. I was right about the smell.

"He's not Joe Harden," I said. "What makes you think so?"

We were drawing a crowd. It didn't help that more than a few soldiers was part of it.

Two of them put hands on Marion, twisting his arms behind his back, and the officer Marion had been talking to was taking his pistol. This unkindly treatment didn't sit well with me.

I was betwixt and between, wanting to stand up with Marion and knowing this would make Maude the last card up our sleeve. She was an excellent card, but it was a weight to carry, I knew.

I said, "Who is this Joe Harden?"

"A wanted man," a fellow in the crowd said. "I seen his name on a poster last week."

"It takes only a touch of bad luck," I said, "and yours could be on one next week."

"What about this one?" the bounty hunter said, meaning

259

me. He had written all over him the likelihood that he was going to set us back some in our hurry to get to Uncle Arlen. Even without that, I disliked the fellow entire.

"A boy," the officer said, and I didn't care for him, either. Boys could be more trouble than he was willing to credit them. "You can't expect me to arrest a boy."

"You can't arrest anyone on the say so of this smelly mongrel," I said.

The bounty hunter said, "Shut it, brat."

I kicked him in the shins.

Somebody grabbed me from behind and knocked the box from my grasp. The cookies fell into the dirt. "Hey," I said, twisting around inside my shirt. I connected with another kick.

I was taken along right behind Marion.

I looked back to see two dogs come from nowhere and start to gobble up those cookies.

The bounty hunters followed, arguing for collecting their money. The officer wouldn't part with a penny until he knew Marion had a price on his head. In this, I could admire him.

We were walked over to a few horse sheds in a far corner of the fort—that is, these were places only a horse could love. Up above, at the top of the fort walls, a guardhouse overlooked the prairie. If the soldiers looked down, they overlooked the sheds.

A foot soldier sat at a small table, his chair leaning back against a wall, pretty much doing nothing until he saw the captain coming. Then he jumped up, saluting and saying, "Sir! Captain, sir!"

One of those bullying Marion along said, "Two prisoners for you."

The foot soldier said, "You can't put a boy in together with these men. Two of them is murderers."

"We can't put him with that fellow who cut three fingers off that little squirt who moved his boots while he was sleeping, either," the captain said irritably.

With the air of a man who was ready for anything, the foot soldier went over and drew the bar from the door on one of the sheds. We were let into the shed, where there were three other men already.

There were pallets strewn about on the dirt floor, so I knew these men did sleep there. Two were standing, and one sat in the corner. I was hard put to figure out which of them were murderers. They none of them looked quite right to me.

One of them had a bad shape to his jaw, part of it missing and scarred over. He didn't look at us as we came in, and it struck me the reason for this was so he wouldn't have to see us looking curiously at him. I made my gaze travel on.

The next one was dressed fancy, but was dirty to a turn, like he had been dragged through mud flats by a horse. Only, if he'd been dragged, the coat he wore would have sustained some damage, so he was just dirty, really.

He looked at us as if we were going to be some personal trouble to him. He'd likely make us sorry for it if we were. I didn't say a word of hello, and neither did Marion.

I looked at the last one.

He was old and dressed oddly. It was going some to stand out as odd in these parts, but he had pulled together a queer kind of riding pants, I thought they were, and a moth-eaten jacket that might have dated from the Revolutionary War.

He was talking to himself there in the corner. He looked at us, but we might have been sparrows or wood blocks for all the difference we made to him.

I'd already made up my mind not to move anybody's belongings.

When the shed door was shut, there came a small scuffle between the scarred fellow and the dirty one. There was no real start to it, more like we had interrupted a dispute. They just fell to the ground in a tussle.

At first this was alarming. I thought it the beginning of something I didn't understand. When it came clear there was some personal difference being worked out, I said to Marion in a low voice, "What's wrong with that one's face?"

"Looks like part of it was shot away," he said. "Most likely the war."

The shed door swung back suddenly, and the foot soldier rushed back in to settle the argument by kicking both men soundly in their midsections. Marion pulled me behind him. The soldier left with a glare at us, as if we might have caused him this extra effort.

We sat in silence for maybe half an hour. Those two didn't look at each other. Only the third fellow whispered into his cupped hands.

In this time I went from being glad to be at Marion's side to being grateful he was at mine. I remembered Maude's words: "If they're not locking the door on you, you're fine."

If Marion felt the same way, he didn't show it through fidgets or sighing.

"How will Maude find out about this?" I said to Marion in a low voice. "She's going to expect us to show up pretty soon."

"I don't know, Sallie. Maybe there'll be talk around the fort, and the word will trickle back to her."

"Word?"

"That Joe Harden has been arrested."

This didn't have a pleasant ring to it.

When my belly began to want the lost cookies, I set my mind to knowing every inch of this prison. No mud or stone, they used half-rotten wood to build it. I suspected it was meant to be a horse shed. Likely the horses had refused it.

We had a pitcher and bowl set on a wooden crate. We also had a slop bucket I couldn't use, with a cloud of flies hovering over it. All the comforts.

"I'm sorry," I said.

"What for?"

"This was my idea."

"The bounty hunters were no part of your idea."

Outside, there was only the muffled sound of life going on without us. Overhead, the shuffle of boots on the catwalk couldn't be separated into a pattern of guard duty.

The door opened again, and that soldier came in, carrying small buckets of boiled potato and a chicken joint. I hoped it was chicken; I was hungry enough to eat prairie dog, but I didn't want to know it. We no sooner began to eat than some manner of biting green midge began to bother us.

It's strange the way the mind works, that being hungry would seem to be more tragic than being jailed, and to forget all in the irritation of bugs.

We were given a lantern at nightfall, which was a comfort

of sorts. It didn't discourage the flies, but if there was a rustling noise, we knew it was one of us made it and not a rat or a snake.

"What did you have to say to John Henry about writing your story into those Joe Harden dimers?" I asked Marion. This question had been darting about in my mind since learning John Henry was none other than John Henry Kirby.

I hadn't wanted to bring the matter up where Maude might overhear. The whole matter could lead to her wondering why Marion had never noticed those dimers and finding out he couldn't read.

"I told him my continuing adventures must happen in Texas or Mexico," Marion said, "but I had other bones to pick with him."

"Like what?"

"I didn't make any money off these stories he was writing, don't forget. The least he could do is make me out to be a good guy."

"You are a good guy."

Marion ducked his head. "I didn't want him to make mention of your aunt Ruthie again."

I said, "Did he agree?"

"He did. He offered to write more honest accounts if I would write him a letter now and again. He said he would pay for the right sort of letter."

"Oh," I said. "That's right fair of him. You didn't have to punch him?"

"No. I told him you would help me write the letter."

This pleased me well enough I almost forgot the flies.

From the other side of the wall I heard a cat hiss.

FORTY-NINE

AT LEAST I BELIEVED IT TO BE A CAT THE FIRST TIME. The second time, I wondered. And when my name was whispered, I stood up. I stood up rather suddenly, then looked around.

The man with the scarred face watched me from his pallet. I could see he wanted to know what I was up to. "Believe I'll try to get some air on my face," I said somewhat loudly.

I could just see through a crack in the wall. It was dark to begin with, except for our lantern light, but also this little shed was backed up to the corner of the fort. With walls on two sides, the torchlight from outside didn't creep back there.

I heard another whisper. "It's me, Sallie. Maude."

I strained to see her, but I said nothing. I didn't dare.

Behind me, the dirty fellow got up. He might could have been on his way over to peer out through that crack where I was, but he had to cross in front of the scarred one.

That one was still mad, their tussle not forgotten, because at the last moment he stuck his foot out and tripped his enemy. The lantern went over, spilling oil and flame that was somewhat soaked up by the dirt floor, but not before it had teased a bite out of the wall.

They fell to it just as before, a silent struggle but for grunts and wheezes.

"What's happening?" I heard Maude say; she'd forgotten to whisper. "Sallie?"

"It's a fire," I said, in not much more dire tones than I would have used for "it's a rat."

"Do you have a pitcher of water in there?"

"Yes."

"Dip a rag in the wet for you and Marion," she said. "I'll be waiting. Macdougal, too."

I wondered if I'd heard the last rightly.

"Do it, Sallie."

I made a quick inventory and decided the only likely rag was the torn-off piece of Maude's petticoat I had put in my pocket as a change of bandage.

"Tear off a piece of your shirttail," I said to Marion. He had stepped over to the door as if to bang on it, but after one look at me he thought better of letting them outside know what was happening.

I dipped the bit of ruffle in water, and the piece of Marion's shirttail. We stood quiet, but clapped the wet rags over our noses.

Those fellows went on pulling and tugging at each other. It took maybe two minutes before the backside of our shed lit up some.

Someone outside yelled, "Fire!"

As if discovery hurried it along, the smoke and flames

slipped across the wall and climbed to the roof of the shed. The wood began to snap and crackle. Outside, the cry went up, and I heard the heavy tread of men running.

Smoke collected under the roof faster than I would have believed it could. Those wet rags did cut the smoke some, but my eyes stung and tears ran down our faces.

It was bright as daylight in there by then. The old man began to rock back and forth, but he didn't move away as the flames climbed higher and reached out in his direction.

The door opened and two soldiers rushed in with buckets and threw the contents at the wall. Sand, that's what it was, and it didn't discourage the fire much. The two on the floor abandoned their fight and were gone before the buckets were emptied.

Everything happened fast.

I saw those fellows on the move and knew Marion and me should be right in front of them, never mind behind. But Marion ran across to that old man in the corner instead, and I followed him.

The soldiers rushed out, maybe for more sand.

We tried to get the man on his feet, but he only commenced to screaming and fighting us off.

His shirt caught a bit of fire. I saw it and shoved him back to the ground and tried to stomp it out. The old fellow took to shrieking like something wild.

Marion rolled him over to smother the flames.

"Get out!" he shouted.

I shook my head.

He'd lost his wet shirttail and started to cough. But he

reached down and snatched that man out of the corner as if he was a sack of feed. "Go on," Marion said to me, half carrying and half dragging him along.

There were soldiers rushing in, yelling orders at each other. We didn't make a speedy exit, but no one put down a bucket to stop us.

The officer was standing only a short distance from the shed. Marion lifted that kicking, screaming bundle and set it into his arms. The officer took the old fellow before he thought better of it.

The fire was taking the shed down and had leapt to the next one. Men in the guardhouse had been turned both bright and shadowy as they ran along the catwalk to other corners. Smoke wafted through the night air like draperies.

Someone yanked at my hand, and I didn't resist. I ran. In the next few seconds, I realized a strange woman had taken hold of me, not Maude.

"Follow your sister," she shouted over all the other noise. She held my horse and pointed me in the right direction.

I looked back as I swung a leg over. I saw those soldiers who had rushed into the shed were rushing back out, but I couldn't quickly find Marion in the crowd.

That stranger slapped my horse and I was on my way.

It had been no more than five minutes since the fire started, probably less, and we were on horseback. When I cleared the smoke, I saw the white of Maude's bonnet in front of me as she rode straight for freedom.

We couldn't gather any real speed with so many people and a few dogs about. But the way was cleared when men saw a horse coming at them.

At the gates, more people were pushing their way into the fort. It gave me a bad moment. The way the torchlight played on their anxious faces, it felt like that night when things had gone wrong, and the mob attacked Dr. Aldoradondo.

My horse fought our way through when I faltered. And in another few moments, we were outside. I could still see Maude a ways ahead of me, winding her way through the tent city.

I leaned into the horse's neck and shouted, "Git up!" But there was no clean row to ride, and we had to be satisfied with zigging and zagging around the tents.

A few shots were fired into the dirt nearby as we rode away. I saw the clods fly. The shots brought Maude up short.

At first I feared she might have been hit, but I saw she wasn't riding off till she knew she had collected her people. Marion and another rider were bringing a string of horses along behind. They were dark shadows against the pale tops of tents and wagon.

We all rode away from the fort together. A thought made me smile, even as another shot bit the dirt near my horse.

Maude did have a gang.

FIFTY

WE WERE SOON OUT OF RANGE OF THE BULLETS.
That last rider put up a hand to signal us to slow down.
"Pleased to meet you, Sallie, Marion. My name is Ellie Mac-
dougal," she said.

I saw right off this was the Macdougal who sent the
telegram saying her father had been shot and her dog killed.
"Let's all of us spread out," she said. "We don't want to leave a
good trail for them."

We rode in this order: Marion, Ellie and her horses, me,
and Maude, strung out across the high plains. Now we weren't
being shot at, I worried about being followed.

We made those horses run.

As we rode, I was turning it over in my mind. I added
started a fire to the list of accusations that might be made
against Maude.

I thought *broke jail twice and broke loose her gang* sounded
more serious than burning down that shed. But if it turned
into a big fire, that might be a whole lot worse than breaking
loose from Fort Dodge.

We would just have to wait and see how the papers wrote it up.

Riding at about twenty yards apart, we went south for a time, and then west, and then south again. I rode tense, waiting and yet dreading to hear the rumble of the cavalry riding down on us.

We were trying to get away from the river trail. I couldn't see the fort plainly any longer, just a spot less purple on the horizon I figured for the light from the fire.

When nothing happened, we slowed the horses for a time. Ellie, I'd noticed, ran her horses crossways behind us now and again, and I figured it had something to do with breaking up the trail we were leaving.

"You were daring," Marion said to Maude in a tone I thought admiring. "What plan did you have before those fellows obliged you with a fire?"

"Digging under," Maude said. "Although I won't call it daring."

"It's good enough."

She didn't appreciate this compliment, but said to him, "You had my sister in there with you. Could you not get yourself arrested without dragging her into it?"

"She throws a mean kick," Marion said, looking at me. And to Maude, he said, "Would you have left me in there if I was alone?"

"Not once the place was on fire," Maude said.

I said, "She doesn't care to have you thinking she's softhearted."

"You stay out of this," Maude said.

"I could hardly think it," Marion said to me. "More like, she kicks old dogs, and I'm feeling like an old dog myself."

I didn't take his meaning, but Maude's voice went high. "Why would I kick an old dog?"

"There was that new dog around for a while."

"John Henry Kirby is funny and sweet," Maude said, like she was laying down a trump card. "He has a cowlick, like a boy."

"I'm surprised you didn't take him up on his invite to see New York City," Marion said. He gigged his horse and rode off a ways, like Ellie had encouraged us to do.

I hadn't known about any invitation. I didn't like the tone of this. None of the things Maude pointed out were what I would have used to describe John Henry.

"I never noticed the cowlick," I said to her.

"He had one," Maude said. "Likely Aunt Ruthie wouldn't think highly of it."

"What do you think of it?"

"You might offer him some of your boot black," she said to me with a grin. "That's likely to kill it."

"You can't fight with Marion the way you fight with me," I said.

"And how is that?"

"To have the last word," I said.

Ellie had just finished one of those diagonal runs and brought her string of horses near. Riding at this slower pace, I saw Silver Dollar among them.

"I'm glad you brought Uncle Arlen's horse along," I said to her. "How did you happen to come across us?"

"It wasn't accidental," she said.

"You were looking for us?"

"Your uncle Arlen got your telegram and sent me back here to find you."

"That's where she watched for us," Maude said. "At the telegraph office. We came looking for you and Marion and found your horses hitched to a post. We waited for a time, then Ellie asked around. It didn't take long to find someone who knew there'd been a man and a boy arrested."

I said, "Where is Uncle Arlen?"

"Back at the ranch," Ellie said. "Doing the job Daddy can't do since he got shot. I couldn't do it."

"We got your second message," Maude said. "We started out as soon as we could."

There was more to the story from there, but Maude decided to save it, for Marion shouted that we should all be riding apart. Ellie took her horses off in another direction.

Maude said, "I wonder if Uncle Arlen has got himself a girl."

"Wouldn't he tell us?"

"I don't believe he has yet told *her*," Maude said, "so you can't repeat what I said."

It may have been hours later that we came back together, close enough to talk. At first we only wondered aloud. Were they tracking us, chasing us? Or were we scot-free?

"Maybe we burned the fort down," I said to Marion.

"Too much rock for that," he answered me.

I was back to *broke jail twice*. Why, they might not even know Maude was there. She wouldn't get blamed at all.

We ate on the move, right out of the cans, cold beans and then peaches. The crackers were broken, but we might later roll the cheese across them and eat well enough, so we didn't throw them away.

Later on I remembered the string-tied box of molasses cookies with great longing. We rode with the sunrise behind us, satisfied most of the miles we'd put in took us further west.

FIFTY-ONE

WE DIDN'T RIDE BACK NORTH TOWARD THE RIVER FOR three days. We laid low, sparing our water, always keeping our eyes open for any bands of soldiers that might be on the hunt for Joe Harden and his boy sidekick.

We had run out of food when Ellie judged us to be nearing the border, we aimed once more for the trail we had been at such pains to avoid. We rode hard and long.

As dark fell, we hadn't seen any sign of life at all, except for the four-footed kind, and birds.

"There's something up ahead," Maude said. "Like fireflies."

I couldn't see them, and it bothered me something fierce. "I can't believe you can look that far away and see a firefly."

"Oh, hush," Maude said. "You're just hungry. I see lights, Sallie. But they twinkle like fireflies."

"How many lights?" Marion said, wanting to tease her.

Maude said, "Don't pester me," but her tone sounded near to cheerful.

"C.T.," Ellie said. "We'll find a well there."

I would have liked to hurry my horse, but he was at least as thirsty as I was, although he wasn't so hungry. I hadn't been eating grass all day.

We could've found this town in full dark, even if they didn't burn lamps. The piano and banjo music, the laughter and shouting, carried on the night air for some distance.

I'd grown used to hearing such rowdy goings-on, standing on the street in front of the Aldoradondos' wagon, and it didn't bother me much. I was tired, which can make a body slow to worry.

But we did go in with a care. The place was mainly a camp of whiskey bars, one after the other, with such names as the Satin Slipper, the Blue Goose, and Rory's House of Cards.

None of them looked to be painted up prettily or securely nailed together. The only upstairs porch sagged like a hammock. I didn't believe anyone would dare to step outside on it.

"Look for a place like George Ray's," Maude said.

We found one, only not so busy. There was no one up front serving customers, some of which were eating, some weren't.

"See what you can do about rustling up some biscuits and coffee," Marion said. "I'm going to look around."

I knew what he was looking for. Soldiers or that bounty hunter, who might be feeling cheated out of his money.

We went inside to stake our claim to a table.

"Chicken dinners for four," Ellie said when the fellow came to take our order. "We'll put a hurtin' on anything you can bring to the table right away."

"Are we in Colorado Territory proper?" Maude asked Ellie, but that fellow answered.

"Oh, you are," he said. "We're half a day from the Kansas border, give or take a few hours." This was news good enough to bring tears to Maude's eyes.

It brought tears to mine, anyway.

"Come a long way, have you?" he said, wiping the table with a damp rag. "Everybody out here has come a long way."

"How far to Liberty?" Maude asked when that fellow had gone away again.

"Two days' ride," Ellie said.

We were nearly asleep in our chairs and were grateful when the fellow brought cups of coffee out to us. "On the house," he said.

Marion came back there to find us.

"We can put our horses up at the livery," he said. "There's a young fellow over there promises he puts on a real good feed bag."

Maude got up and stacked the dirty plates on a table. At first this made me stare, wondering what she was about.

Then she took the newspaper someone had left behind, walked back past me, and dropped the paper in front of me.

While she took the plates on to the kitchen, I noticed the paper came from Memphis, Tennessee. It was only a few days old, so I didn't expect to find much that interested me—I got a surprise.

Ellie leaned in to read with me. One article claimed Maude had robbed a general store in St. Joseph, Missouri, a long way from where we had been at the time.

MAD MAUDE ON THE RUN!

—◆—

Latest reports hold that that wily madwoman who
has made a name for herself, none other than Maude
March, has been riding hard and long. She and her
gang of five burlies showed up in a general store south
of the Missouri border, guns a-blazing—

"Every crazy Mary Jane in the country is wearing her
name," Ellie said, as if her breath had been snatched from her.

This wasn't news. Right next to this ran another headline,
and I skipped over to it:

GRANDMOMMA VOWS REVENGE

—◆—

Black Hankie's grandmomma claimed he always
had a romantic nature, as she folded and refolded his
dusty mantilla, the scrap of lace he wore at his neck. It
was delivered to her today at her home in Tennessee. It
is her opinion this weakness for the ladies caused him
to be led astray by that wicked madwoman, Maude
March.

I flipped the paper over, thinking that couldn't be all they
wrote. However, there was nothing more said on the matter. I

would have read it out to Marion, but Maude came back to the table with a plate of biscuits.

Her eyes flicked to the paper. I was quick to fold it over. I kept folding until I could just about hide it under my dinner plate.

"This looks good," I said, sounding to my own ears like Dr. Aldoradondo.

"It's only hot biscuits."

Marion reached for one. "Like the boy said, they look good."

There was no jelly, but they came with a dish of apple butter. I hoped the nervous feeling that felt like it jumped from my fingertips would be taken for hunger.

We ate for a few minutes before Maude said, "What's in the paper?"

"You ain't still dead."

"Picture any good?"

I said, "Not really. The good thing about so many Maudes running around, they don't all look alike."

Maude got her incensed look. "How many are there?"

"Maybe three, not counting the ones we met personal. All of them in different states than we are."

She looked down to spread a little apple butter. I hoped this meant she didn't find the idea of three more all that offensive. Nothing like six or eight more. Eleven. Nor anywhere near knowing Black Hankie's grandmomma blamed Maude for his misfortune.

Ellie said, "Your uncle told me something about your troubles. I admit, it's more disturbing to read these stories than I thought."

"I don't know what's worse," Maude said, "the stories the papers make up or the women who pretend to be me so they can be in them."

"It's worse to be the one lied about," Marion said, "but John Henry is going to help you with that."

I hoped this would smooth things over. But then I noticed something—"Maude, look at your hands."

Her fingertips didn't look like puffy little pillows anymore. Her fingernails had grown out. They were dirty, but they were long enough to just cover the tips of her fingers. "You don't bite your fingernails anymore, Maude."

"Looks like I don't scrub them," she said, but she was halfway to smiling.

"You could go to the law with your story," Ellie said, for she didn't understand the interest I took in Maude's fingernails.

"They've already tried that," Marion said.

"Lawmen are deaf to pleas of innocence," I said. "They have their job to do."

"Let's us just eat up and make our way to Uncle Arlen," Maude said. "There's nothing we have to decide tonight."

"You have the right of it," I said. "Let's don't bother with the hotel. It's not like we need a bath all that bad."

This put a grin on Maude's face and Ellie's, and the mood lightened a good deal as forks were lifted. The bird was cooked crisp and tender, the potatoes were plenty, and there was a green sauce to dip everything into, should we care to. That sauce had a bite of its own.

We slept in the loft at the livery.

FIFTY-TWO

WE STARTED OUT AT THE BREAK OF DAWN. THE NICE thing, we found dew on the ground. I hadn't noticed the lack of it until I saw it, felt it again. Even then, I wasn't so sure.

I touched a vine growing up the wall of the livery. "Did it rain a mite?"

Ellie said, "It's morning dew. We aren't quite so dry out this way as they are on the lower plains."

The land made a nice change. I saw now the gradual slope to it. If we only overcame a series of treeless grassy ridges, at least we had something to look forward to. The rise wasn't hard on the horses, and a dark blue line we saw on the horizon was easier on the eyes.

"Mountains," Ellie said when I asked about it.

Near the end of the day, Ellie led us off the trail to follow a trickle of a creek for half a mile before coming to a worn path that climbed the backside of a low bluff.

This looked to me like a chopped-off hillside at the front, atop which we could see an adobe-brick building. We rode for a time around it and then uphill at the backside of it to reach the top.

Once there, I found it to be more of the same, flat grassy plains. I had to walk right up to the broken-off edge to know where the grass stopped. The advantage to this place was it looked in every direction over the plains.

The land sloped away from us in a way that made me feel like we could roll downhill for miles. But this was only a trick of the eyes.

"There was a family here when I was a little girl," Ellie said. "The Osgoods. We stayed the night here once."

"Looks like they've been gone for some time," Marion said.

"A long time," Ellie said. "But the roof's still here. The walls stand. The porch is good."

It was no surprise the walls stood, for they were thick as tree trunks and not overly broken up by windows. The two at the front had been boarded up, and the one at the back still had unbroken glass.

The place didn't have much to offer but shelter from rain or wolves, and there was no rain. A ragged corral had been built up out of flat boards that might have come from a wagon bottom—more than one wagon bottom.

These were worn down some by weather, and there was a gap on one side, where the gate had gone missing. But grass grew over the earth in there, and the horses would graze. We could rope off the opening.

It took us better than an hour to get them all tended to, for Ellie was more careful of horseflesh than Uncle Arlen. I carried the saddles over to the porch and hung the blankets over the rope.

We carried water up from the creek and made ourselves

comfortable for the night. By the time we were settling, the stars twinkled hard and bright overhead.

We would sleep inside, so we wondered if the chimney was still good. This was a short discussion because Marion came inside wanting to show us all something.

We walked out to the place where the bluff overhung the trail. He pointed back east of us, where two campfires could be seen as beacons some distance away.

They were far enough from each other, and down low, so each may not have known the other was there. "What do you figure?" I said to Marion. "Anybody looking for us?"

"Hard to say. But making a fire isn't a good idea."

We ate cold food, but it didn't feel like any great hardship, for the night was warm. We turned in early, talking like we would be on our way before daybreak.

That was the plan, but we slept a ways into the morning.

Marion was up first, and out without waking me.

Ellie roused me and Maude, but she wasn't truly moving at a pace. She sort of drifted toward the coffee makings and then remembered there was to be no fire.

I felt as if I could sleep longer. But Maude reached over and pinched me so I wouldn't fall back to the soft pillow of my folded pants.

"We need a bath," Ellie said.

"What good is that?" I said, not wanting to get roped into this. "We'll only be dusty again after we get on the trail."

"Just a spit bath," Ellie said. "It won't take ten minutes and we'll be refreshed."

"I don't need refreshing."

Maude grabbed me by the shirt. "It'll wake us up."

I consented to a face-and-neck wash, but I wouldn't allow myself to be talked into wearing my dress.

"Why, look at you. Under all that dirt, you're as pink as one of Betsy's pigs," Maude teased, and tried to run the cloth over my face again.

"I wouldn't know her for the same boy," Ellie said with a grin.

"We'll be riding up to Uncle Arlen in a few hours, Sallie," Maude said. "You have to wear the dress."

"You make it sound like he'll fall over from the shock," I complained.

This made them both laugh, and for a moment Maude looked like an ordinary girl, leaning up against Ellie. She still looked weather-tough, but her manner had softened in a way I did like.

I grabbed the cloth and scrubbed myself as near clean as I could get. I even wiped it over my hair. Maude and Ellie went on making little jokes to each other and giggling as I put on my dress and beat it for the outdoors.

I wanted to please Maude, but I wouldn't consider wearing the bloomers, for I didn't care if I showed a bare knee. Those bloomers would be ruined from saddle dirt; I would have to take great care with my skirt.

To his credit, Marion didn't blink when he saw me in a dress. He nodded a "Good morning."

He'd already been up long enough to bring our horses over to the porch and saddle them up. We had not much grain left for them, and they were eating the grass down to a bare patch.

They looked to me thinned out through the neck, their flanks too flattened. Maude and me were thinner, I reminded myself, and we weren't suffering awful much. In only another day or two, we could let the horses rest up properly.

"Them women ready to go?" Marion said to me.

"Ten minutes," I said. I dug through my sack and found the bonnet. It was none the worse for my having loaned it to Maude, but I sort of promised it a good wash and starch as soon as I could manage it.

I shoved my hair back and tied the bonnet under my chin. It didn't have quite the smooth feel as when I wore braids beneath it, but my hair was too tangled for braids.

I sat down on the porch.

Beside me, Marion said of the horses, "They've mowed it down here worse than if they were goats. The grass may not come back."

"It'll come back," I said. "All it needs is a good rain."

"Let's move them to a fresh spot," Marion said, chucking me on the shoulder. "Give me a hand with them."

I'd no sooner wondered if I was going to regret putting on my dress than I heard a racket of horses. It didn't sound like many riders, but they pulled their horses to a stop out there on the trail. This brought us to our feet.

Marion went to the horses, soothing their laid-back ears, shushing them, and I moved quick to help him. Horses did want to call out to each other sometimes.

Clear as if his voice were a bell, one of the riders said, "There's a house up there on the hill."

I stood stock-still, half-turned to warn Maude.

And in answer, the words "There's no smoke coming up the chimney. We've lost the trail, if it ever was one."

The first one said, "Don't think I'm pushing for it. I'm not of a mind to get myself shot at by another war vet. I'm ready to go home."

There was some muttering over this. My heart pounding, I inched forward, ignoring Marion's frantic waving me back. I could see just the faces of a couple of those fellows, and they weren't looking back at me, which was good, for they were the bounty hunters.

Another voice, as travel-weary as the one before, came from a little distance. "This path looks to be used recently."

I yanked my bonnet lower and made myself stroll out to the edge of the bluff as if my curiosity had got the best of me. "Who're all you fellows?" I called, letting my voice go high.

"We're a posse," one of them lied. "Looking for a fellow has broken out of jail over at Fort Dodge."

I wanted to tell them a posse from Fort Dodge would be lost if it found itself this far west, for we were well out of Kansas. Only I didn't want to look like a smart girl.

"Well, come on in, then," I said. "My granny will want to hear about that. She will give you all some of her rhubarb tea. You should not be too polite about drinking it, a full cup will give you the runs."

This invitation was met with a stony silence.

"I'll go tell her she has visitors," I said, and turned on my heel.

"Girl!" one of them shouted. "Tell your granny we are sorry to have to turn down the invite, but we're in a hurry."

I let my shoulders slump hard, and for a moment I wondered if I'd overdone it. For one of them said in a kindly way, "Looking forward to a little company yourself, were you?"

I said, "Granny is enough company for anyone. Her hearing is so bad I have to say everything twice at least."

"Give her our good day," one of them said, and started out of there. The others followed, the kindlier one waving at me as he went. In only a minute or so, we were alone again.

I walked back to where Marion stood with the horses. "Bounty hunters," I said, though he had heard the whole thing.

He said, "You're a pistol."

Maybe I was, for I had the shakes like I had just shot a pistol. I had to sit down on the porch. Marion dropped down into the grass at the edge of the bluff and watched until he was sure those fellows had really turned back for the Kansas border.

When Maude and Ellie came out a few minutes later, they were scrubbed to a rosy glow, both of them. They hadn't heard a thing from the outside world through those walls.

FIFTY-THREE

WE COULDN'T HOPE TO REACH LIBERTY MUCH BEFORE the middle of the afternoon. We wouldn't push our horses. They were tired. I remembered I had a dimer in my sack.

The title read *Rusty Nael, Blacksmith at Large.* Since there was little talk, I kept everyone up on the developments of the story as I read.

The land was rugged, but dust didn't fly awful bad. It struck me the other, dustier trails had been real cattle trails. The dirt clods had been worn down to near powder.

We were looking at more hills. Once into those hills, the trail got kind of rocky and rough-trod. We crossed more than one dry creek bed. Some of the cracks in the ground were no doubt due to the dry weather.

We came to a place where the trail split and rode through a dry creek. "This is it," Ellie said. "Macdougal land."

Ellie intended to make a detour to deliver those horses, except for Silver Dollar, to a neighboring ranch. Silver Dollar was on a long tether wound around Maude's saddle horn.

"Ride south there," she said, pointing to another split in

the trail. "You'll be at the house in an hour or so. I'll see you at the ranch this evening."

"You can't ride on alone," Marion said to Ellie, for we had already heard enough about her father's troubles to know she was not let to ride around on her own.

"Go with her," I said. "Me and Maude can follow this trail without any difficulty." I glanced at Ellie. "I want to lay eyes on Uncle Arlen."

Marion said, "I don't think much of this idea."

"It's only a couple of miles," Maude said, already moving along the trail.

"Don't let your guard down," he said.

We struck out for the ranch; Marion and Ellie took the other trail.

I said, "I'm glad to have a little time alone with you, Maude. There are a few things we must have out."

"I know it," she said. "We can't go home with Uncle Arlen."

"We can't go back to Missouri at all," I said. "At least not until we don't have to worry about getting arrested."

"That's the corner I can't get around," Maude said. "Ellie's easy to get along with, but I don't know we can ask to stay at the ranch. Uncle Arlen owes her father his life already. I don't want to make him feel more beholden."

This was just the line I'd hoped not to hear. "I might could help out with the horses," I said. "And you could do the baking."

"Well, that's all ahead of us," Maude said. "We'll just have to wait and see what Uncle Arlen has in mind."

"We have to be in one place long enough to hear from John Henry."

"I'm not counting on John Henry."

I said, "You don't care if your name gets cleared? You don't want justice?"

Myself, I was guilty of shooting Willie, so this was not fresh territory to me. It made me more of an outlaw than he was. Maude had never been that kind of outlaw. She deserved justice.

"I think we have to change our idea of what that means." She gave me a thoughtful look. "I think I can live without seeing justice done as we used to think of it."

A question kept running through my mind—what would become of us? I didn't consider us lost, just at loose ends.

"How are you going to feel, Maude?"

"So far, I don't feel bad," she said. "Bad*ly*. I've had some time to get used to the idea there's more than one way to see a happy ending to this."

"I'm not so sure," I said. "I don't like giving up Uncle Arlen now that he's found."

"His happy ending may have changed more than ours," Maude said. "Try not to worry about it until we have to. This isn't the kind of thing you can plan for."

I thought this a remarkable thing for Maude to say. Not because she knew me for being a planner, or because she wasn't so much of one. But because she'd always had clear ideas about how things should work.

Not half an hour later, we were climbing a hill at an easy pace when, on the other side of it, we heard a shot. Me and

Maude pulled on the reins as if we were one, bringing our horses to a standstill.

"They weren't shooting at us?" Maude said, half in surprise. I knew how she felt exactly.

I'd begun to think of gunshot as a sign something had gone wrong. I saw that other people reacted differently. They thought a gunshot meant someone *else* was in trouble. Sometimes they could think of perfectly good uses for a gunshot.

"Could be somebody popped a rabbit," I said. "Or a bird."

Another three shots rang out, one right after the other.

I headed my horse off the trail. Maude went for the other side, so all we could do, when the shooting stopped, was look at each other. I, for one, felt a little silly. Scared, but silly, too.

When more gunshots didn't come, I rode over to her. Maude said, "What do you think?"

"Bandits?"

There were two more shots, just far enough apart to think somebody might have been taking aim. Our horses snuffled and blew, wanting to run. I whispered quieting words to them, but they weren't in the mood to listen.

"I'll have a look," Maude said. She dropped her horse's reins over the low-hanging branches of an oak tree. I pulled off my bonnet and hung it over my saddle horn.

"Go slow and try not to make a lot of noise," I said, for I couldn't go fast. I wished I had stayed in pants.

Maude was already on the move, carrying her rifle. I hadn't yet taken mine out of the boot. When I caught up to her, she whispered, "Go straight up, and I'll work my way over a little."

Thinking ruefully that Maude had good instincts for someone who had never meant to be a range rider, I picked my skirt free from a stickery branch, some kind of weed. I hoped there wouldn't be many of them.

Maude hadn't gotten far away, and she came back to say, "They aren't going to be wearing masks out here, Sallie. Who's to say which one caused the trouble?"

"Exactly right," I said. How were we to tell which of them would be the one needing help?

After three or four minutes of climbing, we were nearly to a point where we could look down the other side of that hill. Maude started moving away so she would be able to look down from another angle.

"Wait right here," she said. "Wait till you hear me whistle like a bird."

"What bird?" I said, for there wasn't a sound of birds on the air.

"That's how you'll know it's me," she said with a lift of one eyebrow.

I said, "You'll be careful?"

She said, "I swear it on my fingertips." And she kissed three fingertips, as if she were perfectly willing to kiss them good-bye.

"Don't show yourself," I said, the short hairs on my nape all aquiver.

I took up a position behind some blueberry bushes while Maude crawled away. I plucked a berry and popped it into my mouth. Still a mite tart.

Several blueberries later, I hadn't heard a whistle.

I leaned through the bush and couldn't see Maude. She

had gone further on than I thought she would have to. I decided it couldn't hurt to go around the bush for a better view.

But there I still couldn't see her. I could see the road down below us and a dead horse in the middle of it. Behind that, a buckboard with two healthy horses harnessed to it. Those horses didn't want to stay there much longer, judging by the way they were switching their tails and pawing the ground.

I couldn't see who had done the shooting.

I moved forward, trying to be quiet.

A whistle brought me up short. Maude had found a hiding place in the hollow of a tree. She sent me a look that said simply, I knew you couldn't do one thing I asked you to do.

Beyond her, someone slowly poked their rifle out from behind a tree. Directed away from us, it still gave me a start.

I pointed the fellow out to Maude right quick.

I hadn't expected to find anyone so up close, and I was glad she was well hidden.

This fellow put a shot across the way. The bullet whizzed near enough to those horses to make up their minds—they started pulling that wagon up the trail in our direction.

I didn't blame them. They weren't looking for bee stings.

Somebody yelled, "Stop those horses," but nobody tried.

The team skirted the dead horse in their path—it may have been the prospect of getting around that horse kept them from running amuck any sooner. That and the load of dried skins they were carrying in the wagon.

Once started, those horses ran for all they were worth. Nobody could have stopped them, not even in a dimer. "They'll stop when the trail flattens out," somebody else shouted as the wagon crested the hill. I tried to know where those voices came from, but there was no telling.

The same fellow shot again. I tried to catch a glimpse of him, but he leaned out on the side away from me.

It did prove, however, the two sides in this fight were separated by the trail between them. One shooter couldn't rush the other without being in the open long enough to have the period put on the end of their sentence.

Maude had worked her way back to me. She was good at being quiet. "I wonder whose horse it is that's dead," she whispered.

"Lemme get my skins," the shooter called out, "and I'll call it a day."

Maude looked at me like I was a fellow jury member. I could not disagree. This did seem to make them the injured party.

"You got those skins by poisoning our cattle," the other fellow behind a tree called back. This statement did cloud the issue, and it inspired a few more bullets to be traded.

Ducking down when shots were fired, and then peering out through the underbrush, me and Maude played the parts of silent witnesses, unnoticed by either side.

Behind us, the wagon noises didn't fade away but stopped abruptly, so I didn't have to look to know the horses had quit running.

"Where's that fancy shooter of yours now, Wa—ers?"

Maude said, "What did he say?"

"Where's your fancy shooter," I said, believing this might be a clue. "In many a dimer, it's the bad guys who hire a gunman."

"No," Maude said. "The name. Was it Waters?"

"I don't know," I said.

Maude shushed me, for somebody was shouting something back. We missed it while I was talking and Maude was shushing; they didn't have awful much to say.

It was apparent cause for more shots to be traded.

I began to get some idea where the other fellows were hidden. Then, seeing one of them slip from tree to tree, something about him looked familiar. My heart leapt at that familiar sight.

"That's Uncle Arlen," I said.

FIFTY-FOUR

WHAT WITH THE SHOCK OF IT, I SPOKE OUT LOUD. There was a rustling in that nearby hiding spot directly after. Me and Maude ducked low. We stayed low for what we judged to be long enough.

"Don't call out," I said to her when we were giving each other a go-ahead look. "It might cause Uncle Arlen to make the mistake of showing himself."

We bobbed up, and Maude said, "Where?"

I pointed. In a few seconds, he made another dash between one tree and the next. "See?"

Maude whispered, "Uncle Arlen doesn't wear buckskin."

"He could change his shirt. And you did hear that other fellow call him Waters."

"You weren't so sure what that fellow said. What makes you sure it's Uncle Arlen down there?"

"The way he moves," I said. "Watch. He's trying to get up here, I think, to come around behind them, like."

We were both of us with our gaze trained on the tree, waiting for Uncle Arlen to show himself long enough for Maude to recognize him.

I saw out of the corner of my eye that down below us another of those fellows was on the move. They knew somebody was up here, and they had decided to find out who.

Uncle Arlen moved, and Maude drew her breath in sharply. She had seen him well enough. I pulled on her sleeve and made her notice the fellow crawling our way through the bushes.

Maude didn't hesitate. She drew a bead and shot a branch off a tree so it fell right in front of him. He jumped about a mile and scooted back into the brush.

"Uncle Arlen," I called, so he'd know where the shot had come from. "It's Maude and Sallie up here. One of these wranglers is trying to climb the hill."

There was a moment when nobody said anything. Then Uncle Arlen called out, "That means we've got 'em surrounded."

Maude broke into a grin. She pumped another shot into the trees, although I saw by the way she turned her rifle she was careful not to hit anyone by accident.

Another branch fell in front of the nearby shooter.

"All right, all right, let's have a little parlay here," he called out. "You've got ree-inforcemints, you've got our skins. How about if we call it quits? We'll jist walk back aways from here and fergit the whole danged thing."

"My horse is dead," Uncle Arlen called back.

"So's mine," the other fellow answered. "I been riding a mule since one a you fellers killed it last week."

"We don't make war on horses," Uncle Arlen said. "You probably killed it yourself with a careless bullet. But someone who shot a dog shouldn't worry over a horse, either."

"Here now, don't be insulting," another fellow in the brush said. "We didn't shoot the dog a-purpose." It sounded to me like wherever there was a gun, there was an accident waiting to happen.

"You shot old Macdougal, too," Uncle Arlen yelled back.

"That's another story," the fellow in the brush said. "He had it coming."

"Are we letting them run for it or not?" Maude shouted out. "I can pick off two of them from here without any trouble at all."

There was a great rushing about in the underbrush below us. When they mounted their horses, which were hidden as well, beneath a skirt of pine trees, we saw there were no fewer than five of them. Because Uncle Arlen didn't shoot, we didn't shoot, either.

It took maybe five minutes for them to clear out and get far enough away to cause no trouble.

In this time, we listened to the sounds of their leaving and did a little talking back and forth.

"Uncle Arlen, is everyone down there all right?" Maude asked.

"Dabney. His shoulder is broke," Uncle Arlen said. "He landed funny when the horse fell."

We clambered down the trail to have a look at them. Apart from Dabney, I saw only an old codger Uncle Arlen introduced as Whistler. He looked hard at me and Maude.

"Whooo-ee, pretty girls," he said. "What'cha don't see when you ain't lookin' through a gun."

"You silk-tongued flatterer," Dabney shouted. "Give the rest of us a fair chance, why don'tcha?"

"Don't get yourself all in a lather," Whistler said. "They're pretty, all right, but we've any of us got about a fair chance at playing granddaddy to them at Christmas."

To Uncle Arlen, I said, "How many more of you are there?"

"We are it," he said. "We didn't want to take too many hands from the ranch, not knowing these fellows were waiting to ambush us."

We hugged each other all around, even Dabney, who squeezed our hands. Whistler had gotten Dabney splinted up while the shooting was going on.

"We ought to get Dabney back to the ranch," he said. "There's no sawbones, but Dismal will take care of him."

I said, "Dismal? There's an odd name."

"Cain't say if he has another. He used to be a dismal trader. Getting the dead ready for a last review has made him a fair hand with repairs."

"That sounds all right to me," I said, thinking I'd rather have an undertaker to fix a broken bone than a doctor too easily referred to as a sawbones.

We double-timed it back down the other side of that hill and brought the buckboard back to carry Dabney. Those pelts made a soft bed for him, and likely the trip wouldn't bother him near as much as it would have without the padding.

By then, Marion and Ellie had come in answer to the sound of gunshots. "I told you this wasn't a good idea," Marion said to Maude.

"What was that he said?" she said to me, teasing. "My hearing is suffering from the noise of gunshots. Did he say he was glad to see we aren't shot down?"

I put my hands around my mouth like an ear horn and shouted, "I believe that's what he said."

FIFTY-FIVE

AS WE RODE ON TO THE RANCH, UNCLE ARLEN HAD A little reunion with Silver Dollar. I wouldn't have known to say that horse was down in the dumps while we were leading him, but he did look to me to be a great deal more cheerful with Uncle Arlen on his back.

"I've been worried about you girls," he said to us next.

Uncle Arlen was determined to hear my side of Maude's jailbreak. I concentrated Uncle Arlen's interest on John Henry and that maybe, once Maude's true story was known, her name would be cleared.

He was moderately cheered by this. I'd hoped for more enthusiasm, but he only said, "Tell me about the trip from Independence. Did you run into any trouble?"

Maude told Uncle Arlen how we traveled with the Aldoradondos for a good part of the time. I promised to put on my button shoes, but of course we left out the part having to do with tar and feathers.

In fact, there were so many parts we felt it prudent to leave out, me and Maude were down to pretty much, "Hot and dry. No rain at all. We saw a lot of grass, and then more grass."

I figured we could get together later to decide exactly how we should tell our story. Because we were for sure going to have to tell everything all over again.

Uncle Arlen had given Dabney a flask filled with something golden-colored and potent, it being our uncle's intention to medicate him against the pain. Dabney had three or four swallows together and pretty much passed out.

It looked to be some more potent than anything Dr. Aldoradondo kept in his wagon. I watched in some suspense as Whistler sipped at it and choked, but he didn't pass out.

We topped a rise and saw there was a ranch in a hollow of the land—a house made of cedar and pine, with green shutters, behind which there was a sizable garden patch. A new barn was being raised alongside the spot where another one had burned to the ground. I thought I wouldn't be run out of this place without putting up a fight, either.

Another old fellow was sitting on the porch in a long chair made of picket-fence slats. "Right nice chair you have there," I said to him after we were introduced. Mr. Macdougal, I was to call him.

"A convalescent chair, my daughter calls it," he told me. "Lets me lay back like a pasha."

I didn't at that moment ask him what a pasha was, for my eyes lit on a little stack of dimers on the table at his elbow. He said to me, "I like to read about this fellow, Wild Woolly. Have you heard of him?"

"Is he still lost out there on the icy plains?"

"Well, now," he said, but the door opened, and out of the house came an older woman with strong features and graying hair pulled to the back of her head in a thick broomtail.

"You found them," she said to Uncle Arlen.

"They showed up in the middle of nowhere," he said, "just in time to save our bacon. Dabney's been hurt." Dabney raised his good arm as if to make little of it. However, he didn't raise the injured arm.

"She hurried out to the wagon to look him over.

"It's not too bad," Uncle Arlen said. "He's had a strong dose of medicament, is all."

Her attention was drawn back to us as Uncle Arlen said to Maude and me, "This is Maria, Ellie's aunt."

"It's about time," she said. "Once we knew you were making your way here, I made them go over the map and over it, figuring out where you ought to have been, day by day."

"She was like a mother lion," Macdougal said. "Sent her own niece out there to bring you through the wilderness."

Maria said, "I thought for sure something terrible must've befallen you. But, Arlen, he said you two girls were like corks in the rapids, you always bob to the top."

"I like to hope so," Maude said, being led into the house.

"They are not just girls," Uncle Arlen said. "In a tight spot, they have the Macdougal touch. They can be counted on."

I rode to the barn with Uncle Arlen, feeling myself tall in the saddle.

The undertaker was in the new barn, keeping himself busy with a wooden puzzle, a small box with parts that had to be put together just so. He looked relieved to hear we needed him to set a bone.

We put Dabney on a worktable littered with wood shavings, trying not to jog his shoulder. It pained him something awful. Uncle Arlen poured more of that medication down his throat. Dabney whooped and coughed.

"Easy there," Whistler said. "We don't care to drown him."

Dabney, still gasping from the drink, said, "Am I getting ready to die?"

"I don't believe your shoulder is broken," Dismal said. "It's just dislocated. I believe we can have you right as rain in only a moment."

He instructed Uncle Arlen and Whistler on holding Dabney just so, then yanked his arm, causing Dabney to give a yell, but the whole thing was over quickly.

"That feels some better," he said after a minute. Then he passed out again. The stuff in that flask more than beat the liquid Dr. Aldoradondo measured out with a dropper.

"He'll sleep through the night," Uncle Arlen said. "Let's go up to the house and let Maria fuss over us."

FIFTY-SIX

MARIA MANAGED TO BOSS EVERYBODY ABOUT WHILE she made them feel welcome. "Come on in here and let me fatten you up a little," she said to us, and we weren't reluctant.

When I had nearly done with eating a cake with blueberries running through it, I started to think about questions we had traveled with. "In your telegram, Ellie, you said it was too late for you," I said to her. "I thought you must be in much worse shape, somehow."

"I wanted to go home," Ellie said. "Daddy didn't want me to get caught up in this fight. Then they shot him, and truly I'm glad I was here to care for him. But they also killed my dog, the devils."

Maria said, "This ranch is your daddy's dream, not your own. You ought to have been safe home with your momma."

Maude looked to Ellie. "You don't live here?"

"No. Daddy went west in 'forty-nine to make his fortune in gold," Ellie said. "The wonder was, he lived to tell about it. That we all lived to tell about it."

"Oh, I see," Maude said.

"No, you don't," Maria said, sitting down and leaning across the table to us. "Her momma is now living in California while her daddy is following a different dream. He wants to be a cattle baron, and he has to be east of the mountains and the worst of the deserts to do it."

Ellie took up the telling. "Momma wants to create a fabulous vineyard, like her poppa had in Italy, where she hails from. She's trying to grow grapes out there in a place called Rutherford."

"Have you seen the ocean?" Maude asked her.

"Many times," Ellie said. "We're two days' ride away from it, in a wagon."

I could see this information being tucked away in Maude's heart. "Are you going back?" I asked Ellie.

"I'm in no hurry just now," she said, glancing across the room at Uncle Arlen. "I want to see Daddy through this rough patch."

"Uncle Arlen will see him through," I said.

At this, Ellie smiled, and so did I. Me and Maude weren't going back to Independence, and Ellie looked like one more reason why Uncle Arlen wouldn't go back, either.

"I believe the West has begun to agree with him," Maude said.

Some time later, after supper, we settled out on the porch for a spell. There were crickets singing, and an owl hoot-hoot-hooted every so often. The air was cool and fresh.

One of the ranch hands had brought over a fiddle, but hadn't played it yet. There was much recounting of one adventure and another. After a while I took a seat on the steps and pulled my boots off. It hadn't yet been said in so many words, but I could see we were going to be calling this place home for a time.

Maude came to sit beside me. I said, "Did you like Independence?"

"It was noisy and smelly and dusty," Maude said. "But I liked it now and again."

I pressed my toes into the cool of the dirt. "Do you like it here?"

"It looks fine to me," Maude said. "We haven't been here long."

I said, "Let me know if you decide to really like it."

While the conversation going on behind us didn't miss us, Maude said, "You have to take things as they are and just go on living, that's what Aunt Ruthie used to say."

I said, "Do you think of Aunt Ruthie very often? Think about what she taught us and how useful those things are?"

"Every day," Maude said.

"I wish I could tell her how smart she looks to me now."

"That would give her a laugh," Maude said.

"Likelier she'd make that little 'hmph' sound, like she was holding down a sneeze."

"Same thing," Maude said.

Well, it was, since we were talking about Aunt Ruthie.

The full moon hung above us, low and large in the east, and made it nearly as bright as before the sun went down. I could see my shadow.

"I dreamed once that she laughed out loud," I said. "It looked good on her."

"Sallie, I feel like I'm making myself new."

I walked barefoot out into the grass. I liked the feel of

grass between my toes. On the porch, one of those fellows lifted up his fiddle and began to play a reel. The music looped through the air like a hawk in flight.

Maude followed me, saying, "It's all right with you, isn't it?"

"It's all right," I answered, putting into my voice lilting tones I had copied from her. Maude had many a good point, and the lilt that showed up in her voice now and again was one of them.

She must have liked hearing it. She led me into dancing ring-around-the-rosy under the moon. A light rain began to fall, pit pat, and in a minute, settled into a gentle mist, just enough to cool the skin.

Marion stood leaning against a porch post. He tipped his hat back and watched. Ellie sat with Uncle Arlen, but she got up from the couch that was only big enough for the two of them and came to join hands with us, so we were me and Maude and Ellie weaving in a circle, heads thrown back, laughing.

ACKNOWLEDGMENTS

A great big WAVE and an even bigger THANK-YOU to Brittany and all her gang at Drauden Point. You have no idea how long a compass was on my wish list.

Thank you, too, to the readers, reviewers, and booksellers of *The Misadventures of Maude March* for their generous reception of and enthusiasm for two girls gone kinda wrong. 'Preciate it.

Let me express unflagging gratitude to the staff at the White Sands Chicken Ranch for their warm welcome of two city dudes. Thank you Richard and Arnola Hall in Accommodations and Pat Dannemann, chief lookout and border guard.

And hey, Kirby, your name is in this book.

Shana Corey and all the hardworking people at Random House are fast becoming my usual list of suspects, acknowledgment-wise. This is a warm blanket and a big comfort to a writer sleeping under the stars, and most writers are. I am so lucky to have you all as pardners, and I know it.

I have an ever-deepening well of appreciation for my husband, Akila, who makes this easy for me. I thank him a thousand times a week; I hope he knows it.

Ditto the friends who help me and put up with me and, I am grateful to say, know how hard this is. May they be equally fortunate.

Last, not least, still thanking Jill Grinberg and the friend who drew me the map to find her.

About the Author

AUDREY COULOUMBIS'S first book for children, *Getting Near to Baby*, won the Newbery Honor in 2000. She is also the critically acclaimed author of *Say Yes* (2002), an IRA Children's Book Award winner, and *The Misadventures of Maude March* (2005), a Book Sense 76 Pick and a National Parenting Publications Award Winner. Before becoming a full-time writer, Audrey worked as a housekeeper, a sweater designer, a bookseller, and a school custodian. Today she lives in upstate New York and Florida with her husband, Akila, and their dog, Phoebe. Audrey and Akila have two grown children. You can visit Audrey's Web site at www.audreycouloumbis.com.